NIGHT WOLF

Syndra Jones

Contents

[1.1] SLAVE

"RUN, RUN AS fast as you can Keffer!" The voices of the Night moon Pack kids echoed behind me mockingly as I ran barefooted, weaving through the forest trees, my heart a rampant beat within me.

"Run Keffer!" They called out laughing in their sickening amusement, their taunts prodding through my mind as they chased after me. Their footsteps ran light and fast through the forest.

They were built for this; it was like a walk in the park for them.

Not for me.

Never for a Keffer.

My vision was a teary blur, my body shaking in fear, yet still ignoring the tiny little cuts the fallen branches and dry leaves made through my skin with every step I took, my breathing harsh and hollow, as I pushed through the forest, the afternoon sunlight barely scraping through the dense trees to light my way.

The voices of the taunting kids vanished, and so did the sound of their footsteps but my heart only sank. I knew what came next. The sound of bones cracking behind me only meant one thing.

They were shifting.

Soon the taunts were replaced by growls and, their human figures were replaced by their wolves. Howls began to echo behind me more deadly than their taunts had ever been, animalistic promises of what they could do to me if they caught me.

I pushed forward as best as I could, running into an opening in the forest, the wind in my face as I swatted through the large field of high grass, where the sunlight shone through harshly.

They knew I couldn't outrun any of them, not even skinny Douglas, the weakest one.

Not in their human forms and much less in their wolf forms. They were better than me in every way- faster, stronger, good-looking- d yet they found the utmost pleasure in scaring me to death.

They loved the chase and I was always going to be prey in this world.

Keffer, they called me.

Wolfless.

Tears blinded me further and I tripped, falling and scraping my knee on the hard ground, but that was the least of my worries.

My eyes quickly darted around me, my heart pounding, fingers shaking as I heard the sound of their growls closer than ever before.

I crawled backward on the ground, head darting in every direction I could hear a growl. They were circling me now, I noted, catching glimpses of the musky brown fur of their wolves as they stalked the middle, sealing every route of escape until they finally came into full view, creeping noiselessly through the grass, growling and barring their sharp white teeth at me.

Trying to make myself as small as possible, I hugged my bruised knees, hands shaking as my eyes trailed the wolves.

They were only omega wolves, but still much bigger than I could ever be.

My eyes darted around the five wolves that encircled me, stopping as the sixth one emerged through the middle. He was bigger than the others and behind moved another wolf.

From his mere size of him, as he was bigger than some full-grown omega wolves in the pack, He could only be one wolf.

Gabriel, the Alpha's son. And behind him was the Gamma's son, Lawrence.

I gulped slowly, shaking my head, pleading softly whilst moving slightly backward as the large Alpha wolf stalked forward until he was standing over me, his large paws on either side of me.

My back lay flat on the ground as I stared wide-eyed into the beady eyes of the Gabes wolf, filled with hate and distaste I saw mirrored in almost every pack member of Night Moon Pack whenever they looked at me.

I was a walking curse.

The seed of bad luck. The moon goddess forsook. A keffer. I was wanted by no one. I was no one.

That was what the wolf hovering over me was trying to say as he growled deeper, his sharp fangs grazing my face, hot stenchy breath fanning my skin as my fingernails dug deep into the soil, eyes shut tightly closed in fear, awaiting the sting of the bite-

Then I heard it.

A howl so deadly deep it rattled my very bones.

A growl so powerful that it seemed to shake the earth itself. The sounds of birds launching from the trees in flight, followed by the wolves' whimpering as they suddenly scampered away, the feeling of the large alpha wolf hovering over me vanishing in an instant.

My heart stopped within me, as silence followed.

I was too scared to see what it was, what could have made that sound.

A soft wind grazed my skin as I found the courage to slowly open my eyes, one at a time, coming face to face with nothingness, nothing but the open field.

My eyebrows arched, quickly sat up and drew my knees to my chest as I looked around the grassy field, only now-

-now there wasn't any grass.

Everything was ashes.

Burnt to ash.

Something grazed my skin, and I looked up, watching as bits of ash fell from the now grey, darkened sky.

I reached out a shaky hand into the open, a piece of ash falling into my open palm, a sudden flashback of buried memories melting into my mind.

A figure of a blurry woman tugging a child along as they run through tall trees. The fire crackled around the flame-lit forest, howls, and screams echoing behind them.

I shook my head, tears now spilling freely from my cheeks, hugging my knees tightly against me, shutting my eyes as I tried to stop the flashbacks.

"No, no, no," I whimpered, shaking my head until everything suddenly stopped, and silence returned.

I forced myself to be still, sniffing as I tried to calm my heart. Feeling a hand suddenly rest on my shoulder, my whole body stiffened. But I was way too scared to open my eyes until a gentle voice whispered right above my ears.

"Go my little flower," it breathed softly as if it was out of breath.

"Go find your Alpha."

I opened my eyes, staring straight ahead into nothingness as the words echoed through my mind. I stared down at my bruised knees as if in a trance, watching as the bruises on my knees healed in a matter of seconds, the ashed fields around me growing flowers again as the sun showed through.

I wiped my tears, getting up to my wobbly feet, sniffing again as I stood, blinking to get a clear vision back, eyebrows arching when I noticed the most peculiar thing.

The whole field I was in had the bright harsh sunlight of the afternoon, but as I looked back into the forest I had come from, it had been overtaken by the darkest blackest night.

It was as if I was standing in the place where Night and Day met for the first time.

From the depths of that Night, I saw a huge shadow move, larger than I had ever seen, two bright red eyes glowing from midnight.

The growl I had heard before sounded, shaking the earth once again as it barred the sharpest fangs I had ever seen-

I sat up in bed with a gasp, my heart thudding within me, eyes wide as I came face to face with Vale, her bright shy blue eyes and thin blond hair bounced lightly against her shoulders as she shook me awake, her face only illuminated by the small candle beside my bed stand.

"Nightmare?" She whispered lowly, moving back slightly.

I stared blankly for a minute, trying to recollect my thoughts. My eyes traveled around my surroundings, recognizing my small room with a relieved sigh, eyes trailing back to her,

"A-as always," I whispered back, pulling my sleeve over my exposed arm, covering the numerous bite scars on them.

Vale glanced at the action for a moment, her eyes catching mine again, before falling to her lap, silence looming between us.

It was the same dream I had been having for years now. The bullying, the ashed field, the voice in the forest, and the creature that brought the night- it was a mixture of both memories and nightmares I figured because some parts felt like I had lived them before and whilst others were just replays of what had already been done.

I didn't want to dwell on it too much, at least not now. I was bullied every day, and I was used to it, and so was Vale.

I was a keffer, and she was a rogue's daughter.

Neither one of us were wanted in our pack.

True, I got the brunt of the bullying and the insults and the hate, the stones, the chases through the forest, the bites- it was because I was worse than a rogue, worse than a servant.

At least rogues had wolves, their only crime being traitors but I was cursed, cursed to be wolf less and therefore mate less. Denied the gifts of the moon goddess and shunned by her.

I pushed those thoughts away. All that didn't matter now. What mattered was the future. The future of Vale and I.

"I'm fine, Vale, I promise," I grinned softly pushing the light sheets off me.

I was as quiet as a mouse as I trod across the small room grabbing a woolly coat and throwing it on before tiptoeing back to my bedside, where I pulled out a packed bag from under it quietly, placing it on the bed.

I glanced up at a nervous-looking Vale as I studied her figure. She too had a packed bag under her arm, her body covered well enough to be shielded from the cold of midnight outside.

"Are you ready?" I whispered.

She paused, gulping but nodded quickly, though I noticed the shake in her hand as she pulled her bag tighter.

"Vale-" I whispered, my tone harsher than I intended, noticing her unfocused gaze.

"P-perhaps we should stay," she suddenly blurted, "j-just f-for a day or two," she stuttered out, hesitantly.

I moved to her, placing a hand on her shoulder.

"Look at me Vale," I prodded, her scared gaze holding mine.

"If we stay, bad things will happen to us. Do you want to slave to some other territory?" I asked slowly.

She shook her head, gaze shifting to the ground.

"That's what's going to happen tomorrow. We're going to be sold, Vale- sold like pigs. Alpha's only been waiting till I turn eighteen like you- that was his only promise to AMA. That he would take us both simultaneously," I reminded.

"We can't. Stay. Here." I gritted, taking a rolled brown paper out of my sleeve.

I looked back up at her. "This map will get us to the harbor, then we can get on a ship and finally be free across the sea-" I continued, "I understand it's risky but trust me, it will be much worse if we stay- Do you understand Vale?"

She pursed her lips for a moment, her eyes searching the urgency in mine, finally nodding, as she took a sharp breath in, cooling her nerves.

I took out my shaky breath, trying to steady my hands as I squeezed her shoulder reassuringly.

If we got caught trying to escape it would be worse for us but staying was simply not an option.

I smiled softly, nodding toward her.

"Come on, it's time to go," I breathed, blowing out the candle.

In the darkness we moved, Vale, trailing like a shadow behind me, down the hallway. We tip-toed even slower past the familiar door right outside our room before heading toward the front door-

I glanced behind me, stopping when I noticed Vale had frozen before the wooden door looking at it skeptically.

"Vale!" I whispered lowly.

She looked back at me, her eyes sad, permission in them. I knew what she asking, why she was sad.

We weren't saying goodbye to AMA. The one woman in this godforsaken pack that showed us kindness and took us under her wing, called us her family, her daughters- probably the only woman in the whole cursed continent of Valcane whoever would.

"W-We need to go," I whispered.

She looked at the door one more time, her fingers lightly grazing over the wood before moving silently after me, finally walking toward the front door.

I was about to open the door when Vale's hand clamped on my shoulder causing me to turn, eyebrows arched.

She put a finger to her lips, pointing towards a window where a spot of light vanished in the darkness of midnight outside, only lighting up a second later.

I moved to the window quickly, catching sight of horses. My heart beat loudly as I moved rapidly toward Vale, grabbing her bag and throwing it behind the door-

"S-shade?" Vale whispered as I took a shaky step back from the door, pulling her with me not a second later as the door suddenly swung open, banging against the side by sheer force.

Both of us moved backward as Gabriel walked in, behind him, the light of horses and Lawrence, his gamma, accompanied by a few other pack warriors.

He didn't seem surprised to see both of us standing before him, despite randomly barging in.

Gabriel Sindor was soon to be Alpha, his eighteenth birthday only a week behind mine, where he was to finally ascend as Alpha of the Night Moon pack, and one of the 13 Alphas under the Night Wolf territory.

With brown eyes and blonde hair, he if anything should have looked mismatched and yet the combination did wonders for him.

Standing at an Alluring height, with broad shoulders and a face that had all the unmated females praying to claim him on his eighteenth birthday, it was a shame his heart did not match his beauty.

"Shade Shadows," he stated eyes staying on me, a smile that made my blood crawl curving his face. Vale moved instinctively behind me.

"Gabriel-"

"ALPHA Gabriel!" Lawrence corrected, trying to sound intimidating I assumed. He was the complete opposite of Gabriel. Green eyes, and brown hair, and though he was decent looking could not be matched to Gabriel despite his unique features.

He always tried too much.

Maybe it was because he was to become Beta the next week after Gabriel ascended as Alpha.

He had to live up to that title besides being the Gamma's son.

Simply put, the Night-moon pack had no current Beta. Beta Samuel died a long time ago leaving his widow without a pup or heir to carry his name.

Despite all my misfortune, I found it humorous how I still felt pity for Lawrence. It was a lot to bear especially being a beta to Gabriel.

"He isn't an Alpha yet," I gritted out, surprising myself.

"How dare you speak to your Alpha like that, Keffer! -"

"Where were you going?" Gabriel cut, holding up a hand to stop Lawrence's babble.

My gaze locked back to him, heart beating wildly within me, Vale reaching for my hand, holding it tightly as she stood behind me.

"W-what do you mean?" I stuttered, my voice shallow.

"It's the middle of the night- and you're out here-" he paused closing the door behind him, my heart dropping as he moved to the bags.

"You really thought I wouldn't hear this?" He said grabbing a bag and dropping it to the floor.

The sound.

Of course, his Alpha ears would have picked it up.

"You sure can't be stupid enough to plan to escape your fate?" He mocked though his tone was calm with the same creepy smile on his face as my throat run dry. His brown eyes held the depth of hate he never failed to unleash.

He moved closer, eyes trailing from my face to Vales.

"You wish to be a Rogues daughter and a traitor? Isn't the world cruel enough for you?" He huffed, before looking back at me, he moved closer pulling my chin up to meet his eyes directly,

"And you- a keffer?" He grinned.

I held my position. "Perhaps it's as low as it gets-"

"The clothes are mine." A voice stated.

We all turned to look behind us.

There stood AMA. Grey eyes, healthy Raven hair, and a face still youthful despite her age.

"Austria-" Gabriel began

"You may call me Austria when you're Alpha, Gabriel," she paused, "For then I will no longer be the beta's widow."

Her eyes trailed to Lawrence's who looked to the floor.

Gabriel's jaw hardened, hand dropping from my chin as he moved to AMA.

"AMA- " he stated, eyes searching her steady ones.

I often admired AMA's courage. She was a pack warrior till she retired a few years back, hence she knew no fear, despite looking into the eyes of the future Alpha.

"What are you doing in my house?" She growled lowly, her wolf's amber eyes flashing for a second.

Gabriel's eyes darkened, his jaw clenched but softened after a time, stepping back.

"We're simply here to collect-"

My heart beat loudly. Collect.

Collect us.

"The day has barely begun," Austria gritted.

"But it HAS begun, has it not?" Gabriel grinned. "Besides, Alpha Darren was concerned there would be...attempts to escape so he permitted us to collect now," he stated.

"Additionally- an urgent letter came from the Night Wolf court-"

My fingers froze at this, unable to breathe.

No. No.

Please- not there. Anywhere- but NOT there.

"A demand for all slaves no matter the rank- those almost and already eighteen summers before the crack of the second Dawn-" he paused, eyes staying on Vale and me.

I couldn't breathe and I could feel Vale's fingers drain cold in mine.

"T-The N-night Wolf?" AMA stuttered.

She never stuttered.

"Take them," Gabriel commanded with a low growl, the pack warriors behind him moving on command as they walked into the house, grabbing Vale and me.

AMA immediately moved forward.

"You cannot take them!" She yelled. "Leave my daughters alone!"

"They are not your daughters. They are a rogue and a keffer," Gabriel growled back, tone deadly.

"The only reason my father ever allowed them in our pack is because of his respect and love for his Beta, Samuel. He could never deny you anything no matter the disgrace to the pack, but now even this is out of his hands-" he drawled out maniacally as we were pushed into the metal cages.

He was not wrong.

Even Alpha Darren could not go against the Night Wolf's orders.

Gabriel moved forward as AMA rushed to our silver cages, holding the metal bars, reaching out for our hands desperately just before the carriage prison prepared to move.

"I'm sorry AMA, I'm so sorry," I cried, tears gushing down my face. Vale cried along beside me.

Her face was filled with sadness, and her grip tightened around us urgently clasping both our hands, "This is no time for tears my dears. I-I need you to listen."

I nodded sniffing as she spoke, trying to calm my nerves.

"I will find you both, I will-" she emphasized, her hands gripping ours tightly, her eyes traveling to me-

"Till then, I need you to be a nobody-" she stated gravely, a hidden meaning in her eyes.

"I already am-" I countered softly.

Her eyes fogged for a minute at my response, before staring down at our connected hand, "just till I find, for your protection." She begged.

Finding confirmation in my eyes, her own, clouded with tears as the carriage yanked alive our grasps on each other slipping.

The single lantern that hung above us swayed back and forth as we stared back at AMA and the place, we used to call home in despair, till her figure was swallowed by the darkness.

Vale held on to me as we stared blankly down the darkened road. It was then I realized something.

I was not only a nobody-

I was a slave.

•~•Please leave a comment! I would like your thoughts on the chapter! Don't forget to Vote!•~•

[2.1] THE NIGHT COURT

|•|•"Now little ones, go to sleep. For the Night Wolf brings the Shadows, and he has fangs that breathe death."•|•|•

I KNEW I was cursed long before I ever knew I was a Keffer. AMA said she found me buried in a pile of ash in the forest that bordered the Fire Wolf Territory as she and her pack warriors watched the borders.

I was hiding was all that I remembered.

Six and scared to death, fire and ash falling from the sky in that half-burnt forest, only the sounds of horses and screams echoing in my mind.

Staring down at my skin I ignored the yank of the carriage beneath us on the harsh gravel road, our backs leaning against the silver bars of the cage.

Vale had fallen asleep at the crack of Dawn after crying a while, her head slumped against my shoulder, but her arm remained wrapped around me on instinct.

There was a huge contrast in our skin tones. Another curse of mine. I was the only one that was different in my pack, they had never seen anyone quite like me. Neither had I, though I was sure my parents must have been.

Whilst Vale's skin was milky, only blotched by the dirt of the cage, mine remained as dark as night, the dirt blending into the tone.

Shade they named me. Because I was the absence of light.

Vale's hair was long and light, whilst mine was short, dark, thick, and stubborn, unable to flow down to my shoulders.

I pursed my lips, looking out of the cage. The sun was high up ahead, soon would be scorching. I grabbed a rag in the cage throwing it over Vale. Her pale skin would surely fry as I noticed it did in direct sunlight.

Mine was already too dark to fry.

I swallowed softly, I needed to wet my throat, dry from the lack of water. My head leaned against the bars closing my eyes. We had a full day's journey to get to Night Wolfs Court, but sleep would not come.

The Night Wolf.

Of all Courts we could have been taken to, sold or traded, that of the devil himself? My chest tightened as I glanced down at Vale.

Of course.

I was cursed.

It was the reason I had no family, why I was a Keffer and why I was headed to the home of the most feared Arc-Alpha of the 4 territories.

There was only one comfort I had. As a Keffer, I would probably not be allowed to even stand in the presence of his royal blood. That is if they didn't kill me before that.

Either way, I would never have to see that monster, but Vale-

My eyes opened looking down at her, tears glazing my eyes. Slaves died every day in that court, all victims.

The Night Wolf was known to be unforgiving, heart as dark as his Arc-Wolf. It is the only reason why his territory was the largest among the 4 Arc- Alpha, and why he was feared the most despite the many mysteries turned into myths about him.

Perhaps I should appreciate the safety it brought being a pack under his rule, but that too evidently, came with a price.

"Do you think we will survive a night there?" Vale asked, indicating she had long been awake.

I glanced down at her with a soft sigh.

"AMA said the Night Court is a big place. They'll probably have hundreds of slaves, we will never even see the Royal," I encouraged.

She didn't reply right away, sitting up in the cage, her eyes puffed up from crying, but her tone was dead.

"I was scared, but I'm not anymore," Vale stated, leaning against the cage as it rattled roughly once more, her head turned my way, pale blue eyes catching mine.

"But I welcome death Shade, with open arms. It is not like this life has anything to offer. For even if we died, it wouldn't matter. We will never see AMA again, we will be slaves for the rest of our lives, bound to the walls of the Night Wolf's Court," her voice skipped, tears clouding her eyes again.

"We have no saviors to prey or hope for. You have no mate and mine..." she trailed off, laughing sadly, her tone dripping in spite, "would never want a traitor's daughter and a slave."

My hand clamped over her arm, "we will surely escape, Vale. We will make it over the sea, so we can live normal lives with the humans- " I encouraged.

She scoffed at this, pulling her arm away, "that's a fairy tale Shade, and even they died out centuries ago. Look at where we are."

Her tone was bitter, as her eyes trailed around the trees that lined the bumpy road.

"Maybe we had a shot at home but now? The sea is 8 packs away from the Night Court! - that's 8 territories to cross barefoot- with a rogue's scent-" she added pointing to herself, "and even if we magically escaped, what makes you think the humans won't treat us any differently?"

"Because I'm basically human," I huffed, "and AMA knows things. She said humans have no way of knowing what we are. They can't smell you or know what you are unless you shift. They don't have mates; they fall in love freely."

I let out a shallow breath, "we could have good lives there. We could marry, have pups of our own..." I trailed off.

Her wet eyes stared back at me, dead of hope, "I wish I had your dreams Shade, but when I close my eyes, all I see is darkness."

"There are rogues that have escaped and lived among them, freely-" I prodded on, "some had to travel farther than we have to."

I sighed, "Vale you don't need to have dreams. I can dream for the both of us."

Leaning back against the metal bars, I watched the trees, "I want to live, Vale. There is too much of this world to see. All we need to do is find a way to escape- "

"Even if we could... live." she paused, glancing at me, "how on earth are we going to escape the Night Wolf's court?" She huffed.

"We're going to try-"

"And die trying probably-"

Our eyes met, and we both burst out into laughter for a moment, tears filling our eyes, as we grinned.

I sighed taking a deep breath, glancing back at her, "We are nobodies Vale, no one is going to miss us. Let death come for us, we have nothing to lose."

I felt her eyes linger on me for a moment before looking away.

Letting out a shallow breath, I rolled my head to the side as I studied her features, "but" I began, "we do have everything to gain if we succeed."

Her eyes caught mine at this, a low glow in her dead eyes- and I smiled.

———

"Eyes low, blend, always obey, ask questions... but not too many, gain trust, show loyalty... That's all, right?" Vale whispered counting her fingers as she listed them.

I nodded, "that is all."

She sighed, tucking a strand of her thin hair behind her ear before glancing back at me, "are you sure you'll be fine without me? I can't leave you all alone Shade."

I smiled at this, "You'll have to while they're watching. I'm a keffer Vale, most of the other slaves there will be rogues and servants disposed of by their Alpha, maybe some Omegas who were rejected. But even the lowest classes have their own hierarchy. If you stay near me, they'll shun you too, and you need to be close to them if we should ever find an escape from that place."

She nodded at this, as we approached the glowing light of Yulis, the oldest City in Valcane and the Capital, glowing in the Night.

The lantern swung above us, lighting our way through the dark city street, before turning into a backway alley, coming to a halt near a large black door. Vale and I stayed close together as the doors to our cage swung open, an old lady dressed in all black standing beside our handler, Geoffrey, the man who had been driving the carriage.

"This is what you bring for the Royal?" The old woman hissed, "A rogue and a.." she sniffed the air, her face turning in disgust, her black eyes turning grey as her wolf growled.

"A keffer? You dare bring a breathing curse to the Night Court?!" she spat throwing the angriest look at the man.

"Just following orders," Geoffrey merely stated, shrugging as he tucked his hands in his pants, "on a request sealed by the Night Court. Their kind is demanded by the crack of Dawn."

I never liked Geoffrey. He was the man that Alpha Darren sent to transport slaves. Tall, skinny, and creepy was all that was needed to sun him up, with hair that fell to his shoulders in thin strands, slightly covering his brown eyes.

The old woman scoffed at this, turning towards us with the ugliest grin.

"Then they must be the entertainment," she replied. "After the ceremony, there's always a hunt."

My blood ran cold at this. A hunt? What ceremony?

"Get up slaves," she growled.

We moved out of the cage, our handler slapping chains on our wrists and feet. Vale hissed at the impact of the chain on her tender wrist whilst Geoffrey only scoffed, "better get used to it."

My jaw clenched, eyes darting to the chains around my wrists.

Silver, I noted. Wolf's poison. It did not affect a wolf-less wolf.

I glanced at the woman as she grinned grimly.

"Forward slaves," she grunted pushing us in front.

We walked through the doors, the stench the first to reach me, before the hundreds of whispering voices that sat in the room, chained to the floor.

"Stand here," the woman continued before moving to the front of the room, grabbing a candle from a boy.

She soon separated all the slaves into 4 notable groups, placing our group in a second carriage.

"Off to Night Court," she gritted out to the driver of our new cage, moving backward to face us, an ugly smile on her face.

"Savor the sun slaves, for the Night wolf, brings the shadows-" she cawed creepily, her grey eyes glowing in the moonlight as the carriage began our journey to the Night Court.

"And his fangs breathe death," a girl whispered, clasping her hands in prayer, staring aimlessly into the darkness.

I shivered at this, glancing at Vale who seemed scared too. Silently watching the city of Yulis pass us by, we delved further into the midnight. We would be at the Night Court at the crack of Dawn.

———-

I woke up to the jab of the carriage as it hit a bump, grunting as my back banged against the silver steel of the cage. Vale still slept soundly near me, but I noticed the other girls had huddled away from us.

My eyes met that of the darkened irises of a girl watching me from the farthest corner, her brown hair draped over her face, a cut on her lower lip.

"What are you looking at Keffer?" She snarled.

I pursed my lips looking away, staring out in the fading darkness- There, I saw it, as we moved down the stoned pathway.

Night Court.

The largest thing I had ever seen. The large castle-like building towered around us as dark as night in the fading hours. It had numerous towers and the breadth of it spanned farther than I could ever imagine.

So large, I was sure it already held hundreds if not thousands of slaves and servants alike. I shook Vale awake, pointing at the sight.

She seemed confused for a moment before her eyes widened, drinking it in. The large heavy gates, painted midnight black were already swung open, carriages of slaves pouring in from all directions.

For the new influx of slaves, one could only agree there was going to be some sort of ceremony or event taking place as the old lady handler had said.

The carriage moved in further and I admired the elegant court grounds, even though the grass was brown and airy, a light mist hanging in the air-

They pushed us out of our cages, making us move in a line, filing into the Night Court, where we all knelt on the courtyard stone, hundreds of us.

I watched as the guards walked among us, some booting slaves to the ground, grinning and mocking but my eyes focused on the front, watching a well-worn lady take center stage, looking through the row of slaves whilst saying something to a guard perched at her side.

After a few moments. She addressed us.

"Midnight pack slaves," she began as she walked through the front slaves.

She stopped before a young male slave. "Spare this one, Artemis and the lot need an extra help in the barn," she stated, moving through the line again as the guards brought the boy to his feet, taking him out.

She stopped once again, at a female slave. "Go to the front," she casually stated.

She kept this behavior, selecting slaves until she reached our pack, "Night moon pack," she paused her eyes on both of us, a sparkle in them when they met mine-

"A keffer-"

I swallowed staring down at the stone.

I was not going to be chosen or spared. Of course, my journey would lead me to the depths of despair, only the worst fate awaited me. My end.

I pursed my lips feeling all eyes on me.

"Your skin..." she trailed off, "were you burnt as a child?"

I shook my head gritting my teeth, "I was born this way-"

"Even the moon's light couldn't shine on this one, only her shadow," the guard beside her chuckled, grabbing my arm roughly, jutting forward as tears filled my eyes.

Vale gasped beside me, a panic set in her eyes.

"Please! Mercy!" I pleaded as I was dragged along, another guard grabbing my side, as my wide gaze shifted to the woman.

"She will do well in the hunt," the guard growled, accompanied by the laughter of the other guards, but it was his hand wrapping firmly around my waist that scared me more than that ever could, his fingers hard against my hips.

My tears fell down my cheeks, begging.

I couldn't go out like this. Not like this.

"Wait-" the woman began, green eyes narrowing on me.

"The chef needs a help," she paused as if contemplating her statement, "I believe she'll blend right in with the ash."

The guards paused at this as I pushed out of their arms, falling to my knees.

"You plan on keeping a keffer in the Night Court?" He hissed, "Do you not value your own life, Madam?"

She paused, eyes narrowing on the guard.

"I know you fear for my Life Zura," she smirked, though it did not reach her eyes, her tone dripping in authority.

"Do not worry my dear guard, I have years till I depart from this world, " she paused before looking down at me, then at Vale.

"Both of you, to the front."

I tumbled forward supported by Vale, kneeling with the other selected slaves in the front. After a few more selections, the rest of the slaves filed out. Where too? I dreaded knowing. They were too many to be kept that I knew.

The guard left us alone with the strange yet familiar-looking woman. She had these familiar eyes I couldn't quite pinpoint.

"There are only three rules as you serve in the Night Court," she began retaining her polished stance.

"Do as you are told, serve the masters, and listen to Catherine," she paused, a shimmer in her eye. "I am Catherine, but you will refer to me as Madam. I keep the Night Court slaves in the main Quarters in order, and run most of the household, obey me and live, disobey and ... fade." She finished.

"Understand?"

"Yes Madam," the slaves echoed, and I swallowed.

— ———

We were shown to our quarters where we changed, the soot cleaned from our bodies.

Standing in a line Madam inspected us, pausing at me.

"Keffer," she commanded, "You must know that you cannot show your face or your scent anywhere but in here and the Kitchen," she stated.

"Blend with the coal, that is the only way you'll survive."

I nodded at this as she pointed to the door leading outside.

"Kitchens that way."

I nodded bowing before walking toward it.

"Tell My dearest Lucy, I sent you," she grinned after me.

Bowing again, I moved in the direction of the kitchen, still counting my blessing for being alive. I walked into the kitchen, bigger than anything I had ever seen, but it had to be, for everything in Night Court was huge.

It was rather busy as people cooked and moved with platters of food out the other door, but the moment I stepped in, everything stopped.

Wolffish eyes trained on me, and my breathing lagged.

"What in hell's name is that smell in my kitchen?!" Someone growled.

A hulk of a chubby man moved in, a small apron around his waist.

My eyebrows arched at this. Was he even able to shift?

He looked down at me as he sniffed the air.

"Keffer!" He growled, "what are you doing here?!"

"L-Lucy?" I echoed, pausing as I gulped slowly, feeling dumb.

This was a man, not a woman named Lucy.

"Luciferous!" he growled back- eyes growing darker.

I gulped at this.

"I-I was sent by Madam Catherine, I'm your new help-" I stated, bowing low.

He paused at this, as whispers echoed in the kitchen.

"Shut up!" He growled causing the kitchen to quiet.

"A keffer? She sends me a keffer? Am I supposed to kill you then?" He asked.

I bit my tongue at this, my heart pounding.

"She's the help, Lucy," Madam's voice gritted out, walking out from behind me. "You asked, here she is. She is for the furnace. She'll blend right into the ash don't you think?"

"But she's a keffer..." he growled out.

"You can keep her, or leave her to wander... it's your funeral," Madam stated casually.

Lucy's eyes darkened, growling at her before they snapped at me.

"You-" he barked, fiery eyes raining down on me, "furnace now!"

I nodded quickly rushing in the direction of the furnace, ignoring the eyes of the others on me. Here, I found a large man leaning against the wall. He stood straighter, walking to me-

"Scoop, throw... " he grumbled, throwing me the shovel.

I nodded, my finger shaking, getting right to work. My shovel dug into the heap of coal, throwing it into the large burning furnace.

It was better death.

It was surely better than death.

•~•Please leave a comment! I would like your thoughts on the chapter! Don't forget to Vote!•~•

[3.1] ARC WOLVES

● |•|•"Fear the Night Court, my child, for the sun, never shines too long."•|•|•

My back hurt as I lay on the weed mat, the cold biting at my exposed body as I stared up mindlessly into the darkness of the stoned roof above me in the slave quarters.

Pushed tears stung the back of my eyes, taking a calming breath out.

My arms were sore as I silently turned to my side, face twisting in pain, eyes meeting that of Vale. She smiled over at me softly, and I returned it despite the space between us.

She slept huddled with the others on a worn-out yet more comfortable mat, whilst I practically slept on the hard ground.

The other slaves had huddled together for warmth, but of course, they left me out, only talking amongst themselves and throwing me disgusted looks before turning off to bed.

I didn't blame them though. And it didn't matter as long as Vale was safe.

I watched her eyes lids close finally falling asleep. It was after I listened to the sounds of her low breaths that I finally succumbed to my sleep, my last thought- AMA.

She had been alone when the Beta died and now that we were gone, I hoped she was all right without us.

When I dreamed, I repeated my nightmares.

The monster in the shadows with eyes of red, the soft voice that commanded me to find my Alpha, and finally the fields of ash healing back to life in the place where day and night meet.

————

Slaves are supposed to wake up bright and early, just as the sun creams the sky, still overpowered by the night- but that was not the case in the Night Court.

"Heavens above!" Someone gasped, her tone shaky.

"I-it is as they say," Eve stated, as the candles flickered in the dark.

I turned slightly, recognizing the girl. She was the same one who had been with us in the cage, her hands in prayer.

She had thin brown hair and a heart-shaped face. Certainly, tiny compared to the rest of us, and her voice was soft, as soft as her hazel eyes.

"What now Eve?" Haven grunted, her dark eyes settling on the shy girl who stood frozen, frail body rattling softly in the cold of the morning.

Haven was Eve's opposite.

She too had been in the same cage as us. Her cut lip had healed significantly in the last three days, to a scar, however, she still held bitterness in her eyes I had never seen.

I overheard the other slaves talking in hushed tones yesterday, she had come from Greenwood Pack, one of the bigger packs in the Night Wolf territory.

I heard rogues there were treated differently, harsher than what Vale and I had experienced in our small pack. The things I heard were done made me shiver. For if they could be that merciless to a Rogues daughter, what more a Keffer?

Eve pointed out the window with a shaky hand and my eyes trailed to it.

"The never-ending night..." she trailed off.

"That's because the sun isn't out yet. You seriously can't be that stupid," Haven snapped rolling her eyes as she neatly wrapped her hair up in a bun.

My eyebrows arched at this, walking towards the window and staring out into the night, my heart beating strangely at the sight, turning round to face the other slaves in the quarter.

"She's right," I stated. "It's nearly dawn and it's as dark as if it were midnight."

Vale's eyes rose to meet mine in confusion, the other slaves following suit.

"Are you dumb and a Keffer?" Haven growled, her eyes flashing angrily momentarily showing her wolf. "We were probably woken earlier than usual-"

"N-No.." Vale stuttered, she paused when everyone's eyes glued to her.

"It is the same time as yesterday-"

Haven's fiery gaze launched on her but before she could say anything, a voice interrupted-

"The sun will not rise today. This is your first Dark Day, but I assure you, it will not be your last," A uniformed voice explained.

Madam causally walked in our midst as we immediately separated into 2 straight lines.

"The Night Wolf controls the day and the night. When he wills it, he forbids the sun to shine. On days like these slaves, tread carefully. Do not make mistakes as the night has many shadows..." she trailed off at this and I couldn't help but think there was a hidden meaning.

"And when it Storms and flashes of light brighten the dark, do not do more than breathe. For his fury is as harsh as thunder," she paused, straightening her shoulders, "And as deadly as lightning."

Silence loomed among us, my throat running dry as I studied Madam's cool yet somehow creepy tone.

"Off to your stations my dears. Your masters await." She suddenly turned, walking in the direction she had come.

—————-

Scoop throw, scoop throw.

My arms grew heavy after a few throws, the heat blazing in my face, roaring back to life. I dropped back on the stool, wiping the layer of slick sweat off my forehead.

I stared down at my blistered hands, unable to close my fingers.

A week. It had been a week of sleeping on the hard floor, eating scraps, covered in soot to my chin, spots of filth on my face, insults, kicks to my back, and eating the leftover scraps from the servants-

I was so hungry all the time.

"Tired already keffer?"

My gaze traveled from my blistered hands, tucking them away quickly, settling my gaze on the heat of the fire, and pursed my lips.

As a slave, I couldn't say anything to Barnabas, the man whose job I had relieved on my whim. I wasn't Shade anymore in this place. They didn't call you by name- they called you by your status.

Your Highness, My Lord, Madam, Master, servant, slave... and Keffer.

I watched as the flames tossed about, a sudden urge to throw myself into the heat. The longer I stared the more inviting it looked, a dark depressing thought echoing at the back of my mind.

Vale was right, there was no need to fear death- death was better than a life stuck in these walls.

I would be sitting on this stool for the rest of my life if Vale and I didn't come up with a valid plan to escape. And by the looks of it, there was no plan. I had only been to three places in this Court. The kitchen, the slave quarters, and the bathhouse all of which were guarded each night.

"A week and you're already miserable," Barnabas chuckled, hearing him sway into a seat, with a hard sigh.

"Then again, you must have already been miserable. A Keffers life can't be that glamorous."

My jaw clenched but I remained quiet staring into the flames. I had to be quiet and obedient.

That was my place.

"He must be gloomy," Barnabas suddenly stated, causing my eyes to snap to him, watching as he took a swing of the ale he held, his eyes settling on the only window in the furnace room, high above us.

My gaze traveled toward it, spotting the blackest night only lit by lanterns in the night court glowing lowly in the howling wind.

This was the fourth day and the sun hadn't risen. I missed the sun because, at night, one could really tell what time it was, and how long the day had taken. Minutes felt like hours and I felt like I was trapped in hell, only the flames were burning brightly in the furnace before me.

My eyes found the fire again, watching the heat dance.

"What does the bastard have to be gloomy about? He is a fucking King. All he does is wake up, sit, eat and shit."

I couldn't help but agree with the drunk, despite my better judgment, as the man usually said things like this when he was wasted.

From my week with him, I could describe Barnabas as a man with nothing to lose. He was not a slave but a servant which meant he had some kind of freedom and got paid coin- no matter how little.

But that was just about where his luck ended.

From the rumors I heard, he had lost his mate to the hunt, years ago- since then, he had become a miserable bastard. Not that I blamed him.

As much as I had once wished for a mate of my own, I was quite aware of what happened when one lost the other half.

AMA cried herself to sleep every night. However, whilst she found some little comfort in Vale and I, save a few drops of tears each night, Barnabas had found his way to cope with his loss at the bottom of an ale bottle.

He talked whenever he liked, he cursed, and by Selene, he was certainly not kind in his words. But somehow, I noticed drunk was the better time to talk to him.

Maybe this was my chance, my chance to ask questions. Vale was doing her part, growing closer to the other slaves.

I had to do my part.

I had to get as much information from drunk Barnabas as I could from this place. But I had to be careful-

"How do you know?" I whispered lowly, turning to him.

His eyes snapped to me, and my heart stopped, seemingly studying me. It was the first time I had directly talked to him. I couldn't back out now.

"How do you know he's sad?"

His eyes hardened, and for a moment, I regretted saying a thing to him. However, after a lingering second, he pointed a rough finger at the window.

"He takes away the sun when he's angry so we can be as miserable as him."

His eyes turned to the fire chuckling, "As if our lives aren't miserable already, aye Keffer? Might as well just put us out of our misery."

"I-is that all he does?" I asked, gaining a bit of confidence, his eyes snapped back to me, and I sucked in a breath.

"I-I heard each Arc Alpha has a gift and their wolves are... different-" I trailed off. "Different than ordinary Alphas."

"No shit," Barnabas growled.

"I've been here for 12 years," he continued, eyes trailing to me as he took another swing of ale, "I was here on the last Tribunal, 5 years ago. All 3 Arc Alphas came back home, to the Night Court." he trailed off.

"I saw 3 Arc wolves, that night... one that was shaped like fire..."

"The Fire Wolf," I blurted.

He glanced at me nodding. "Another wolf who was bathed in dazzling light, so bright I simply could not tell the difference between it and the sun. And the last Arc froze everything his claws touched." he chuckled for a bit, "I would like to have a beer with him in summer."

He described the 3 other Arc Wolves exactly as I used to hear from AMA and the other kids in the Night moon pack. The Fire Wolf, The Light wolf, and the Ice Wolf.

The three other Arc Alphas of the 4 territories in Valcane.

"Y-You didn't see the Night Wolf?" I asked, my eyes trailing his face as he took another swing of ale.

He shook his head.

"I count it a blessing every day. No one sees the Night Wolf and returns whole..." he grunted his rough fingers pounding against the side of his head.

"He does something to your mind girl; he plays with shadows..." he huffed looking down at his open palm.

"The night wolf doesn't just control the night, but even the monsters that hide beneath the shadows," he glanced down at me, seemingly returning to normal.

"Dig Keffer," he growled getting to his feet. "Your fire burns low."

I nodded, watching as he walked toward the door.

"Ought to get me another ale," he huffed, mumbling something incoherent under his breath.

I pursed my lips at this. grabbing the shovel, taking in some coal, and shoveling it into the dying flame as I contemplated our conversation.

I counted it a blessing I hadn't seen him yet too.

I was sure the Night Wolf would kill me if he ever knew a Keffer was in his court. I took out a short breath relaxing my beating heart. It didn't matter. there was no way I would ever see the Night Wolf.

If Barnabas had been here for 12 years without ever seeing him, it was more than likely I was safe here. The rest of the day was long and harsh and the sun remained hidden in the veil of night.

•|•|•Enjoying the story? Let me know by voting and leaving a comment! Thank you!•|•|•

[4.1] THE EYES IN THE SHADOWS

● |•|•"Watch the Shadows, pup, for there are monsters hidden beneath
."•|•|•

The darkness echoed all around me as I pumped hard on the lever, my breathing short and airy until water is poured into the bucket on the other end.

I kept pumping until the light of the lanterns that some of the other slaves held, revealed that the bucket was finally full. I let out a quiet breath, my eyes reaching that of Havens.

She grinned cheekily, grabbing her now-filled bucket, "perhaps you are good for something Keffer."

I remained silent, watching as she took the bucket, handing it over to Idah, another one of the slaves who whispered a small Thank-you, to which Haven only smiled at. The kind of smile that didn't quite reach her eyes.

Idah's gaze moved to me momentarily but quickly dropped, taking her bucket to the lower bath house.

The other slaves had a lot to fear. From the whips of their masters, from the mere fact that they were residing in the Night Court and yet somehow, Haven was even more frightening.

No slave seemed to want to go against her. I hadn't seen anyone stand up to her viciousness in the two weeks I had been in the Court.

"Keffer," Haven grunted, placing a new bucket beneath the pump.

"Fill it up."

I glanced at the empty bucket, then at the guard who stood watch as we pumped our water.

He was a young boy, maybe a few years older than me, with clear grey eyes, his hair hidden by his helmet. He side-glanced my way for a minute but he too didn't say or do anything.

I went back to pumping, trying to keep my head off Haven's hawk-like eyes. I hoped to bury myself in my thoughts, but I only felt despair. Every morning it was like this. My arms hurt long before I shoveled piles of coal for hours upon hours for Lucy.

I mean... Luciferous.

When the bucket was filled Haven took it, walking to the bathhouse without a further word or even an act of gratitude.

"I-I'll pump mine," Eve stuttered, quickly moving to the pump as I stepped back.

"Thank you" I replied, rubbing my sore arms. I had pumped water for over twenty slaves. Now only the three of us stood here.

Eve, Vale, and I.

She nodded shyly, her eyes shifting to the sky, a small smile on her face, "he's released the sun today," she noted, her hands on the lever.

My eyes traveled to the Night sky above us that had begun to fade slowly- a small smile crowning my face. It was true, the sun was coming out.

It had been a continuous week of Dark Days and now, the sun was finally coming out.

All three of us grinned, Eve pumping out her water, before slipping into the bathhouse.

Vale and I remained, Vale moving to the pump, "I'll do my own too," she offered with a cheeky smile.

I smiled gratefully, glancing at the guard before moving closer to her, my tone hushed, "Any word?"

She, in turn, glanced at the bathhouse.

"Yes actually." She whispered back, whilst I kept my eyes on the guard. Her tone was low as she pumped slowly.

"There are only two entrances," she began. "The one we came in from, and the other is in the garden court. The housemaids say the first one is heavily guarded at all times, but the garden..." she paused seemingly breathlessly.

"Well? What's wrong with the garden?" I asked quickly, my tone was impatient.

She took a short breath out, pausing- her eyes darting to m.

"Very few use that entrance because it leads into a forest. A forest where the Night Wolf hunts..." she trailed off, shivering.

My eyebrows arched at this.

That was a valid reason not to venture there. There was no need for guards if the Night Wolf himself shifted in there. No one in their right mind would step foot there. Not even desperate slaves.

Which is why it was perfect.

"The Night Wolf can't possibly hunt every night... I would have heard his howls," I reasoned thoughtfully. "A being as powerful as that... I would have heard something."

"-Shade, do not tell me you're thinking about..."

"Is that all?" I quickly interrupted glancing at the bathhouse. My heart pounded within me.

"It's just the garden and the Forest?"

Vale studied my face for a moment.

She shook her head. "It's impossible to use that way, Shade. The risk of meeting the Night wolf, especially as runaway slaves..."

She seemed to freeze at this thought, a shudder coursing through her.

"You didn't think freedom would be easy to attain, did you?" I argued watching her face.

"It is something we need to fight and take risks for. As I see it, the Garden is our only way to escape. We have a one-in-a-millionth chance of actually meeting the Night wolf. We could make it-"

"No, we could not." Vale gritted out rather harshly and louder than I had expected.

My gaze snapped to her notably stressed face.

She took a calming breath out, trying to be lower, her eyes darting from the guard to me.

"It's the Night Wolf Shade. This is not a mere Alpha- this is not Gabriel Sindor." She scoffed.

"By Selene! You seem to have forgotten why people fear him. Do you think we are the first slaves to risk an escape?" she huffed-

My eyebrows arched at this statement, moving closer. My tone lowered.

"You mean to say that they have been others then? K-killed by him?"

"Not technically. The housemaids speak of a maze," she sighed softly as she pumped.

"A maze winding in the garden. Slaves are not allowed there, but to reach the forest that is the only way..." she trailed off moving to her bucket, looking up at me.

"Escape slaves get lost and die in there long before they reach the forest. The slaves say... it is filled with monsters that hide in the shadows. His pets. The worst kind of shadow demons."

I spotted her shaky hands at this.

"T-They say, their cries are heard- and that is why they know they are dead. And when morning comes, their mangled bodies are left in the garden. No one knows how- Just that they died soulless and Wolfless."

My heart pounded at this throat dry.

Of course, it wouldn't be that easy.

My eyes traveled to the looming Night Court. I stared up at it, venturing past its vastness until it suddenly stopped at an open window at the highest tower.

An idea wavered in my head.

I looked at Vale.

"Have you been there?" I asked knowing as a court maid, she was sent to clean in the court.

Her gaze followed mine, before recapturing it.

"No. That area is abandoned. Not even cleaning maids are allowed," she stopped glancing at the top again.

"Janice told me that it's falling apart so no one goes there anymore. Why do you-" she paused as she studied my face, suddenly growing more serious.

"Shade do not-"

"I will not," I replied, helping her with her bucket.

"I'm not stupid Vale."

She paused at this, as if unconvinced.

"Hurry, before they think you've made a friend of me," I smiled softly.

Vale muttered a soft goodbye grabbing her pale and walking off to the bath house.

I looked at the guard, whose eyes were mysteriously watching, only looking away when we held contact.

I moved to the pump, getting my water. My eyes traveled to the dark room in the tower, my heart a low beat.

I was getting out of here. If it is the last thing I do.

———————

The ash clung to my fingers and I set the shovel aside against the wall, eyes turning to Barnabas who lay fast asleep in a corner, leaning against the wall, his broad shoulders relaxed.

I contemplated leaving him there without a word, but I decided against it- moving towards him.

"I know what time it is Keffer," he grunted eyes still shut, as I stopped in my tracks.

"You may take your leave-"

A smile wedged against my lips.

"Thank you-" I replied moving out of the furnace room, through the kitchen, and out the door. Guards moved around the courtyard in the late evening and so were slaves.

It was Dark outside as the sun had gone down already.

I made my way to the slave house, settling in my usual spot whilst ignoring the whispers of the other slaves. I turned slightly watching as Vale talked with the others before I let my eyes find the stoned roof, the seconds passing until it was quiet, very quiet. The last candles went off as the slaves went to sleep.

I gave it a full hour until I turned, watching Vale sleep peacefully. I said a prayer for her and myself, for luck. I needed all the good luck I could get, all the luck Selene would be merciful to give a Keffer, before getting up, quietly maneuvering around the slaves until I got to the door.

Turning around, my eyes settled on a still-asleep Vale, swallowing for a moment.

I had to do this. For her. And for me.

We have to try I told her, but this part only I could do alone.

Without looking back, I slipped into the veil of night. My skin blended into my surroundings, so even a passing guard didn't bother to look twice my way.

I made it to the empty kitchen, glancing at the closed door of the furnace room, before turning to the only other. One that led straight into the Night Court.

Taking a deep breath in, I pushed the door open, a low glow in the distance as I stepped back immediately closing the door, the sound of guards passing by not a moment after.

My eyes dashed around the kitchen, stopping at some stone root. It was a common ingredient in the kitchen I had noticed and yet few knew of its other uses.

I happened upon it in the woods when I was being chased by the other kids in the pack.

Stone root affects werewolf senses, something that made me smell like a wet stone instead of my scent.

I quickly rubbed this across my body, grabbing a few which I slipped into my pocket before trying again, pushing the door slightly open.

This time there was nothing but darkness. This was good.

Blending into the darkness, I kept to the walls, my heart ramming with me with every courageous step I took up the winding stairs.

This was stupid and reckless, but I tried to keep a level head. I didn't want to be found by a guard or even worse, a lord or the Nigh-

No... that could not happen.

I was sure the Night Wolf was situated in the West Wing. The slaves say that part was off-limits to everyone but Madam and a few higher-ups. Yes, the Night Wolf had the whole west wing to himself.

Lucky for me, I was headed in the east, the hallway now long and dark. There was no need to worry- I reassured myself sucking in a breath when a lantern suddenly appeared and I hid behind a pillar, my heart pumping.

A guard stopped by the pillar, sniffing for a moment. His eyes turned yellow, a growl escaping his lips, as my body shook, watching his figure as he turned slightly.

"Do you smell that Lucas?"

Another guard appeared sniffing the air before gagging.

"Wet stone..." he grunted. "There must be a leak somewhere. We'll tell the Madam in the morning if the sun rises that is," he chuckled moving past him.

"Come on, do you wish to stay here forever? With the shadows?"

The guard scoffed at this, walking away with him.

I let out a shaky breath, quickly moving along, this time even more carefully as I climbed yet another flight of winding stairs.

This one was narrower and the stones here were notably colder until I broke out into a hallway.

It was cold, colder than I was used to and I shivered, goose bumps running up my skin. Rubbing my arms for warmth, I noticed the dusty floor and old stone against its walls, a ripped red carpet lining the floor.

The East wing.

I swallowed at the airiness. Vale had been right.

This was abandoned.

It was creepy, especially at this time of night. I took a deep breath in, plunging further into the darkness and finding a wooden door at the far end. Taking out a short breath, I gently pushed the door open, cringing at the loud squeaky noise it created.

I sneezed at the dust that poured through the room. There were broken ornaments littered around it, and ripped pages laying around the small room. At the far end sat a window. I smiled at this, nearly running toward it, looking down, gasping at the height of it.

I could spot the small water pump on the ground floor, barely visible in the night, with small lights beneath, wandering about. I couldn't believe I had made it.

My eyes quickly darted to what I came for, turning my eyes toward the garden court. It was as I expected. The maze lay sprawled before me, but since the window was placed at a particular angle, I could not see all of it.

However, I could tell it was quite large, the forest starting even further out.

I quickly grabbed a fallen piece of paper from the littered ground, flipped it over, and took out the ink that I had tucked into my dress, dipping a finger into it, and quickly drawing all I could see.

I had 3 problems before me.

The maze, the monsters, and the Night wolf.

Firstly, I needed to find a route out of the maze, and this window was high enough to at least see part of it. The moon was bright enough to illuminate the way.

I sketched over the brown paper, my heart pounding with each lingering second, almost done when something came sizzling by my head ramming behind me with a loud thud.

My heart stopped as I abruptly turned, my eyes settling on the Raven that had somehow flown in with incredible speed and hit the door, falling to the floor where it tried to flutter painfully, cawing loudly.

I was scared for the noise it made would surely bring unwanted attention. Moving swiftly toward the animal I picked it up as gently as I could but it only cawed louder. With more care, I settled it on the window sill.

"Let me see, be still little bird," I whispered calmly in a low hushed tone.

It immediately stopped, taking the command, beady eyes looking at me.

I inspected it, noticing the most peculiar thing.

A claw mark on its right wing. It was so deep it had almost ripped off the bird's whole wing. I was amazed the raven had even been able to get this far. I glanced out of the window in the direction the bird had flown in.

The Maze.

I gulped as the bird shivered, beady eyes watching me.

"D-don't worry. I'll fix you... but you cannot tell anyone. I promised AMA-" I paused, shaking my head.

I do not know why I was talking to a bird.

Studying its peculiar eyes for a bit, I took a long deep breath in, blowing softly on the wound. My breath grazed the feathers, then the open wound softly. I watched as the wound healed up in a matter of seconds, bones and flesh reforming.

I kept my steady blow until it was fully healed.

Gasping for air, my hand grabbed the window sill, the other around my throat as I struggled to get a breath in, my eyes wide open, before I collapsed on the floor, finally able to breathe.

The bird cawed stretching its wing and flying around the room.

I smiled from my sitting position on the floor. The Raven perched on the sill again.

"See, you're all right-" I grinned still a little bit dazed as I tried to regain my sanity.

It hopped to the floor, standing a hand away from me. I petted its head for a second.

"You should go, now little bird. Why would you ever stay in the Night Wolf's court when you can be free?"

It cawed softly again, and I shook my head.

"I better go too."

I got to my feet, tucking my drawing back in my pocket before heading toward the door, giving one last look at the raven still perched on the window sill, waving goodbye before moving back into the night.

I moved down the hallways, and down the narrow stairs, but the sound of guards coming up them made me turn in the direction I had come from, moving fast heart pounding, finding the nearest door I could to hide.

My ear was against it as I heard them talk.

"In preparation for the Council of Courts, Madam wants to ensure every area of the court is guarded for the pre-inspection."

"I hate roll calls," another guard grunted.

I froze when they stopped right outside the door, and I stepped back from it, my heart pounding.

A slight push against the door was all that was needed to reveal me.

"We should start here first," A guard began.

My heart beat louder, shaking my head-

"No- not there. That area is strictly forbidden. Madam was specific about the crimson door- " my eyebrows arched at this.

My mind flashed back moments ago.

It was a crimson door I had entered.

And now I was frozen on the spot when I realized the coldness of my surroundings. The darkness filled it to the brim and only one streak of moonlight darted across it to my feet.

I slowly turned, noticing the shadows first. But when my eyes steadied, they only widened at the sight.

It was a library, filled with books as far as the eyes could see. The room was massive- rows upon rows stacked to the ceiling and in the center was a large cushioned chair in velvet.

My eyes traveled upwards because from the shadows that crossed it, were two bright red eyes glowing darkly, a dark shadowy figure seated in the middle, hidden from head to toe, eyes focused right on me.

I held a breath, blinking and suddenly the shadow was gone. My eyes darted around, my heart thumping within me, my skin crawling as the strangest feeling whipped my insides.

I could feel a the shadow behind me but when I turned there was nothing.

I was staring at the door now, my heart pounding.

I almost died when I felt a low breath right against my neck followed by a deep sigh.

•|•|•Enjoying the story? Please vote and leave a comment to let me know!•|•|•

[5.1] THE ARC ALPHA

● |•|• "A keffer? Do not speak of those curses unless you wish to be cursed yourself." •|•|•

[Kayos]

Peace.

The darkness was my home and I reveled in the quietness that accompanied the midnight as I casually flipped through the book I was reading in the dark. Despite having no candlelight to see, I was quite able to read the words as clearly as if it were day, only looking up when the door suddenly opened.

I stared blankly as a shadow moved in, the door shutting a moment after. Pausing I wondered if I had hallucinated the action, gaze focusing on the figure that stood by it, its breaths shallow and quiet, its body shivering slightly.

It wasn't one of my shadow creatures. This one had a heartbeat and a smell- a smell that was covered in stone root it seemed.

My curiosity peaked, eyes unable to leave the figure, for who dared to walk into my sanctuary uninvited?

I narrowed my gaze into the shadows, allowing myself to see more of it until I realized the darkness clung onto the figure as if it were a part of it, a shade of its skin.

My heart froze. Something it never did.

There was only one being I knew that looked like this. My breaths became low as it turned suddenly, feminine eyes searching, until they settled in mine, widening, a hitch in her breath as I held my own.

She blinked and I moved in the darkness. Watching from the safety of the shadows, my heart pounding at the sight in confusion as she turned, panic in her eyes, searching for what she had seen.

She would not be able to find me.

I stared at the frightened girl in the center of the moonlight. She did not look the same as I remembered- she was older, her body more defined, her scent-

Without proper thought, without hold of my actions I moved closer, unable to contain my want, as quiet and as invisible as the shadows I moved behind her, leaning forward and taking a deep breath in, a sigh escaping my lips as my wolf growled within me in familiar want.

She froze amid a breath, her heartbeat slow, too afraid to turn as she bolted out the door, her scent growing dimmer the farther she run but I could not move.

Intoxicated- poisoned- it was all the same. The sudden event made me lose my balance.

I leaned over a hand on the door as I tried to push my wolf back in, fangs out sharp as ever, throbbing and aching as the strongest feeling of absolute want overtook my body, dark veins running up my arms. I turned to the side, eyes set on the moon hanging through the singular open window outside as if laughing at my fate.

"Screw you, Selene."

————————————————————————

Pacing.

I hated the action, and yet I did it often.

My study was darkened only a singular candle flickering on the large oak table as I continued pacing- my ears picking up the soft anxious chattering of people in the hallways leading up to my study.

"I-Is there a reason he called for me?" Gregory asked. His voice was stale but low.

"I do not know Master Gregory, he has been quiet all day, but the sun hasn't risen this morning, it can't be good-" Elias replied.

The guard has been Gregory's informant, I know he tells him of whatever I do.

I did not like spies, but I understand fear. It had been around me since my birth. Gregory did not wish to do me harm, he simply feared for his life- he feared that if he breathed the wrong way- or said the wrong things he may not live another day.

I heard a squirming noise coming from across the room, and I caught the shadows moving, a creature moving along the walls in its shadow form. I sighed and moved toward my desk I grabbed a single gold coin and tossed it to the shadow. A dark cloudy hand emerged from it, taking the coin, and whispering its gleeful thanks.

"Go and find her-" I growl.

"Yesss, master," The creature hissed, moving away and disappearing beneath the doors.

Not a second later a knock is heard.

"Come in."

I caught a sharp intake of a quiet breath and watched through the reflection of a glass vase as Gregory walked in slowly, his head slightly bowed.

The white in his hair was more than it had been a week ago, but his beard was clean.

"You called Your highness?"

His voice was blunt, without a shake. Something he had mastered over the years.

"There is a keffer in my court."

I hear his heartbeat decrease, almost as if it wishes to freeze.

"Y-your Highness?" He stutters in disbelief. I turn to him, his eyes wide, heart beating faster-

"A keffer-" I repeat, eyes narrowing down on him. "Do you not know of her presence in my court?"

His breathing was quick and shallow.

"M-madam Catherine would not let a keffer in the court, I assure you, your majesty-" he huffed. "She would not dare bring a living curse into the Night Wolf's very home."

"But she did."

His eyes met mine, a quiver in them, his lips pursed- at a loss of words.

"You are supposed to know of these things, they should never reach me first-"

He bowed low. "Forgive me, your highness, she will be quick for beheading, or placed in the hunt for your mating ceremony- whichever you desire."

I pursed my lips at the sound of the ceremony. Something I had not put much thought into a year ago, as my mother set the date- but the closer it drew- the more my wolf misbehaved.

"Where is my mother?"

"The Queen Mother is still busy with the preparations, and the announcement to the Council of Courts."

The Council of Courts would be arriving in a few days. And that would be the beginning of the mating ceremony- my wolf growls within me, and my fists clench as he struggled to break free from my ever-stiff hold of him.

My eyes shoot to Gregory whose eyes are on the floor- his breathing as irregular as his heart. It's only now I realize that I had been staring at him whilst I held down my beast. I must have looked furious then.

"Gregory."

His eyes shot to me, a low panic behind them.

"Can I trust you?"

His eyebrows arched. Confused for a moment.

"I am your royal adviser, my lord. You have my uttermost loyalty."

I was not pleased with his answer. It's uniformed. One that is expected. But I knew Gregory to the depth of his deepest fears. He could be trusted.

Taking a deep breath, I take a seat behind the oak desk, shrouded in shadows.

"Do you remember the night of the Mate hunt?"

He paused for a moment but nodded. "Your eighteenth birthday my liege. You spent 5 days in search of your mate-"

"What do you remember from that day?"

"I remember the Queen, praying that you would find your mate in your absence-" he spoke truthfully.

"That you would be as lucky as your father," his jaw ticked at this.

"Forgive me my liege, I did not mean to open up old wounds."

I ignore the last part of his speech. Apologies are minor.

"I said I did not find my mate-" I replied as he watched me.

"When I came back-" I added, "I claimed I had not found her-"

His eyebrows arched at this.

"D-did you?" He suddenly asked as my eyes wandered to the window where the darkness hung in the dark day.

"I don't know, I thought I did for a weak moment," my breathing drawled as I whisked into a memory of that day, my tone slightly lofty.

"For if it is anything my father taught me, the scent that drives your mind delirious, the sweet- sweet musk-" I trailed off shutting my eyes, picturing the day I ran into the farthest reaches of my Kingdom, in the pack bordering the Fire wolf territory.

"The scent led me to a Forrest, and the Forrest to an opening. In that opening was a gathering of shifted omega wolves. They seemed to be surrounding that delectable scent."

His steady breaths let me know he was listening and listening deeply.

"I sent a warning, and they fled. And behind them- she lay."

"W-who was she?" Gregory stuttered, his voice dripping in intrigue.

I ignored him, picturing the day in my mind.

"When she sat up, her hair was wild, her skin was dark. No, it was darkness itself," I clarified.

"And her eyes, her eyes were large and beautiful, lips full. She was young- but not too young-her gaze melted into mine as she stood to her feet-"

"Her wolf recognized you."

My eyes opened at this, turning to him, reality wrapping around me in a cold embrace.

"She had no wolf."

His jaw dropped, running out of breath, eyes wide. "M-my Liege, forgive me but it is not possible."

I run a hand through my thick locks, some tumbling over my face.

"It is for the Night Wolf," I hissed, "Everyone knows Selene has never loved this part of the Prime Wolf our blood carries. She has hidden and killed our mates, and simply not designed any for some of us, and for me," I scoffed.

"She went out of her way to create a scent, to laugh in my face- " my gaze zeroed in on Gregory.

"A keffer is a keffer because she has no wolf and therefore no mate," I gritted out the basic physics with growing frustration, "Tell me advisor, how then is possible that she carries a scent that drives my wolf to the border of destruction?"

He paused at this, as I kept speaking.

"Perhaps it is my fault," I growled getting to my feet.

"As the day of the mating dawns closer, my wolf grows anxious. All he ever desired was someone to call his, someone truly designed for him," I paused, turning to Gregory,

"He will never have that; this I know for certain but somehow even that divine knowledge did not stop me from praying-" I chuckled darkly.

"For hell's sake, I did not think she would listen-" I huffed glancing at the place the moon should have been in the darkened sky had this been night. It is not like Selene would ever listen to the prayer of a Night Wolf.

"What did you pray for my liege?"

"That my mate would come to me if she was the one." I blankly replied, noting that his eyebrows seemed to arch at the statement.

Was it hard to believe that even a Night Wolf desired a Mate?

"I made a decree in secret with the order of new slaves. I sent an additional letter to the pack that borders the Fire Wolf territory. That all slaves-no matter the status be delivered with the new batch. Of age, or almost of age-" I paused turning to a wide-eyed Gregory,

"I did not expect that a keffer would journey from our farthest border and be accepted so easily within my walls, For Hell's sake, it was supposed to be an assurance that a keffer couldn't possibly be destined for me. She should have died long before she reached my dark gates. She shouldn't have been able to live this long and yet..." I trailed off, a dark chuckle escaping from my lips, "She wanders freely into my sanctuary."

Gregory listened with a crease in his forehead, his lips pursed in a thin line.

"Tell me, Gregory, is it wrong that I wish to have her close despite what she is?"

His eyes snap to me, his wise eyes often hidden in fear slowly resurfacing.

"I wish to say that it is wrong- that she's a keffer, a curse, and most likely a joke Selene is playing on your mind, as she often does with your bloodline. But I know of your greatest longing my lord, it is a wish for every wolf. I cannot fault you for that."

I nod at this with a sigh, "She dies then?"

"It would be easier than to entertain it, truthfully. However, I believe in destiny. Perhaps there is a mystery behind a keffer who made it behind the walls of the Night Court. One who lived to see the night wolf in his sanctuary and still breaths."

My sanctuary was a place no one was allowed in. Not even my mother.

"Maybe there is a reason why she holds a scent without a wolf so close to that of one your mate could hold. Maybe there's another reason why your wolf is so fond of her. Surely a mystery as great as hers does not deserve to simply die."

My eyes peer at him, and he lowers them.

"You defend a keffer?" I asked curiously.

"N-no my liege. I enjoy mysteries, that is all. She may be a clue to finding your true mate."

I raised an eyebrow at this, "You think Selene would be that cruel? To place a clue in the one thing I cannot stand?"

"Selene has done much worse to Arcs of your Bloodline."

My wolf presses inside me, a deep plead. I turn slightly away, eyes settling in the darkness outside, "True. But shall I grasp onto twigs? Shall I hope once more? Become a fool to play her game?"

"Do you believe you will lose your majesty?"

My eyes snapped to him, "It is not possible."

"Then you cannot be the fool in this equation."

I stared at him for a moment, studying his face. I tried to think about this with reason, to ignore the additional message my wolf sent to me.

"Very well," I sighed, "I do enjoy a good mystery after all there is nothing to do in this court."

From the corner of my eyes, I caught a small smile Gregory released through the reflection of a glass and I roll my eyes.

"Perhaps we can answer a few mysteries now. Bring Catherine to my presence."

"Yes, your majesty."

Gregory left not a moment later, the door closed behind him, and in return, a shadow dashed back beneath the door, moving against the wall, till it reached behind me. Its shadowy form emerges from the shadows taking shape of a dark creature, smaller than those in the maze, its fork-like tale, and monkey-like figure moving toward me, crawling up my chair, hanging off it as it whispers in my ear of its discovery.

"Is that all?"

"Yesssssss master."

My eyes dropped to the gold coin on my desk. "It is yours, Alchest,"

A gleeful screech echoed and my wolf grunted at this. The creature grabbed the coin slipping back into the shadows, just as a shaky knock came against the door.

———

"A keffer?" Catherine repeated, her voice shaky.

Gregory stood a little further behind her as she knelt before my desk, eyes refusing to meet mine.

"The one you keep in the kitchen, with the coals," I grunt at this, my wolf growling.

"Or are there more you hide in my walls?" I snicker.

Her eyes snap to me, before snapping back down in horror at what I suppose was a mistake. No one meets the eyes of royalty without permission.

She shakes her head, "T-there is only one, your highness. Forgive me, I do not know what made me keep her. She will be sent for the hunt; I will not waste a further second."

"You dare lie?!" I growl the sound of it fuelling the coals of anger within me.

"You do not know what made you keep her? Was it the note that was delivered to you by the raven?"

Her eyes widen, though her stare remains glued to the floor in disbelief. She is baffled about how I know of her secret note. But the shadows tell me everything I need to know.

She shut her eyes, tears running down her cheek as she clasped her hands together.

"My sister," she finally confessed. "Whom I have not seen for many years. She adopted the keffer and the rogue's daughter after the death of her mate, a beta of the Night-moon pack. Her only wish was that I keep them safe. Forgive me, your highness." She grieved.

My eyes trailed to Gregory who looked at Catherine thoughtfully. I knew what he thought of.

How can a cursed keffer be so lucky?

Such things were too strange to be mere coincidences.

I stood from my seat walking to her. Her body shook whilst my mind ran rampant with many ways to kill her. I shut my eyes at the blood lust, though I knew to kill and dispose of her body would be easy.

The creatures of the shadows would take her in a second if I willed it. I could hear them whisper, and watch, patiently waiting for their meal.

I raised her chin to meet my eyes and I see fear wrap around them in a soul-stealing embrace.

"Lie to me one more time and not a single soul will ever know of how you died."

Her skin crawled with goosebumps.

"You will do, exactly as I say."

•|•|•Enjoying the story? Please vote and leave a comment!•|•|•

[6.1] A GIFT OF A CURSE

● |•|• "You dare look into the eyes of the dark ones? Do you not value your soul?" •|•|•

[Shade]

~Last night~

I was going to die!

My heart raced and my body quaked in fear as I bolted my way down the stairs, barely remembering that I needed to be quiet.

I couldn't stop, and I wouldn't stop. My legs ran of their own accord from mere instinct, heck, I would rather be caught by guards at this moment than-.

Oh, Selene, I saw him! My brain was a melting mess. I saw the Night Wolf! The bloody Night Wolf!

My mind was racing with dark thoughts, not able to even risk looking back, too scared he might be right behind me though basic logic assured me that if indeed it had been him, he would have caught up with me before I even got to the door. Before I took my next breath.

But I was sure it had been him.

Granted I had not seen his face, but the mere presence in the room, those amber eyes glinting in the shadows, the figure hidden beneath the veil of darkness-

It was the Night Wolf!

Dear Selene I was going to die!

My feet couldn't keep up with how fast I was moving, dodging behind a pillar just before a couple of guards passed by, talking lowly amongst themselves.

As soon as they moved out of sight I bolted toward the Kitchen, moving to the furnace room where I covered myself in ash, from my forehead where my sweat glistened to under my armpits, fingers shaking.

This was the only thing I could think of that would dull the scent of my sweat and hopefully my paralyzing fear.

Peeking through the doorway, my heart a hard bang within me, I bolted back into the kitchen and into the darkness, arriving in the slave quarters.

I sucked in a breath glancing down at the heaps of bodies on the floor fast asleep.

As calmly as I could and despite my inward panic, I sifted through the bodies finding my worn-out mat in the farthest corner, immediately dropping to the floor like a sack of potatoes, petrified to the bone.

"S-Shade?" A voice called out in a low whisper.

My eyes snapped to Vale, who was apparently wide awake, her pale blue eyes staring at me in confusion.

"Where on earth did you go?" She huffed sliding her body toward me.

"Shhhh!" I hushed a finger against my lips, lightly pushing her head down as I spotted a light behind the doorway. My breath hitched, eyes wide as the door creaked open, fear gripping me in anticipation.

Low whispers came from the door and I shut my eyes.

My body shook and my heart was a rampant mess within me, but I tried my best to regulate my breathing

Remaining motionless, I could hear two guards talk in low hushed tones as they looked in, inspecting the room for any non-present slaves I assumed.

One sniffed into the room before sneezing, his voice light and airy.

"Ash... and wet stone," he mumbled as he closed the door.

"Slaves stink."

I let out a loose breath at this finally able to relax for only a moment, turning onto my back, staring into the darkness of the high roof above us, memories of what happened flooded my mind.

"Shade?"

My eyes shifted to Vale staring at her wide eyed. I was unable to say a word, my mind paralyzed, so scared that I would suddenly see those amber eyes peer out from the shadows.

My frightened gaze remained in hers, tears falling from my face, before I looked up at the ceiling again, a hand over my heart as I shut my eyes.

————————————

"Can you be any slower?" Idah asked rather impatiently as I pumped water in her bucket. My sleep filled eyes trailed to hers and I failed to care still deep in my thoughts.

I finished and she took her bucket, not without the last harsh comment.

"Sleeping in her own filth," she snapped, finally leaving in the direction of the bath house.

I pursed my lips, getting back to pumping, knowing she had been referring to the ashes that still clung to my body.

Idah hadn't been one to talk much, but she had been spending a lot of time with Haven which must have rubbed off.

"What happened last night?" Vale hurriedly asked in a low tone, leaning forward slightly, as the last slave left the pump and headed to the bath house.

"You looked like you had seen a ghost."

I didn't reply, numbly turning back to the pump. pumping more water into the bucket, remaining tight lipped. My heart beat rapidly within me, hands stiff as a board I kept on pumping, trying to bury the growing panic beneath me whilst blurring the visions of yesterday.

Ever since the events of last night my mind, body and I was sure, my very self-seemed to be stuck in a loop of fear. Fear that took hold of my very being.

I had looked into the Night Wolfs eyes. And I couldn't sense a soul. I don't know how but it was just darkness.

Barnabas was right. Staring into those fiery soulless orbs did something to you, as if multiplied your deepest fears a hundred-fold, and now I was a shaky mess.

She circled the pump to me, taking over with firm hands, glancing at the guard that stood posed a few feet away, eyes never breaking away from his firm stare toward the Night Court.

Her tone was hushed when she spoke. "Come on Shade, you need to talk to me."

I kept my eyes low, my throat running dry.

She pumped down water in her bucket, her eyes low as she glanced down at me, her tone a rugged huff, "I know you went to the tower last night. Where else could you have gone? You've always been so stubborn."

My lips shook at this, tears pressing behind my heavy eyelids.

Why was I so stubborn? Why didn't I just listen to Vale? Now I was a panicking mess, my anxiety was through the roof and I couldn't stop thinking-

I remembered those eyes that seemed to pierce through the depth of my soul searching for my darkest fears, and I couldn't shake the feeling that I was being watched. My skin crawled as my eyes shifted to the tower high above us, a shiver crossing my spine.

"What did you see up there?" Vale pressed, her tone breathless as she spoke, her gaze following mine, wind in her face.

"What did you see that made you look so-" her eyes found mine, pausing for a moment, her eyebrows arching.

I could see her mind work and I looked away, blinking rapidly at the stones that littered the ground around the pump trying to keep my heart under wraps.

"No-" she gasped, her eyes wide as she stared right at me, "You couldn't have-"

Tears swelled beneath my eyelids swallowing harshly, but I nodded. She was smart. She knew there was only one thing that could make me this way.

"T-The Night Wolf?" She whispered her tone so low and uncertain it felt like she was struggling to say it out loud.

I stared into her eyes, allowing her to read my panic and my tears all at once.

Her large pale blue eyes traveled to the highest tower that sat in the darkened sky, a shade of fear crossing her own eyes as she gripped her cloak tighter, fingers moving back to the pump, lips pressed together breathlessly.

She pumped for a few more times before suddenly looking at me, disbelief and fear mixed in her voice.

"Are you sure it was h-him?" She stuttered, "I mean, how are you still alive then?"

It was a valid question, one I racked my mind all through last night, unable to get proper rest. I was so scared he would come out of the shadows and kill me.

I didn't know where to begin and I couldn't reassure her of what I had seen as my brain had been in shambles since the incident.

"I-I saw these eyes in the shadows," I finally stated, my voice sounding raspy and dry to my own ears.

Those were the first words I had spoken since last night.

I didn't have to rack my brain for the image, it had been replaying in my head like a broken record, all I had to do was describe it.

"Amber, bright yet dead." I trailed off, my eyebrows drawing together.

"It was just a dark figure, a d-dark shadow just sitting there, reading me."

My eyes snapped to Vale who was listening with wide eyes, her knuckles growing white as she tightened her hold on the lever.

I let out an exasperated breath, my body growing limp as I leaned against the pump.

"Vale it was like my deepest fears were there in his eyes, gifted for me. My frickin body was a shaky mess, shivers crossed my skin, my heart felt like it would give out- Selene, It was so dark..." I trailed off glancing up at her.

"Too much darkness."

She pressed her lips at this, but her unstable eyes betrayed the fear behind them.

"I don't know if it was him, I did not see the Night Wolf. I cannot describe his face but that feeling, and those eyes," I shivered.

"I cannot shake the feeling that I had seen the Night Wolf. What else could have looked like that?"

Vale seemed to have paused at this, her breath short. I could tell what was running through her mind.

Growing up, tales of the Night Wolf had been plenty. Some called him the Master of Shadows, the Prince of Demons, all titles and all stories had one thing in common.

He was an Alpha that should be avoided at all times.

Vale shook her head finally turning back to the pump, pushing a strand of her thin blond hair behind her ear as it blew in the wind, before sharply glancing back at me.

"IF it had been him, you would have been dead. It makes no sense whatsoever that he would let simply let you live."

"What else could it have been?!" I snapped unable to contain the anger that stemmed within me.

She was trying to brush it off. I knew what I saw- hell I could still feel those eyes on me.

Vale shook her head, swallowing for a moment and shrugging.

"I don't know, there are many masters in the Night Court perhaps you met one of them. You were in the east wing. The night wolf resides in the west," she explained.

"Maybe you saw a creature of the shadows, for if it was the Night wolf he would not have let you simply walk away."

I pursed my lips knowing arguing with her would be fruitless.

Besides, I had been thinking about that too. Why on earth I was still breathing if a keffer like me wondered in the very presence of the Night Wolf?

The only two explanations that I could come up with that were somehow killing me was not on his Agenda.

Had my curse become my savior? It was no secret that Keffer's were thought of as insignificant beings. Perhaps he had better things to do that bathe himself in the cursed blood of a keffer.

The more logical reason was Vale was right. I had simply seen things or mistook it for something else. That the breath I had felt on my back was just the wind, the eyes could have been mere fireflies.

Extraordinarily larger and brighter that was for sure, but still fireflies.

The figure could have been a lingering shadow.

But even at the most logical reason, I could still feel a fear growing deep in my bones, my eyes shifting to that of Vale.

"I know, but I can't shake the feeling that something's wrong Vale, something's terribly wrong."

Her eyes snapped back to me, a brief display of annoyance that hid her shaky fingers.

"Don't be ridiculous!" She suddenly snapped, "You're alive which means all is well and that's that!"

She let out a loose breath after this sudden outburst but she couldn't fool me. Whenever she was afraid her fingers would shake.

"The sun hasn't risen today and Madam didn't wake us up this morning," I replied calmly.

She froze at this, her bucket full.

Dread echoed like a low whisper in her eyes, she moved to me, quickly glancing about before taking my hand/

"It's nonsense Shade! There have been many, many dark days like this one since we came into this god-forsaken place," she hissed.

My eyes met hers and she sighed, looking at where our hands connected before capturing my gaze again.

"You need to promise me you can't be that reckless anymore Shade, I-" she froze, a hand over her heart, her voice was shaky, "in this god-forsaken world, I only have you, and you only, do you understand me? To me you're not a slave or a keffer, you're my sister. My only sister. If I lose you I will be utterly alone here in this... this place! Do not be selfish Shade, I beg you. Surely you cannot be so cruel as to abandon me here, in this Nightmare."

Silence rained between us as she gulped, breathing in and out loudly, before grabbing her bucket. She turned slightly, her tone calm but sad, "I know you seek our freedom but freedom is of no importance if you're already dead."

I watched as she moved away, guilt racking my body.

My eyes blurred but I turned blinking the tears away, sucking in a deep breath, and refocused on pumping my water into my bucket before walking into the bathhouse.

—————- My heart had cooled down to a steadier beat as I dug my shovel into the coal, throwing a heap of it into the fire. It blazed as if thankful to be fed, and I kept my gaze in the heat of the flames.

As the morning dawned to afternoon without any occurrences, I started to doubt what I had seen. Vale must be right. I probably mistook what I thought I had seen.

The fact that nothing of major importance had happened so far was a green light. Everything was fine, everything was plain and normal. All I had to do now was tackle the fear in my bones, fear that something was going to happen.

I yawned, scolding myself for not getting enough sleep last night, for fooling myself into being afraid of closing my eyes when I had seen nothing.

Gradually, my head stooped, rolling forward, taking short breaths in, heated by the warm blaze of the fire. It felt like a warm blanket lulling me to sleep.

I suddenly rocked forward as I dozed off, a rough hand suddenly stopping me from toppling over. My eyes widened when I stared at the close flame, looking deadlier than how gentle it had been before I dozed off.

"Do you wish to die so soon, Keffer?" Barnabas growled, his wolf showing momentarily.

One of his large hands steadied on my shoulder, stopping me from toppling over into the large flames.

I was this close to losing my face. This close.

He pushed me back and I landed backward with a hard thump as the chair legs tilted back, my heart beating faster, eyes wide.

His eyes snapped to me, studying my face. "You had no sleep last night?"

I was still rattled by how close I had come to burning my face off, glancing up at him with wide eyes but nodding.

"I-I couldn't sleep."

"Well Of course you couldn't sleep, not whilst sneaking around the fucking castle."

My eyes darted to him, my heart dropping to my feet. He... how did he-? His hard glare took me in, whilst I stood wide eyed and frozen in my seat.

How did he know?

"You should know Stone Root is hard to wash off, it's scent remains..." he sniffed the air, "Pungent. Few know the uses of Stone root. I must say, I am impressed..." he trailed off, eyes darting down to my soot-covered feet.

"Who would have thought that the Keffer has balls?" he drawled.

I gulped at this, not sure if he was actually impressed or 2 seconds away from telling Luciferous, I had stolen some herbs from his kitchen, and eventually Madam Catherine that I had snuck into the castle.

Before I could beg for my life, the door suddenly opened and my gaze locked with Madam Catherine. She looked rather out of it, not as collected as I was used to seeing, her breath shallow.

I immediately stood up; eyes set on the floor.

"Keffer," she began and I noticed a slight shake in her tone she covered up when she cleared her throat. I looked up at her, my heart racing. Her lips folded into a thin line, the usual light in her eyes was dull, and her voice monotone.

"Follow me."

•|•|• I was given a Nonexclusive contract for Mated to the Night Wolf on Good novel, can't say I'm too thrilled by it, but on the bright side, I can keep posting this book here so- win-win . Please vote and leave a comment if you're enjoying the book! •|•|•

[7.1] THE MASTER

● |•|• "There is a whole world out there pup. Read to learn for wisdom is your greatest asset." •|•|•

[Shade]

Madam Catherine said nothing further, turning around robotically the same way she came and I watched her quizzically. My heart began that fearful beat within me, so many questions spurring in my mind, of why she would want me, or where she was taking me too.

My gaze lingered on Barnabas whose eyes glinted in an unknown emotion but I quickly moved after Madam Catherine.

My feet moved behind her trying to read her aura as I stared at her straightened back. She didn't seem particularly angry however there was a dread about her I failed to understand.

I was supposed to be the one who was afraid, so why did I sense fear in her?

I moved into the kitchen the smell of roasted meat immediately tackling my sense, my eyes remaining low, knowing feasting on the sight of Luciferous well-done meat would do nothing but pile hunger over my growing fear.

Following Madam Catherine, I was caught unaware when she turned toward the door that led into the court and not the one that led outside to the slave Quarters.

Warning bells rang in my head.

I was going into the Night Court! She was leading me into the very heart of it.

My heart began to beat faster with this realization, noticing that random pairs of eyes kept trailing to me, owned by the uniformed guards and the slave maids that wondered about me.

My eyes flashed back to Madam Catherine.

Hadn't she said I should blend in with the coal? That my life should consist of only the slave quarters and the furnace? Why then was I exposed to the Night Court?

My heart sank as I realized the reason. She must know what I did last night. She must know I sneaked into the Court. Could she smell the stone root coming off me? Was she headed to punish me in the abandoned towers of the west wing?

My fists tightened, trying to relieve the shake.

We climbed a flight of stairs, silence looming between the two of us as I tailed her into another large hallway, here slave court maids were scrubbing the huge floor with large brushes until it shined so bright you could see your reflection through it.

My eyes met that of Vale, who slowly looked up at the intruders from her scrubbing position, her eyes widening as I passed her by and so did that of Eve and Haven.

The only thing I could do was throw her an apologetic tear-filled look as we passed through the walls and to another set of stairs. I may not come down these stairs. I may be made an example.

I should have listened to Vale and now I was going to leave her alone in her worst Nightmare.

My hands clasped together to the front now, fingers shaking as I stared at the back of Madam Catherine's head. Her calm cool nature remained intact, walking with precise posture further up the stairs.

Stairs I began to recognize.

I froze in my tracks as the memory flashed, sucking in a breath. This couldn't be right. - Could she? - Wait, could she be taking me back there?

She turned the corner out of sight, and I recollected myself, pushing my shaky body forward, catching up to her as she moved into what seemed like an abandoned hallway.

It was dark and airy, the torches more spaced out drawing out the darkness and the hallway thinner.

My eyes stuck to the front, settling on the crimson door we were steadily approaching, my heart an empty beat within me.

She was taking me to the Night Wolf or the creature of my imagination, the bloody thing!

Whatever it had been. She must know!

How else could I explain this? How was I back here? I paused a few feet away, my body now visibly shaking, feeling like a lamb being led to the slaughter.

Utterly helpless whilst watching as she paused right before the door.

She calmly pushed it open, coughing for a moment at the slight rise in dust but did not enter, her eyes turning to me.

I lowered my head, my body shaking. I mouthed a soft prayer, one that would make my transition to the afterlife calm and peaceful after my death.

For I was to die like this, and I hoped it would be quick. Arc Alpha's were fast and agile. He could get the job done without wasting time.

Madam Catherine stared blankly back at me, her hands behind her back.

"You've been assigned a new task keffer, you must clean these quarters."

My eyes snapped to her, blinking blankly.

"Cleaning equipment is inside," she continued prodding me to go inside.

My eyebrows arched at this, my voice shaky.

"C-clean?" I echoed, too afraid to ask if that was a code word for 'jump out of the darkness and kill her.'

"The library is large and will take weeks to clean thoroughly as a one-man job but these quarters are off limits and the masters do not want more than one slave to do this job. Therefore, for the next few weeks, you are tasked with cleaning it. You will blend quite well in the shadows when the masters come to study. They would rather not see you as they work, see to it you remain quiet and unseen."

My body was numb but I felt myself nodding, unable to understand what exactly was happening. My mind slowly registered this as a cleaning job and not my doom.

"The sooner you begin the better child."

My eyes flashed to hers nodding frantically, my brain an eager mess, too grateful to say another word. My shaking body moved past her.

Her hand suddenly clamped around my arm as I passed by holding me in place, her tone low and fast with an under threat of warning as she whispered hurriedly-

"Whatever you do Shade, DO NOT look in his eyes and for the LOVE of Selene, always obey."

My body froze at those words, as she let go, hearing the soft click of her shoes as she walked off. My body remained numb, my head replaying one word.

Shade.

She had called me by my name.

I turned slightly catching a glimpse of her skirt as she disappeared round the corner, before turning back to the crimson door.

I studied the door for a moment, the crimson paint fading, my body shaking as I pushed it open, and walked in.

Immediately, I was surrounded by darkness. A dark shiver crossed my spine as I tried to see through the darkness. The window was open at the far end, and my mind flashed back to last night, noting that beneath it, on the velvet couch was where I had seen that figure.

Shaking my head, whilst massaging my tempos, I repeated to myself that those were just silly mind games my brain had been playing with me.

With that, I turned on my heels walking back out the door.

Either way, creature or no creature, Night Wolf or no Night Wolf. There was simply no way I was staying in that darkness.

I couldn't even open the curtains to let the light come in. It was a dark day- which meant no sunlight and no moonlight either.

My footsteps echoed across the empty hallway, sounding loud to my ears, reaching out for the closest torch, and taking it off its mount.

Now armed with a little bit of light, I sucked a breath walking through the crimson door again.

The first thing I did was stare at the large velvet couch at the center of the vast library beneath the open window perched on a platform.

It was empty. No figure in sight.

This however didn't seem to calm me. The fear though deep in the pit of my stomach now still brought about the feeling that somewhere within this darkness I was being watched.

I moved further into the library looking around till I noticed something peculiar. It was a thick glass tube that seemed to go through the library.

Curiosity got the best of me, my fingers sliding against the tube following it to the end. My fingers suddenly dipped into a watery pool. I brought it up to the light, examining the liquid.

Oil.

Without further thought I brought the torch to the liquid and immediately a flame sprouted, following the glass tube to another oil dip until the whole library flicked to life.

Light flooding in.

I stared in awe, setting my torch against a hanger, hobbling to the center of the vast library, eyes set on the ceiling following the lit flames till they cackled to the top revealing just how large this library was.

It was massive!

Mountains of books packed neatly, a staircase winding to the left opening to further rows of books on another floor, balconies of books on either side of the vast room.

I blinked at this. Madam Catherine was right.

This would take weeks to clean, it was not meant to be a one-man job. My fingers trailed against a wooden bookshelf, dust sticking to it in thick pastes.

Needed a thorough cleaning.

Suddenly, I caught some movement at the corner of my eye causing me to spin around, heart rattling within me, curious gaze searching, but there was nothing but more books.

Taking out a deep breath to stop the irrational thoughts clouding my mind, I tried to calm myself, focusing on finding my cleaning equipment.

Tops had to be cleaned, and some books that had not been put back on the shelf had to be restocked.

I was never an avid reader, but I wasn't sure if that was simply because I had no interest or because there were few books to read back home. This library, however, seemed to host every book ever recorded in the history of Valcane.

After letting the awe of this place subside, I finally searched for the equipment, found it, and went right to work, dragging the ladder as I began to dust and pack books.

As time drifted off the stiffness in my shoulders relaxed, and I was able to breathe without my heart pounding, retreating to its steady bit. I began to hum along as I dusted, the song was old, one I always hummed when I was trying to stop being nervous.

I never knew who taught it to me. It had always been just at the back of my head. The words had long faded but only a few lines had remained intact over the years

lay weeping ... mmm mm.

Begging to the moon, Mmmmm.

For a heart to rest his soul

"The song of the first Wolf."

My head immediately snapped in the direction of the stale blank voice, startled at the sudden intrusion. Not registering the fact that at this height on the ladder I could only be caught in direct eye-line, successfully shattering Madam Catherine's first warning.

Stunned was much too shallow of a term to describe the feeling that trapped me in my very body when my eyes locked with his, a soft breath escaping my lips.

His eyes were a kind I had never seen.

Green and blue.

I couldn't decide which color they were, for they seemed to sit at the very center of a deep sky blue and a shallow sea green. His gaze was as stale as his voice, however, hooded beneath tensed eyebrows. His hair fell in short straight strands over the frame of his face, a deep midnight black with unique streaks of blood red littering his head.

His face was molded as I would have imagined a god. Blemish free except for a singular beauty spot right below his firm pink lips.

He was simply beautiful, a breathtaking being, one that left me entranced and breathless.

His youthful face was sculpted to perfection, standing at perfect posture and height, a regal air of authority around him in the flickering firelight that danced around the library. Dressed in all black, except the golden embroidery of a wolf that traced his jacket, he stood neat and posed.

"The song you were singing," he continued, voice blank but firm, his eyes holding mine prisoner like a trophy though his voice remained stale and lifeless.

"The tale of the Prime Wolf," he finished drawing me out of my trance.

I wasted no time in dropping to my knees, my body in a cold panic, my mind reprimanding myself for my foolishness. My voice was a hurried ramble as I apologized profusely, eyes set on the floor.

"F-Forgive me, master, I did not mean to disturb your study. I did not know you were already in here. I should have remained quiet. I-I will be punished as you will."

My voice was a shaky mess, my head low, eyes to the floor, a panic low within me.

Since my endeavors, last night all I desired was to remain unseen.

Madam Catherine had told me Masters study here and liked their privacy. Here I was, singing for the world to hear, lighting this place up like it was mid-day.

Perhaps he had been studying quietly somewhere in the corner of this vast library, maybe he had his candle, reading silently before I had begun my shenanigans.

I was such an idiot and I was getting justly punished for my numerous mistakes. Part of me wanted to be punished as if that would fix what I had done last night and take this fear off of me once I had paid the price.

My body tensed at the lingering silence, afraid of what he would sentence for me. But when he suddenly spoke again, his the stale tone seemed to have a bare undertone of surprise.

"Master?" He echoed.

•|•|• Please drop a comment if you're enjoying the story and vote! I'll appreciate it! •|•|•

[8.1] DECIEVER

|•|• "Perhaps you do not understand your power my little night wolf. You will be feared always, that is your gift and your curse."•|•|•

[Kayos]

The question hang in the air like grapefruit as I studied the girl that knelt lowly at my feet.

The air around us held mystery, a mystery that piqued my interest. Her scent seemed to hide a lulling effect because for a moment all I could do was breathe and capture the moment as I had done for the last two hours since she was brought to the doors of my sanctuary.

All I could do was study her as her eyes traveled around my sanctuary, walking between the shadows, stalking her like prey.

It was easy, way too easy.

Without a wolf, the keffer was as I had already known, vulnerable and weak. Had I decided to kill her, she would not know of it till her head rolled to my feet.

She had no wolf to warn her that she was in the presence of an Arc Alpha, no way to know who I was by a mere sniff.

Master, she called me.

She thought of me as those beneath me, as my council subjects that come to me with tales of what occurs in my kingdom shaking and hyperventilating.

Unbeknownst to them, the shadows keep more of an eye over my region than they would ever be able to.

That is why she was able to stare right into my eyes longer than any without understanding the authority hidden in them, why my subjects couldn't last long staring in the depths of them.

Eyes were the mirrors of the soul. Mine was certainly not a soul to behold, not one that mirrored darkness itself.

Without a wolf to warn her, she fell to her knees in fear of punishment and not in fear for her very life.

It amused me, to say the least, it was a first for me.

To feel a different kind of fear, not one that immediately led to thoughts of death and of painful ways to die.

My wolf radiated a strange low feel, pride. A pride I couldn't quite understand as the person he claimed to be mated to had no wolf for him to bond with and was currently shivering in fear at my feet.

I soon discovered, however, his pride stemmed from the fact that the keffer did not fear us as our subjects did, she only feared the punishment she would be given.

He was beaming in pride because, despite the circumstances, she was the very first being to not cower in fear from our direct presence, all due to her ignorance.

Fear, a new kind.

One that was not aimed at me simply for who I was, but for the punishment that awaited her.

And thus unknowingly, as she trembled at my feet she fulfilled one of my wolf's desires. To have a mate who was not immediately scared to death at my presence, one who was able to look me in the eye without cowering in untold fear.

My curiosity was plagued and my posture became rigid as I battled the strange warmth within.

I did not send her into my sanctuary to find ways to redeem her, but to understand why Selene had given such an abomination the mimicked scent of my mate. Reminding myself of this, I regained my stature.

"F-Forgive me, master," she finally managed to stutter. "I do not know your given name."

I raised a stiffened eyebrow. My name?

The Keffer wished to know my given name. In her head, her crime was her inability to address my title and name.

Master Gregory, Madam Catherine... and I?

No one spoke of my name; they merely spoke of grand titles.

The Night Wolf, Prince of Demons, Master of Shadows, there were many whispers of my nature around my kingdom.

The mere question should have led to her death, for who was she to ask for the given name of an Arc Alpha?

A keffer. One who wasn't even allowed on the doorstep of an omega, and yet here she was, at the feet of an Arc Wolf.

Ignorance certainly is bliss.

Despite the claim my wolf had mistaken her, she would not be allowed to call me by my true name, she was not worthy, and would never be worthy. However, her ignorance would be ignored just this once.

My lips pursed at this, studying her kneeling figure for a moment, fighting the urge to take a deep breath in and bask in her luring scent, whilst her eyes stared blankly at the floor.

"Master is all."

She only nodded at this response, bowing lowly again.

"As you wish master."

I circled the mystery, my lips pursed into a thin line.

I had no idea why I opted to lie, to deceive and not correct her, to say I was a master when I was the very thing she feared as she was brought to the crimson door.

Perhaps her ignorance sparked something in me, a curiosity that needed to be weaned.

Perhaps I was liking the thought of not being feared to death. All my life I had known fear, I was not fond of the feeling.

Logically, it would certainly be easier to let her know who I was and demand why she carried such a scent but I doubted even she knew who she was.

Ignorance was wrapped around her scent like a blanket.

Sweet innocence. Untouched...darkly beautiful-

My loose breath lingered in the air, shutting my eyes for a moment. I would not be swayed by a mere scent. Even one as lovely as this. For she was not my mate, she had no wolf to bond with, therefore there could be no existence of a bond, to begin with.

She, on the other hand, would never know of the slight curiosity she had plagued my wolf with, for she had no wolf to confirm it. She would remain in her ignorant bubble as Keffers do.

I must know where she got this scent, and how it is connected to my true destined mate.

But new thoughts blossomed in my mind, thoughts I never considered.

Here before me lay one of the only beings in Valcane that wouldn't be too swayed by what I was.

That talked to me a little bit more humanely than anyone else had. It was... refreshing and calmed my wolf as the announcement of my mating draws near.

We have darkened the skies on many dark days these past few weeks as the date draws near, anger fouling my mood. It was best to keep myself...refr eshed and occupied.

"Keffer."

She visibly stiffened at the stale sting of her name, her breath hitching.

"Your punishment for your intrusion will be." I paused racking my brain, only now realizing that all punishments I had ever deemed to give ended in death.

Yes, all were spontaneous, creative, torturous ways to die but still, it was death.

My gaze trailed out to an open book sprawled on the table.

It had to be something that would make her talk willingly, and inauspiciously without fear. My eyes narrowed on the book.

"A study."

A moment passed between us in silence, and I could sense the confusion coming off her in shaky waves.

"A-a study?" She echoed again.

"A study I was appointed to conduct," My eyes trailed the darkness of her skin, a certain thirst running through me, dryness scorching my throat. "By the Night Wolf."

Her breath hitched at the sound of the title as I suspected drawing me back to reality, I looked away at this, eyes steadfast ahead, grabbing a brown sheet of paper as the masters did to sell my new identity as I talked.

"One that involves this court. I have taken out a survey of the guards and servants, but I am yet to study- You."

Pausing, I waited for her response. It sounded shaken.

"M-me, master?"

"You are a keffer are you not?" I grunted, harsher than I intended eyes snapping back to her, catching her raised eyes in mine, which took me off balance for a moment.

Perhaps even I had gotten used to not having to meet people's eyes.

She stiffened eyes darting to the floor in a low panic, gulping but nodding frantically, her head bowing even lower.

"I-I am master."

Regaining my sanity, I nodded mindlessly for a moment.

I tried to relieve the authority in my voice this time.

"I was assigned to give a full report on the Night Court, of all its subjects. Lords, masters, guards, servants, and slaves."

My eyes narrowed on her, uttering the question that plagued my mind the most.

"But I was not informed there was a keffer in the Night Court and I doubt his majesty is informed of it either," I trailed dryly testing the waters, "Neither would I have believed one would be accepted behind these walls. Tell me," I paused, eyes training down on her.

"How is it you still live?"

Her breathing lagged, and I could hear the pelting of her heart as it raced within her.

She seemed to be panicking.

This was not the way I intended.

I had an opportunity to not be feared and somehow even with her ignorance of my status, I had managed to distill fear.

Perhaps I needed a change. A different approach.

I knew of only one way to talk, and that was with authority, as the Night Wolf. But if I was to become THE Master, and succeed in my deceit, I had to be a master.

Masters were held in authority, but they talked to slaves and servants directly, which is why she asked for my given name.

"M-Madam Catherine thought I would be useful in the Kitchen, it because of her that I survived, my lord."

That I already knew.

"And before that? Keffers are not known to live long in Valcane, especially in this territory. They are usually starved to death, abandoned."

Her hands shook visibly, her breathing eradicate, her voice even messier under twinned in a growing dread.

"I-I was found by a warrior w-who took me in with Kindness."

"Found?" I echoed interest peaked, and thoughts ran through my mind.

"So you were not born in this Territory," I stated, mainly to myself though she replied with a shiver.

"I'm n-not certain."

"And where were you before that?" I asked, eyes snapping back to her.

"I-"

"Who are you?" I huffed, eyes narrowing on her.

"Where did you come from?" My eyes traveled across her skin that echoed the peace I desired, Questions plagued my mind, her godforsaken scent sucking my mind to irritating madness.

"Do you understand that Deceiving an Arc Alpha is the highest crime? Do you not fear for your life in your deceit?"

"M-master-"

I licked my lips drinking her in, feeling thirsty as I panted. "Why are you so dark?"

"I-I do not know!" She suddenly burst, causing me to pause in shock, her eyes flashing to mine wide in flowing tears, her bottom lip quivering, a glint of strange madness in her eyes.

I should have torn her head off her body.

Never would I have let anyone raise their voice to me, not that anyone who was not my mother had ever attempted, no one was so foolish, and yet, instead of anger a new feeling dawned within me, one I was not particularly fond of.

Regret. One that soon mirrored hers.

Her eyes blinked in shock.

Swallowing deeply, shutting her eyes, and tears trailed down her cheeks that she wiped off rapidly. Her shoulders fell in soft relief. Her body suddenly calmed.

I watched all this curiously having seen that look on a few faces in my lifetime. It was a look of peace. One that came onto the faces of those who had already accepted their fate, their end.

"I-I was found in a forest by a warrior, with no memory of anything before, not even my name. So, I do not know where I came from nor do I know why I was born dark. I simply am."

Her voice was calm, as she crumpled to the floor, eyes set on the ground, sniffing for a second,

"I did not mean to deceive his Majesty, I merely survived. I know I am a curse and should not have been allowed into his Court. I am aware of my fate when he discovers me, what will be done..." she gulped softly.

"I only await my punishment."

She believed it was her time to die. And in truth, it should have been, from the moment she walked through my sanctuary.

She could have died on 3 separate occasions after this, and certainly her outburst even against a master as a slave of her status could only lead to death or things far worse, and yet somehow, equipped with the curse of a keffer, there was no one luckier at this moment.

My questions need to be answered.

I would not get them if she were dead.

Finding my mate was a fading hope I did not wish to rekindle, but with her scent directly around me, the thought of being unable to find out who and where she truly was, is too much to throw away.

Finding my true mate is the only thing that could put a stop to this madness, this bond Selene had made between an Arc Alpha and a Keffer. But if the Keffer was the clue to finding my true mate, deep inside, I would risk everything.

I would play Selene's game. The moon goddess loves to play games with our part of the Prime Wolf, it is no secret.

But this approach would not work. My jaw clenched as I stared down at the defeated girl already yearning for death.

If I was to get the information I so desired, I needed to try something different-

-something strange.

She needed to be comfortable enough to share what she had hidden in the depth of her subconscious. This could not be obtained through force, no, Selene would not make it so easy for me.

Studying her figure, the tight clench of her hands, I spotted fear, the dark kind I recognized beginning to grow on her as they did on the subjects that knew of my true nature.

One that had not been on her when our eyes first met today.

For the first time in my life, I felt I was losing.

Losing a battle. A battle over what? I couldn't put it in words or describe it in thoughts. But Selene was winning.

My mind ran rum-pant, desire flooding my mind in waves, an overflow of emotion so powerful that I did not believe it possible, so sudden that it made me blurt out a peculiar request.

"I need to study you, Keffer, you quite intrigue me. In return, I offer my protection. Do you accept?"

•|•|• Please drop a comment if you're enjoying the story and vote! I'll appreciate it! •|•|•

[9.1] A KEFFERS LUCK

● |•|•"Do you think the Night Wolf has a heart little one? His part of the Prime wolf is dark, tis why the Moon hides his soul.•|•|•

[Shade]

My breath paused low and shallow, my fingers as frozen as icicles clutched around my rag dress, as I stared straight ahead to the feet of the strange master that stood before me.

Confusion flooded my body, one that had been previously relaxed, having succumbed to my fate already.

I had simply made too many mistakes the past few days to deserve to take another breath. I had disobeyed Madam Catherine, let myself be seen by the dark shadow with amber eyes- whether that had been a trick of the light or not.

I had made noise in the master's library, a sanctuary they sought solace. Lit it up like it was midday on the hottest day of summer.

Then I had dared to look into the eyes of a master, not once but repeatedly and now- I had raised my voice, yelling at a ranked lord.

The only penalty that awaited me was death. It was what had always awaited me as a Keffer. No matter how hard I fought- no matter how many dreams I had of freedom, of the land beyond the sea.

I was supposed to be dead or severely punished to the point death would have been kinder, slaves were killed for far less and yet, here I knelt... still breathing.

A master offering his protection.

I blinked blankly at this, unable to comprehend if I had heard right, my fingers tightening around my dress.

"Did you hear me, Keffer?"

My body froze at the voice, drawing me back to reality, eyes clearing into the sight of his blurry robe that covered his sandaled feet slightly.

This couldn't be right.

Why would a master offer his protection? Was he trying to make a mockery of me?

If he was truly interested in me, he should know I have no choice but to be at his disposal, I had no rights over my own body, all he commanded I would do. He didn't have to offer anything in return.

It could be a trap. A trap to what? I couldn't say- but I could not believe a master would simply offer his protection to a Keffer.

My head bowed low, licking my dry lips.

But if he were honest, if his offer was true, what would he protect me from? He certainly had power over a lot of things as a master but from the Night Wolf?

He could only bow and tremble as everyone else did.

"Protection?" I whispered, my voice stale and hoarse, I smiled a little, though my mind was far gone. "A-ask master, I will answer. I am a slave- I will do your bidding. It is my punishment after all."

Silence loomed between us. My knees hurt from kneeling too long but that was the least of my troubles. I simply yearned for peace. I did not desire to leave Vale, but even she would understand that as a Keffer I never stood a chance.

I hated living in fear.

Perhaps the master would grant me a peaceful death.

Even if I was not killed today, if I did not manage to escape, or even worse, was caught escaping I would die a horrible death. Either by the guards or the night wolf himself.

"I know you are a slave-" he gritted out.

My heart pounded at this, he sounded angry-

He moved toward me until he was directly in front of me, my gaze immediately dropped further to the floor, and my breathing was low and harsh.

"And I know what authority I have over you," he continued, his voice slightly softer this time, my eyebrows arching as I took note of this.

A passing moment hovered between us, the sounds of our low breaths in the air. Mine followed slightly with panic.

"Look at me."

The command came strong but calm. I remained frozen. I couldn't understand why he asked this of me, it was against Madam Catherine's rules.

"You've done it more than once; you can certainly do it again."

My heart began that hard pound inside me. I couldn't understand if he desired for me to look up or if this was a reason to relieve my head off my body.

I shut my eyes, burying the panic that stormed within me, reminding myself my fate had always been certain. If I was to die, however, I would die as Shade Shadows, and not as a Keffer slave.

"Keffer?" he sang questionably but softly, his voice hanging in the air.

"Shade," I whispered, lowly to myself mostly, before looking up, capturing those peculiar eyes once more, his eyebrows slightly arched, lips a loose breath apart.

"Shade." He repeated, a dark glint in his eyes as they traveled my face for a moment.

Goosebumps traveled through my skin as he replayed my name. Something about the way he said it, how he played with it, I had only whispered it, but he had plucked it from its hidden pocket in thin air.

Wolves. Of course.

It can only be his sharp hearing.

His fingers moved toward my face, I hated when people tried to touch my skin and my hair, leaving their hateful comments about it, pulling at it.

I waited for that moment, closing my eyes softly, but it never came. I opened them, noticing his fingers had frozen spaces away, his eyes still studying my face, before pulling away, hands clasping behind his back.

I should have felt relieved but I knew, if he didn't touch it, it could be because he was the kind that thought of himself as to worthy to touch a Keffer.

I simply could not win.

"Do you accept?" He asked.

My eyebrows drew together. He was serious then? I could tell from the look in his eyes and the tightness in his jaw.

"Why would you wish to protect a Keffer if you could simply take what you want?" I asked softly, uncertain of the boldness I was displaying.

He rolled his eyes for a second, sighing, as he looked away, his eyes trailing to the bookshelf for a moment, before looking back at me, catching me suddenly as I studied the sharp outline of his side profile, causing me to catch a breath.

"Perhaps I have many slaves to control, perhaps it would be refreshing... for my study to have one to whom I can truly understand," he paused, his head slanting slightly as he studied me.

"If you can offer me that, I will give you my protection in exchange."

"Y-You need willingness."

He paused in my eyes at this, then nodded slowly.

"I need you to be free and open if I am to study you. I have my interests and my reasons. Looking into my eyes, I will be able to read your honesty."

I took out a shallow breath, my eyes dropping to the floor for a moment as I thought this through.

"A-and if I agree-" I began, uncertainty in my voice as I cleared my throat, "You say you will protect me. You have power over the guards, b-but Madam Catherine watches over us, she k-keeps us safe from them-" I paused, gulping, "At least so far," my eyes snapped up to him pausing for a moment.

"I only need protection from one being..."

"The Night Wolf."

We held each other's gaze as I nodded slowly.

"Y-yes but no one can protect me from him. My days are numbered in his court. And if the masters already know of my existence-" I swallowed bitterly.

"I am afraid it will only be a matter of time till he does."

Silence again.

"The Night Wolf will not hurt you."

My eyes snapped to him, nervously chuckling dryly for a bit.

"He will, I am a Keffer in his court. We are not supposed to live so long in his region," I whispered the last part softly.

He held my gaze for a moment, his jaw tightening before suddenly walking past me.

My eyebrows arched, eyes following him, my body slightly turning.

"I will keep the other masters in order, they will listen to me. I am the Night Wolf's most trusted master after all."

My eyes widened at this, my heart beating lowly. His most trusted master? Could I be this lucky? Was it possible?

Could I even trust him?

Then again, he had no reason to lie. I could be safe, at least until I had an escape plan.

"Still, you are right, it has its risks. Trusted or not, The Night wolf does what he pleases," He trailed off, whilst my heart fell slowly.

He turned round again facing me. "Think about it, Shade. I'll return for your answer."

With that, he moved through the aisles, getting lost in the flicker of light.

•|•|• Please drop a comment if you're enjoying the story and vote! I'll appreciate it! •|•|•

[10.1] A KINGS FRIEND

|•|•"You will be silent to your omega's, you will bow to your beta, and kiss the feet of your Alpha. But to your King Keffer? You are not even worthy to pass a breath."•|•|•

[Shade Shadows]

"Oh, Selene! You've returned!" Vale screeched, throwing her arms around me as soon as I walked through the doors of the slave quarters, sweaty, tired with dust littered against my brow.

I could barely breathe in her tight squeeze, a small smile grazing my face, glancing over her shoulder as she spoke.

"I was sure- so sure that you were in some sort of trouble. Thank Selene you're back, I worried about your return," she sniffed, her voice slipping, breathing deep and heavy against me.

My eyes glazed over the slaves that looked our way, whispering slowly among themselves. I pulled away from her, calmly speaking lowly just for her to hear, "I suppose I thought so too, but this is not the place to discuss it."

Her eyes were red and soggy, her eyebrows arching in confusion. She turned slightly, noticing the growing eyes on her as a result of hugging a Keffer. She turned back to me in frustration,

"And you think I care?" She sniffled, wiping her nose.

"I was worried! I thought I would never see you again." she gritted out, staring me dead in the eye.

I swallowed dryly, understanding her pain.

Vale was emotional, but I could barely blame her in such a situation. She was the only person I had to love and so was I for her. Leaving her alone in the very house of the Night Wolf was unfair. But if we were to escape from here, we couldn't let our feelings derail our plan.

I grabbed her by the hand, leading her out of the slave quarters, in the hidden shadows of the corridors.

She pulled out of my grip, frustration laced in her every word, "I want to know what happened! Where did Madam Catherine take you? What did she say? Does she know that you went to the"

I cut her off, by clasping a hand over her mouth, head bowed as an omega guard passed by, grunting to himself about the smell of the slave quarters.

I watched as he disappeared around the corner. She pushed my hands off her face, folding her arms, her gaze square, lips a firm line.

Sighing, with the knowledge that it was my fault I had frightened her, even though to be fair, I was quite worried for my life as well in that instance, I was able to calmly explain all that happened, and she listened attentively. I told her of the strange master and his strange request to which her eyebrows arched in deeper confusion.

"Do you truly believe he is of good intentions, Shade?" She huffed, disbelief in her tone, "it pains me to say, but Valcane will never be so good to Keffer's and slaves. Tell me you have not already forgotten how even omegas behaved towards us, and our fellow slaves! Do you truly think, accepting this offer of his is what's best for you? Since when did the Night Wolf care about the likes of slaves to order a study of us? It could be a trap for Selene's sake! You said he told you to look into his eyes! That could have you hanging in the gallows!"

"And you think I have a choice, Vale?" I cautioned, my voice straining slightly though I tried to keep it low. "A master asks this of me, and he offers his protection, and if I tell him no.." I trailed off.

"How is that of any benefit to me?"

Her lips were pursed in a thin line as I continued to speak.

"Do you not think I have doubts? Of course, I know Valcane has never been kind to me and it will never be to those of my kind but if he truly desires to see me end." I trailed off.

"My answer is of no importance. Yes or no, it's all the same. I am a slave and a Keffer, I have nothing to protect me if he chooses to be malicious. But..." I paused, gulping, afraid of making myself believe in the words I was about to utter.

"If he truly is of good intent. And if he really will protect me, perhaps Selene has found a bit of Favour in me. Even if it is just for a while, it will give us a bit of time for our escape..." I whispered the last word lowly.

"And if the worst is true?" She whispered.

"Then at least I would have gotten some information from him. He claims to be the Night Wolf's most trusted, perhaps I can learn a thing or two to protect myself."

Her eyes studied me for a second, before sighing. "I know you are smart, and I understand you feel this is what needs to be done, but I cannot help but sense a deception. My wolf warns me of this. There is something ... wrong." Her eyebrows arched at her statement.

"Nothing about Valcane is Fair, you know that."

She nodded at my statement, eyes reaching me. "I do not agree, and I wish I could make you see how I see, but you are certainly right about one thing. I don't believe you truly have a choice if a master so highly ranked requests this of you. The best you can do is work with what you have and try to weave it for our benefit."

I hummed in agreement, my hand resting on her shoulder. "I will be careful, I promise."

Her hand laid over mine and she smiled, "That is all I ask, Shade, it is all I ask."

—————————-

I stared at the crimson door for a few seconds, biting my bottom lip. After last night, all I could think of was the master. Would he be waiting for me with those peculiar eyes on the other side or would it be something worse?

The shadow?

I shivered at this, cracking my neck. This was no time to project fear. I had a whole library to clean the size of a grand ballroom. The quicker I would get through it, the better.

Letting out a deep breath, I opened the door, letting its soft creaks run through me, the darkness engulfing the only light streaming from the door. Leaving the door open, I walked in cautiously with my torch, in the direction I knew the oil was placed.

Lighting the place up, I quickly prayed they were no masters studying in there, letting the silence linger for a moment. When nothing happened, I was calmer, moving around the library with my equipment. I came to a standstill before a high window, a good floor above.

Curiosity peaked, and I walked up the stairs, pulling a wheeled ladder along the rows to the large darkened window above. Opening the dark shaded window let the light flood in. Stepping higher on the ladder, I held my breath when I saw the view down below. I couldn't believe it.

It was the maze, the full maze sprawled out there in perfect view. Ripe for sketching. My heart pounded at the sight. It wasn't a partial sketch like the one I could see from the tower, here I could see the exit and the entrance from the splendid height. A victorious smile spread across my face; I couldn't believe I was this lucky. An escape for Vale and me, just waiting.

Suddenly a blurry object darted across from me and I almost toppled off the ladder in surprise when a bird perched against the sill, cawing loudly as if to announce its landing.

My gaze narrowed on the bird as it hopped along the window sill, perching right in front of me, cawing again, flashing its pitch-black feathers, beady black eyes looking at me attentively.

My eyebrows arched, recognizing the creature before me. This couldn't be the same Raven, could it?

"Are you..." I trailed off, slowly reaching out to pet it, expecting it to fly off as a bird would but it stood still, my fingers grazing its silky feathers, beady eyes still on me.

A small grin spread on my face, "It's you."

I paused, drowning in a wave of confusion, "I told you to fly home pretty bird, why would you return?"

It only clicked to the side, hopping closer, eyes staring right at me. I chuckled stroking its feathers.

"Why am I talking to a bird?" I grunted.

"You are so..." my eyes examined the bird noting it was a bit bigger than the average raven, only now spotting the white diamond-shaped spot on its forehead, "peculiar."

"Who are you talking to?"

I almost had a heart attack at the sudden statement, spinning around, holding the ladder dramatically before I could topple over. My eyes only widened, meeting the intriguing bluish-green haze of the master, standing a few feet away, hands clasped behind his back poshly.

I breathed out in relief, which made his eyebrows arch and in turn, made me realize I was staring at him in the eyes again.

I was aware he had encouraged it the last time but by instinct I awkwardly leveled down to just below his chin, trying to sort through my jumbled thoughts.

"Master," I gave a short bow, one hand keeping me up on the ladder.

"I was uh..." I turned back around, eyebrows arching at the sight of the empty window sill, gaze reaching out of the window to the birdless outside,

"Talking to myself it seems..." I trailed off, whispering it mostly to myself, before turning back around, once again almost falling off the ladder due to my unnatural lack of balance it seemed. I held onto the ladder for dear life, heart thudding before I could sway forward.

"Perhaps you should get down."

My eyes snapped to the Master, once again dropping my gaze from his eyes to below his chin before he could catch me, nodding awkwardly.

"Yes, master."

I slowly got down, surely and steadily until I reached the floor. I patted down my ragged dress, turning back to him with my dusting cloth in hand, slightly breathless and also a bit intimidated when I realized I was standing before the master once more.

I couldn't reach his eyes again, instead, my gaze rested below his chin. If his intent was malicious, it was best to play it safe.

Bowing lowly once more, I found my gaze wandering to everything and anything that was not him as the silence reigned between us.

"Have you thought about my offer?" He asked.

His tone was stale but somehow anxious.

I nodded, my fingers twisting around the cloth. My heart was pounding within its cage. I couldn't get myself to say anything past that and I inwardly cringed. But this is how I was raised. I couldn't just speak to a master without waiting for his permission. I was too below him.

"And what is your decision?"

My eyes darted to and from, trying to pluck up some invisible courage, "I-I do not believe that I could speak freely with a master, even if I tried. I was simply not raised that way, my lord. As much as your offer is... tempting, in truth, even if I did accept, I would always be careful in my words. You are my master, I am your slave, and I would not want to anger you."

Silence lingered between us for a moment, and I could feel his eyes on me, but I dared not look up, my breath hot against my skin as I felt him drink me in.

"Is that so?" He asked.

I nodded, biting my lip.

"How unfortunate."

My heart fell at these words, hiding my shaky fingers as I summoned up the needed courage, my eyes slowly trailed upwards, until they reached his, holding his gaze in a moment of defiance, noting the noticeable disappointment on his face that morphed into confused interest.

"H-however," I continued a slight stutter in my voice as my breathing ragged. "Perhaps if we were not master and slave, I could be... free and willing."

His eyebrows arched, staring at me right in the eyes, studying my every word.

"And how do you propose that occurs?"

"There is... a person, I could tell all my secrets, worries, hopes and dreams to. One I could rely on, and trust. Which is needed if I am to be free around them," I explained, my voice staggering in uncertainty, carefully watching his expressions though he seemed to be listening attentively.

"Who is this person?"

I gulped slowly, not knowing how he would react to this proposal. "T-they call such people friends."

He seemed to pause at this while my breath got stuck within my lungs, my heart rattling within me. I could see him process this at quite an amazing speed.

"You..." he trailed off, uttering in disbelief, "You wish to be my friend?"

I could sense the surprise in his tone, one I imagined couldn't be good, for I had just asked a master to lower his status and become the friend of a slave and a Keffer. But I was on a steady roll and I had nothing to lose. I tried to keep up my courage but I found myself rambling.

"Well, to be fair, it is more of a two-sided thing... my friend... your friend... it's not that...uh..." I ended this wreck of a sentence by awkwardly sticking out a dust-covered hand, and pursing my lips closed with one word, "Complicated."

His eyes dropped to my offered hand, raising them slowly to meet mine and I could almost sense the amusement directed at my stupidity and my audacity. To think he would agree to be friends with a slave and a Keffer or even touch a Keffer's skin was laughable enough.

I felt the courage drain me, embarrassment and fear returning in an instant as I stared at my dusty hand, awkwardly perched in mid-air. Who did I think I was to ask such of a master?

I was about to retrieve my hand when something big and warm clasped around it, and I stared in confusion at the contact. Clean hands engulfed mine, a sudden warm feeling traveling through me at the connection, my eyes snapping back to him.

"I suppose this means I agree. Are we friends now with this action?" he asked.

I looked down at our connection still in shock, nodding mindlessly.

He pulled away, but I stared at my just shook, hand awkwardly looking back up at him, mouth wide open in surprise.

"I like this," he stated, placing his hands behind his back once again, eyes narrowing on nothing in particular.

"A friend. I've always wanted one of those."

•|•|• Please drop a comment if you're enjoying the story and vote! I'll appreciate it! •|•|•

[11.1] A TRUST TO BUILD

● |•|•"They Fear me, mother. I approach and they run for the hills. I speak and they remain silent. I am never denied, never refused. I am a child and a god."•|•|•

[Kayos]

The moment passed between us as my eyes strained toward the window pane where the morning light shined through.

There was a strange magic I sensed there but it was light enough to be ignored especially when more important things plagued my mind.

The tingles that danced against my fingertips clasped behind my back were one of those things. It was the contact, the strange flow that had enraptured me at that moment, that still had a brazen effect I was not too keen on ever experiencing again.

However, it was action needed, I was taken by surprise at her countered offer.

She wished to be my friend.

She was the only one who had ever asked, and it was a strange realization that she was probably the only one who ever could.

From the moment I was little, I had desired a friend. I marveled at watching the young pups play in the courtyard, with swords, shifting freely. Father had said I was not the kind of wolf to shift for fun... I should have listened to him.

My wolf brought fear and darkness. My aura was too great for the young pups. I couldn't control my Alpha tone and ended up barking orders always even when I didn't mean to.

I had followers, not friends. As I grew, I had subjects. Even my most trusted adviser, Gregory was not a friend. His loyalty came from his wolf, from his instinct to obey and protect his Alpha.

Only the Keffer before me who had no wolf to command, or to feel loyalty, no way to read my aura, no obligation to obey unless by rank could truly be a friend.

She was smart, rank was what separated us in her mind since she had no wolf, and rank is what she took away. I had thought of Keffer's as ordinary mistakes, this one was a smart one it seemed.

My eyes dropped to hers, still fighting the strange sensation that danced around my fingertips aching for more contact. Her eyes remained wide and confused staring down at her open palm.

I glanced down at it. It was filthy... and yet I ached to touch her once more. It was a strange thought; one I knew mirrored the bond Selene placed between us. My eyebrows arched noting she kept staring at it, her lips sparsely open, and her heartbeat sounded almost non-existent.

"Am I supposed to shake it again? I am not aware of the rules of friendship."

Her eyes snapped to me at my statement, eyes wide as if taken out of a trance, but her gaze immediately dropped to below my chin, withdrawing her hand quickly, fingers rubbing her palm, stuttering a reply.

"No... I ... uh-" she paused, swallowing softly, her eyes slowly trailing up to mine, her voice soft and tiny, "I didn't think you would do it."

I held her gaze for a moment, marveling at the darkest shade of night in them, a breath trapped in my chest. I looked away before they could truly bewitch me, nodding, and clenching my jaw.

"I am committed to my study-"

Her gaze had dropped when I glanced back at her, noting an air of disappointment,

"And I have never had a friend before, therefore I am quite curious."

Her eyes flashed to me, a look of disbelief in them, and then the most peculiar thing happened. A small smile echoed against the corners of her lips making my heart stop. No one smiled my way, if not my mother- it was weird but satisfying to see I was the cause of a smile from someone who would be otherwise a stranger.

"Lying is not the best way to start a friendship master," she warned, her tone light and playful.

I frowned in confusion, and she seemed to note it.

"You are a master, you've had friends."

"I've had subjects," I corrected realizing her thoughts, eyes holding hers, speaking truthfully, "And followers."

My voice trailed off as I remembered my cousins, "I have competitors and enemies to be quaint. None of them are my friends. At least not what I thought friendship was."

Her smile dropped slowly, which made me purse my lips. I could hear her heartbeat slow, and a sad aura around her which I couldn't understand why.

It did not come from fear, if it were, her heart would be pounding.

Still, I was not too fond of the look, it felt like she could see through me, something no one did. Darkness wasn't transparent.

If you looked into the darkness, darkness stared right back at you.

She was looking at me nevertheless, the being behind the darkness. I had no idea how she opened those curtains and revealed what was behind them, perhaps it was I that did it myself.

She was easy to talk to I finally understood. That could be a blessing and a problem.

I turned away from her gaze studying the stacks of books around us.

"Are there rules to this friendship? How does it begin?"

A moment passed before she spoke, her tone was slow and steady as if she wanted me to understand it.

"True friendship is built on trust. I do not believe it has rules but perhaps the logical ones."

"What are those?"

"The holy trinity. Do not betray or lie to a friend, always protect a friend, keep their trust."

I turned slightly, eyes reaching hers, to which hers dropped, right below my chin again. "Simple enough-"

"Perhaps for safety, we could add that our friendship should remain within these walls," she rambled quickly, her gaze trailing the library. "As a slave I-I can't-"

"I understand," I countered.

I was quite aware of how the outside world would look at this friendship I was weaving with a Keffer slave against all conceivable logic. To lower my standards to the absolute bottom would be more than frowned upon. I was also aware of my deceit. As the Night Wolf she feared, it was best she knew only of me as the master and now friend. I reached for her gaze but it remained faltered below my chin.

"Friends always look each other in the eyes."

Her eyes snapped to me at that statement.

I studied her for a moment, wondering if this rule I designed would be for my benefit or my downfall. I could read her honesty in them, but she could see through the veil of darkness and see me in mine.

But she had not mastered her trade, nor did she know of the power she had over me, hence... this was to my benefit.

"That is the rule I wish to add. Whilst we are within these walls."

She blinked as if not expecting such a rule, but nodded, taking a deep breath in, recapturing my eyes. "5 rules for the foundations of our friendship."

I nodded at this, searching her face, "And trust? How do we build that?"

"I'll tell you my deepest secret and you tell me yours."

I paused at this, knowing my secret was not something I ever wished to reveal to her, not if I was to find out why Selene has placed her with my mate's scent,

"I will tell you of a secret, perhaps when we grow our friendship, I'll tell you my deepest."

She thought this through, nodding, "Fair enough."

"Shall I begin?"

She nodded, letting out another loose breath.

"When I was little, my cousins came over to visit," I began. "One of the only 3 times they did. I got into an argument with one of them, an obnoxious wart who was adamant in proving he was the best among us."

Her eyebrows moved along with the story, and her hands propped forward as I glanced at her.

"We were standing at the height of a staircase. He claimed he could jump and land on his feet like a cat because his wolf was so powerful. He was a pompous bastard, and in so doing, I pushed him off the stairs."

Her jaw dropped and I turned to look at her unfeeling, her hands covering her mouth.

"I-is he alive? Did he m-make it?"

My eyebrows arched at the absurd remark, not understanding the actual look of concern mirrored in her eyes.

"Fir is not easy to Kill, unfortunately." I huffed with a roll of my eyes, "When mother asked what happened, I claimed he merely tripped. It's not my fault he was naturally clumsy."

"W-what happened then?"

"He broke his leg obviously, in a way that not even his Alpha wolf could heal as quickly as he should have normally, " I sighed, "and I proved wolves are wolves and cats... are cats."

I was shocked to hear laughter, turning around wide-eyed to a chuckling maiden.

I stared awkwardly realizing I had never been in such a position. Laughter wasn't done around me. Seeing it done because of me was strange...but strangely refreshing.

"All that to prove a point?" She giggled, "You cannot be that petty."

I shrugged and she chuckled again, causing me to fully turn her way.

Not knowing how to react to her laughter, I opted to speak, "And your secret?"

Her laughter died down slowly, but a look of amusement lingered in them.

"My secret? It's not as glamorous as yours, I have few secrets as a Keffer, but I will tell you one."

I nodded at this, eager to hear something, anything that could make me understand the pleasure sinking within me with every moment I remained this close to her.

"I have dreams, strange dreams." She began.

My ears strained slightly.

"I've dreamt of the Night Wolf many times, in one recurring dream. I think it is because I fear him, that dreams of him always seem so real," she confessed.

My breathing was shallow as I listened, my heart a steady but anxious beat within me, "What do you dream of him?"

"I'm in a field, tormented by the pups of my old pack. It's the only game they know how to play well, scare the Keffer."

My heart pounds harder as the memories flash within me.

"They surround me and I'm afraid but then, something scarier than them sends them off. And then, I'm in a field, standing in a place where darkness and light meet."

My breath is trapped and I'm unable to move as I stare at her, and she speaks what I fear.

"And there I see it. The Night Wolf, bigger than anything I thought possible, eyes two embers in a sheet of darkness, and all he does is stare at me. Like he's coming to get me. Like I cannot escape him."

Her gaze drops but my eyes are on a memory of her. I remember the moment that haunts her dreams. Had she been a wolf I would have done just that.

Taken her with me.

Had she been truly mine, she would have never escaped me.

She suddenly smiled, though it did not reach her eyes.

"T-they say fear becomes your nightmares. I think I'm scared of death," she shrugs, her voice a light shake as she chuckles softly.

"They call the night wolf the embodiment of darkness. They sing songs of how the prince of darkness will come to end abominations like mine. I do not know why I fear it. It is death I should embrace as a Keffer, for it never is too far away."

I stared at her for a lingering moment, my heart rampant within me, faster than I ever thought it could pound, and I turned away.

"Fear is normal, but sometimes we fear things because we do not know anything else about them."

She nodded at this, her gaze falling to the ground. "B-but you are the Night Wolf's most trusted, perhaps rumors are rumors and he is not exactly as they say?"

I paused at this, eyes recapturing hers, staring at the ray of hope she was throwing my way.

Flashes of death flooded my memories. Of the hunts I sent my shadows, of the deaths I had dealt with my bare hands, and of the fear my wolf had instilled for his pleasure. The many dark days I give, tormenting my subjects.

Friends speak the truth.

I studied her, shaking my head slowly, "He is everything they say and more."

I could see the light of hope flicker and blow out in the wind and I clenched my jaw.

"I have matters to attend to now, I will be on my way."

She nodded, and I passed by her,

"I-I'll see you tomorrow.... Friend?"

I pause in my tracks at the term, slightly turning. Nodding, I wordlessly promise before trailing into the shadows of darkness where I belonged.

ANNOUNCEMENT!!!

Hey guys! Firstly I hope you enjoyed my double update I know it's been a while but I do have good news. I will be posting chapters of MATED TO THE NIGHT WOLF (MTTNW) every Saturday. However, this will probably be my last DOUBLE update on Wattpad. So expect a chapter (one chapter only) every week on Wattpad.

However, if you want to read more chapters, I have opened up a Patreon account for any readers who wish to support my work whilst having regular access to ADVANCED chapters.

Links to my Patreon are posted on my profile.

Chapter [12.5- A WAR IS WHISPERED] has already been posted up there and DOUBLE updates will be posted there a week before they are made available on Wattpad. Again, I WILL still be posting the book on wattpad, but advanced chapters will be available first on Patreon.

I have also opened a discord channel for anyone who wishes to join my author community for announcements, exclusive content, eventual video and audio content, and direct access to me in case of anything.

Links to my discord channel are also in my bio on my profile.

Any support will be highly appreciated. I hope to have at least 20 people on my discord channel before I start posting stuff, so once you join, just let me know. You are also free to invite other people.

P. S You can earn a rank on discord by joining a tier on Patreon if you wish to upgrade your reader rank.

•|•|•Please drop a comment if you're enjoying the story and vote! I'll appreciate it!•|•|•

[12.1] A WAR IS WHISPERED

•|•|•"The Land Beyond the sea is the land of men. Men have trained dogs to obey their will, and one day, they will want wolves."•|•|•

[Kayos]

I had no reason to be as angry as I was at this moment. Perhaps anger was not what it was, if it were I would have taken the sun out of the sky, released my wolf into the wild forest to hunt, or sent a shadow to harvest a soul.

Frustration?

No. That was not this feeling. Could it? That I had hoped, for one thing, to open her up so I could see the secrets Selene had hidden within her. To control her fear.

I had even become a friend... a foreign word to me. A want I had let go of wishing for YEARS ago, now just offered to me so casually.

Instead of clearing that fear, I chose to speak the truth without any true obligation. Just because I did not wish to lie, I told her the truth about the dark nature within me.

Why was I picking what to give? What obligation did I have to tell the truth? A friend, she called me. I had already broken the rules. I was deceiving her, but somehow, I could not bring myself to tell a single lie.

I was darkness itself, lying is my invention.

I rolled my eyes, pausing my pacing for a moment. I must not get carried away. Selene knows of my every weakness. My lack of patience.

Breathing out slowly, I closed and then opened my eyes again.

Despite everything, I had learned something new about the Keffer. She did remember my visit. Even if disguised as a recurrent dream, it was clear Selene had made her not forget that day. She remembered my wolf, she remembered its eyes, the field of night and Day.

My wolf brought darkness with it wherever it went. Covered the sky in darkness, whilst her side remained in light. Had I approached her, she would have been covered in darkness. My thoughts slipped to the image of her skin, my mouth dry and somehow thirsty, she was already wearing darkness on her like a fine robe.

A scratch-like sound caught my attention and I watched as a shadow detached itself from the wall, crawling quietly on all eight showy legs across the room, pausing in front of me.

"Proceed."

It moved toward me on command, its shadowy finger absorbing within me, sharing its news with me. I could see all it had seen, and hear all that was meant to be heard, my eyes glowing a low amber before it detached, slipping back into the shadows.

I grunted at this, a fire brewing within me, the shadows all ran from the walls converging in the middle of the floor, emerging like a dark cloud.

My eyes flashed amber, gritting my jaw as I walked in, coming out into a bright tent-like room, the sounds of giggles reaching my ears first, followed by two familiar scents.

An open bed came to view and the two naked wolves in it, giggling and, kissing between themselves to my absolute compulsion.

"Is there a reason you seek war Vaeln?"

The two wolves in bed sat up, quite surprised, Vaeln immediately covering his half-naked mate behind him protectively, growling lowly when he spotted me.

"Kayos."

"You dare come across my borders without call and break the treaty? Is this an act of war? Your camp is not many, neither is it guarded."

He growled, his arm still hiding his mate. "For Selene's sake, give us a bit of privacy, how dare you shadow into my private chambers! Keep your eyes off my mate."

"How dare you step onto my territory. Bringing your mate here is your folly. For her Sake, I hope your Arc Wolf is better than the last time we fought."

He growled again lowly, a hideous look in his eyes, turning slightly and whispering lowly to his mate. She nodded as he kissed her forehead, and she moved with a wrapped sheet around her, out of the tent.

Vaeln stared back at me, sighing, before shaking his head. He stood up in all his little glory, grabbing a robe.

"I am not here to declare war Kayos. Kayos, Chaos... perfectly named," he mumbled.

Darkness suddenly engulfed the tent so it was pitch black, my amber eyes the only thing gleaming in the tent as my wolf echoed through.

"Words are minor Vaeln. You are 3 weeks too early for the Council, and you camp by borders in secret. Your actions are very... warlike."

Lightning zapped in the darkness, his arms glowing in light, bolts of light hanging in every corner to light the pitch darkness, his eyes glowing, before growling it all away, turning back to pour himself some wine.

"I was going to send word, I did not want Dane, or Selene forbids, Firdon to hear of it. You might be a pompous asshole, the reincarnation of darkness itself, but I know you are too powerful to want my land."

I watched as he handed me a glass of wine. "Drink, cousin."

When I didn't respond, he scoffed, setting the wine on the table, "there is a war coming, I feel it in my bones. Some rogue packs off my farthest borders to the west bodies were found a couple of weeks ago," he explained, "I would not care if rogues kill themselves, but I have reason to believe this is far deeper."

"Firdon."

He glanced at me, chuckling.

"My thoughts at first, if there was an asshole between the four of us, foolish enough to start a war it would be the Fire Wolf," he mocked, "But they were no markings that fire could leave behind or packs beneath him," he paused.

"These markings were not even Valcanian. They were strange, different. When my scouts reported this, days later, the bodies of the slaughtered rogues could not be found and the forest land was... dying. As I speak, some trees have become wasted bark in a matter of days. This has happened to 3 rogue packs in 5 months,"

I watched as he moved, studying his movements. I had no reason to trust Vaeln. My cousins were as selfish as I was, they cared for no one but themselves. However, if there was an Arc Alpha closest to Selene's light and the first to receive a mate for her favor it was Vaeln, the Light Wolf.

If this was true, then asking for my help could only mean the threat seemed serious.

"Not Valcanian." I repeated, "You believe the threat is from the land of men."

He sunk into a seat. "What do we know of men? Except for the wolf stories our fathers spoke to us. Men are not supposed to have magic, it wastes in their hands and dies. Perhaps these men have conquered our borders and their scents have killed the ancient forests. The scents that linger in the dead forests are foul, unlike any I have ever smelled. Not even the scents of your demon shadows," he spat. "They have tamed wild dogs, perhaps they want wolves too."

"Men are weak and foolish, but they are not stupid," I grunted. "They cannot attack Valcane whilst all four Arc Alphas are in their prime unless all they desire is the end of their existence. I know of the lands of men; they trade at our borders. We have treaties with them, and they do not wander away from the ports."

I downed my wine, placing it on the table.

"This is my first and only warning. Leave my land and return only for the tribunal Council of Courts on my mating, per custom," I turned around, the darkness leaving and forming a dark cloud behind me.

My eyes gleamed amber, "And we are far from wild dogs Vaeln, They can only bite. We wolves destroy and devour."

With that, I stepped through the shadow.

———

"How is the trade at the border?"

"Steady your majesty," Kirion replied, with a short bow. He moved closer to the desk, placing the reports.

My gaze traveled through them, whilst I could feel the middle-aged man, hold his breath as he did every time he brought reports to his king.

Then after, he would look at Master Gregory for his approval.

It was simply because he failed to look at my face directly, and somehow only Master Gregory had correctly mastered my expressions, whether I was angry or I was in approval.

Sometimes he got it wrong though, luckily for Kirion, this was not one of the times.

I could feel him let out a sigh of relief whilst I finished going through the reports.

It was quite annoying at times, that I knew of every fear lingering in the eyes of someone just by looking at them. I paused at a particular report, not because there was something particularly interesting but simply because my mind was far gone.

My little keffer friend was not like that. With her... Shade. I froze as her name repeated in my head. I did not care so much for the feeling that crossed my body. She looked at me like I was human and though she feared things, she was able to treat me like a friend.

I was a friend.

"Y-your majesty? Is anything wrong with the reports?"

My eyes flashed to Gregory, only now hearing the fast heartbeat and the wincing of the wolf of Kirion. I did not look at him, it would only worsen his situation.

Instead, I closed the book, "Everything is all right."

Gregory nodded, his eyes trailing to Kirion,

"Thank you for the reports."

Kirion nodded, bowing lowly before scampering out.

I only looked up when the door closed, gaze lingering on it for a second. "Do you think men would start a war with Valcane?"

"I think men are selfish creatures, but they are not stupid. They are getting all they need from Valcane because of our trade. Your father brokered a deal with the Men Kings in his time and it has served us well. I do not think they would start a war."

I nodded, "My thoughts repeated, but we cannot be too sure. Selfishness sometimes gets in the way of common sense," I turned to Gregory.

"Send word to Vaeln. Tell him I will look at his problem after my investigations."

"As you command, your majesty." He stood up, walking toward the door when he suddenly paused, turning.

My eyebrows arched at his awkward movement, raising an eyebrow.

"Speak."

"If I may your majesty. Any information from the keffer?"

I paused at this, actually surprised he had asked. Gregory was the type to advise and command when asked, nothing more.

Yet somehow, my abomination of my mate had piqued his interest.

"She remembers the day I first saw her. She remembers my wolf. It is a concurrent dream in her mind."

He paused. "Selene bids her to remember. It must be for a reason."

I nodded. "I am sure, but it will take a while if I am to find out what that reason is."

Gregory bowed lowly. "All in due time your majesty."

With that, he took his leave.

•|•|• Please drop a comment if you're enjoying the story and vote! I'll appreciate it! •|•|•

[13.1] A SECRET MEET

● |•|• "And who will I trust mother, since I have no friends?"•|•|•

[Master Gregory]

There was a strange ancient air that seemed to whistle through the trees of Valcane. One that brought in a scent of mystery and an echo of a warning I couldn't wrap my head around.

I looked up from the paperwork as the pigeon landed on the window sill, the sun shining brightly through as it cooed softly.

Getting out of my seat, I approached it, reaching for the bird. It remained cool and calm under my touch even as I untangled the note from its foot.

My eyes glazed over the short words encoded, my fists tightening around the small parchment.

Shutting my eyes at the news, I walked back to my desk, burning the paper into the singular candle fire, and then took a seat once more, and got back to work.

It was nightfall when I walked out of the study, nodding to a pair of guards that bowed in respect when I walked past.

The slight night breeze wheezed by as I turned the corner past the open window of the farthest tower. A few more guards nodded my way as I moved through the dark hallways.

Descending a staircase in the tower, exiting into another empty dark hallway, a heavily cloaked figure stepping out of the shadows.

"Master Gregory," the young lad bowed lowly, handing me my dark cloak.

"Not here, Liston."

He nodded quietly with another bow before following me, our steps in rhythm. I threw on my dark coat and pulled the dark hood up. Shadows in the passageways hid our frames as we slipped between halls. Nothing but the sounds of our short breaths could be heard.

My eyes carefully glazed the corners of each hall, searching the shadows.

Nowhere was too safe.

Pushing the doors open, we descended further into the darkness, down another staircase to the dungeons. Quietly we marched passed the whispering of prisoners and wailing, the scent of blood and rusted metal vanishing as we moved further.

The way became narrower until we reached a barred door. Unlocking it, we maneuvered the old forgotten underground castle tunnels and then slipped into the opening, revealing the darkness of midnight outside.

"The light, Liston."

"Yes, master."

Soon enough the torch flickered in a singular flame. Liston dusted his coat, his face partly illuminated as he held it to his head. Strips of his golden locks pulled back into a bun as his blue eyes met mine.

"The horses are this way master." He continued, leading the way.

We moved further into the darkness until we reached a thicket of trees. As was stated, there the horses stood, neighing softly as we approached.

Wasting no time, we saddled and galloped off.

The wind beat at our faces as we raced through the Veldeon Forest. It took nearly a half hours horse ride to reach the Elders' house, off route from the main path, hidden by vines, lumbering trees, and overgrown bushes. Farther from any city or pack in the Night Wolf's territory and hidden to the eyes of everyone but those who know of it.

Reaching the small abode, we dismantled, tying our horses to the tree. I stared at the image of the lone cabin for a moment, studying its abandoned exterior.

"Is this where she truly resides my lord?" Liston inquired, standing breathlessly beside me. "It looks to be abandoned."

I glanced at him wordlessly and then proceeded toward the cottage.

He followed after, almost tripping over a fallen branch.

Pausing by the door, I let out a loose breath.

The pattern of entry had to be remembered. It had been years but it was one I could never forget.

Three knocks, Pause. Twice more, then once more, steady against the brittle surface of the rotting yet secure oak door.

The door seemed to grow in response coming to life.

A face began to contort shifting the lines of the old wood in peculiar waves as a wooden-faced hag formed from the exterior, wailing shortly as if it had been awakened from its slumber.

Liston to stepped back in shock, wide eyes shifting to me as his torch flickered in the night wind, "U-uncle."

I ignored his stutter, glancing over at the boy, "Have you not seen old magic?"

He shook his head, swallowing heavily, "I don't believe I've seen any kind of magic," he confessed, swallowing deeply as he glanced at the wooden hag's face.

"Yes, Magic is nearly gone save the few that have it," I replied, eyes trailing back to the now fully formed hag, waiting patiently for its question.

"Who livessssss between worlds? What comethhhhh at the end? What fearssssss blindeth the truth?" it hissed, old lines of golden magic trailing around its crooked exterior, jagged teeth forming and deforming.

I looked into the depths of its pale grey eyes without blinking.

"The Mage, Death, and the Mages Curse."

"You live... Thissssss time." It hissed, before dissolving back into old wood, the sound of a clicking following after as it unlocked itself.

The door creaked open into what looked like the darkest room to exist in Valcane. I glanced at Liston who seemed to still be in a state of shock, grunting before proceeding into the darkness of the Cabin.

It was far from what it looked like on the exterior. Inside it was a stoned hall, instead of the wood, it deceived on the outside.

Torches suddenly lit themselves up at each corner as we stepped in.

We came to a pause at the center, standing side by side amid the lightened room, almost as bright as if it were mid-day in the Light Wolf's territory.

"Master-"

"Shh," I quickly hushed, remaining unfazed. My eyes trailed the empty corners, narrowing in search of the elder.

"You dare bring an unchosen to the Council of the Mage?" A stale crooked voice rang around me.

"Do you not fear for your life, Master Gregory?" It spat my title in a drawled hiss as if it was an abomination.

My throat run dry but I remained unmoved.

"Elder, I ask for your forgiveness," I bowed lowly, though remained unfazed.

"The boy is my nephew, and I bring him to pledge," I explained, my eyes shifting to the empty spaces in search of the voice.

"But I assure you, I do not fear death either as I stand in its presence every day."

"You speak of Night Wolf..." the voice trailed off, a figure stepping from the wall, once camouflaged in grey. The wall seemed to peel off her skin as she moved further into the light.

The flames revealed the Elder. Her face resembled the hag from the door but I knew better.

The Elder merely wore a disguise. It was necessary if she was to survive in the Night Wolf's territory and remain undiscovered. There were too many shadows and informants that lurked within the darkness. It would be reckless to reveal one's true self.

Her eyes gleamed in the flicker of light, walking toward a torch. Taking it from its mount, she moved closer to us.

Liston's unsure eyes met mine as she approached him, studying him intently. I stepped aside and allowed her to circle him.

"A pledge..." she trailed off, her pale eyes snapping to mine, "Does he know the truth?"

"He knows it as well as I do. I have taught him my knowledge."

She paused, her gaze holding his. "Why do you wish to pledge, kings guard?"

Liston seemed to be taken by both surprise and fear. I had been in his position once. The eyes of the elder were mysterious and seemed to be looking right into your soul.

His eyes darted to me then to the Elder.

"H-how did you know I was a king's guard?" He asked.

I let out a loose breath at his question. Had he learned nothing?

She took in a deep breath capturing his scent whilst he took a step back in disgust, "I may not have a wolf, but I see Aurae. Glimpses of the past, present, and future." she croaked.

"W-what are you?" He breathed out shakily.

She grinned revealing her crooked teeth, moving away from him, leaving his question unanswered as she turned to me.

"We haven't had a new pledge in 18 years, Master Gregory," she croaked, eyes trailing to mine. "The Mage Wolf is gone, there is nothing to protect. The world is at peace."

"The world will never fully be at peace. Men are too greedy and Wolves are too stubborn," I retorted with a sigh.

Her eyes flashed to mine, "The Mage Council cares less about Wars designed over land and resources," she snapped, hobbling away. "We were created for one war, and one war only. But the essence of that war is long gone. The prophecies spoke of a last and she was born and then she died. And now, the Council rests."

"And yet here you still remain."

Her gaze snapped to mine, her blind eyes holding mine hostage.

"You see glimpses of the past, present, and Future. Tell me, Elder, what futures have you seen?"

She remained wordless but I went on.

"Have you seen war?"

Her cracked lips pursed. "War is inevitable."

She moved away from the both of us, her eyes trailing the ancient markings that lined the chamber walls as if she could see the quite well.

"All I see is death." She began her tone dry and husky, "The fates do not reveal everything to me. Glimpses are what they offer. And all they reveal in those 3 seconds is bloodshed, darkness, and... creatures I have never seen before."

"Creatures?" I echoed.

"It is the only name fitted," she replied.

Thinking this through I took a slight step forward.

"Does that sound like a war over land and resources?" I quipped.

She paused at this, her eyes seemingly studying me. Her gaze narrowed on me, "What is it you have heard, Gregory? What has fuelled your interest so?"

"My informants in the Light Wolf territory say there are rumors of the ancient forests dying. They say wolves have been slaughtered but their bodies have been taken, disappeared as if in thin air."

"I have heard of those stories."

"Stories? So, you believe they are more than rumors?"

"I can sense when magic leaves and I know when trees are dying." She replied with a scoff.

"Well, it is a feat baffling enough that even the Night Wolf wishes to investigate."

Her eyes snapped to mine at this, staring at me. "The Night Wolf has a connection to the shadow realm. If he wishes to investigate there is something truly wrong even if he knows it yet or not."

"As I thought," I replied.

Her eyes narrowed on me, suddenly moving my way, a knowing grin growing against the side of her dry lips, "You wish to say something more?" she growled standing right before me,

"Speak Master."

I studied those peculiar eyes once more, clenching my jaw.

"What do you know of the Night Wolves mates?"

The Elder paused, the smile faltering for a moment, "The Prime wolf was the first wolf created by Selene, Goddess of Night and Moon. He had 3 gifts gifted to him by her. Light, Fire, and Ice." She turned to Liston.

"You must know of the stories. You were taught. What do they mean, pledge?" she hissed.

His eyes trailed to me once more before clearing his throat. "Light, to lead, Fire to protect, and Ice to judge."

When neither one of our eyes left him, he kept speaking.

"3 gifts by which the Prime Wolf was to govern a whole continent for centuries, as he was cradled and blessed with immortality."

"But he died eventually, didn't he?" The hag croaked. "Alexander the Prime."

Liston nodded, "The Mages Curse."

"A mate brought about the end of the most powerful being to exist," the Elder squabbled, "The one thing he desired so much that he lost common sense. That he went even to the extent of consulting with forces from not this world nor this realm."

I listened continuously as the hag spoke even though I knew the story quite well.

"Selene pitied his folly, but when he had his four sons, each inherited a part of him." Her gaze moved back to the symbols on the wall depicting 4 wolves descending from the first. Her wrinkled hands trailed over each one as she spoke.

"The last to see the sun, Ice. The second before, Light. The third before, Fire but the firstborn inherited a gift, not of Selene. Night." She trailed off before continuing.

"He was part shadow, part moon. Son of the darkness and light." She paused around the depiction of the Night wolf, dark echoes of shadows around the engraving, "However, darkness is often stronger and easier to lose oneself into."

I nodded at this, picturing the Night Wolf.

"Selene has held a grudge over that one mistake Alexander made. She has punished that part of the prime wolf with an absolute vengeance. They have been denied the one thing wolves crave from the moment they learn of its existence. She has gifted them, mates with short lives, young brides to discover in their old age, and some unlucky ones..." she trailed off, her tone lower, "Were never found. Some would argue, they were never created.

I watched as her wrinkled hands trailed over a dark cloud that reigned on the throne. I knew what that was.

My throat run dry at this and for a moment I pictured the Night Wolf seated alone on his throne as he normally did.

He had been growing darker by the day, dark days governing the skies for weeks on end.

Had it not been for the mystery of the Keffer that had preoccupied his last two days, I feared soon months will be delved in darkness until it was years on end as it happened centuries ago in the Ever Night.

"You fear the days of Criston the Cruel are near?" She asked, eyes studying mine.

My gaze snapped back to hers. "I feel he was certainly close," I confessed.

"Criston the Cruel," Liston began, as our eyes snapped to him. "The Darkest Night wolf to ever exist. He plunged Valcane in an endless night that lasted nearly 15 years until he was slaughtered by his cousins."

My eyes stayed on my nephew for a bit longer until the Hag spoke.

"He spiraled into the darkest madness. It is what one does when Selene keeps your very soul away from you for 40 years. The current Night Wolf is young but fear indeed strikes harder twice." She trailed off, tilting her head to the side, eyes capturing mine, "But I see something else in your eyes."

I let out a lost breath glancing at my nephew for a bit, "There's a keffer in the Night Court he seems to have taken an interest in."

I could see her visibly freeze.

"I have not seen her yet. But Liston has."

She remained frozen as I spoke, "She comes from the Night Moon pack, from the farthest border that bridges the Fire Wolf Territory."

"How does she look like?" She whispered in a loose breath, her eyes wide.

My eyes trailed to Liston, as he spoke, "S-She has peculiar skin."

"Dark like the shadows of the night?" The Elder breathed, eyebrows arching.

My eyebrows arched at her knowledge.

"Even darker," Liston replied.

Her eyes snapped to his, "What has she done?"

He seemed confused for a moment. "She is a kitchen, Maid. All she does is clean and tend the furnace as was assigned to her by Madam Catherine. Apart from her skin, nothing is out of the ordinary. She's quiet and often gets bullied by the other slaves."

"Nothing? You sense nothing on her, or of her?" The Elder pressed.

"She smells like a keffer." He grunted with a shrug.

The Elder paused, "And yet somehow she intrigued the King and still breaths."

Liston's eyebrows arched at this.

"She mimics the scent of his mate." I began drawing both pairs of yes back to me, "I believe she may be another vengeance Selene plays against him. The Night Wolf Believes the same But-"

"The coincidence is too great." She finished cutting me off. She moved once again toward the marked walls, her old fingers grazing ancient symbols.

"Selene would never...." She trailed off leaving the sentence hanging, "No, she despises the Night Wolf too much. She could not have..." she paused as if something clicked in her.

Turning around she stood poised, "I am led to believe he is either being trialed or deceived."

"He believes she's the puzzle to finding his true mate," I added.

"It sounds like something Selene would do. Perfect really. Bringing the Night Wolf to his very knees. To kiss the feet of the lowest of the low. A keffer. She knows his pride is much too great. Where else best could she hide the one clue to discovering his true mate? He will never crack the riddle."

"I am not too sure about that." I countered, "In truth, he seems to be quite determined as the day of his arranged mating draws closer."

"Desperate times conjure desperate measures," she breathed before turning back to me after pausing on a peculiar symbol,

"She smells like a keffer, and she has no other gifts." She let out a loose breath, "She could be a trial, but there is something that does not fit in this puzzle, not after the loss we made 14 years ago."

"My thoughts repeated."

"For her sake, let her remain a keffer. Death is knocking and a door cannot hold him back. We will have to do what must be done."

I nodded at this. "If she is what we fear. It will be done."

"For the sake of peace."

"For the sake of peace," I repeated

"It is our duty." She continued before turning to Liston, "as it soon will you yours."

I glanced between the two of them, knowing it was time to leave. "I will return when I have gathered more information."

"Thank you, Master Gregory."

With that, I moved toward the door. Liston moved after me but was stopped by the Hag.

"Not you, my dear pledge. You are yet to pledge your soul."

His eyebrows arched at this, but before he could ask, she blew a light silver smoke into his face, causing him to cough and stumble backward.

I studied him for a moment, my hand on the door, pursing my lips.

"Uncle? What is this? I-" he froze as his fingers started draining color as if he had been bit by frostbite.

"Uncle?!-" he panicked, fear in his eyes.

"Please help me!" He screeched reaching out for me but it was too late, life was ripped from him.

I stared at his lifeless body as it heaped to the floor, warm breath caught in my lungs. My eyes trailed back to the Elder.

"A soul pledged."

I nodded, before walking out of the door.

•|•|•

What did you think about this chapter? Please leave a comment down below and I'll be sure to respond!

Chapter [14.1] A FRIENDSHIP TO YEILD and Chapter [15.1] Criston the Cruel are already out on my Patreon! Links to Patreon are on my Wattpad page.

Starting from today, I'll only be updating ONE chapter per week (every Saturday) on Wattpad. Advanced DOUBLE chapters will be available on Patreon for patrons.

I hope you enjoyed the chapter and I hope it left you with questions! Feel free to ask in the comments below or join my discord channel (links in my bio) to toss around theories in the channel I made specifically for MTTNW.

Here's a sneak peek of Chapter [14.1] A FRIENDSHIP TO YEILD on Patreon below.

•|•|•

[14.1] A FRIENDSHIP TO YEILD

● |•|• "What do you know about trust young wolf? You can only trust your soul for she can never betray you." •|•|•

[Shade Shadows]

"How did it go? W-What did he say? Don't tell me he-"

"Shhhh, " I hushed softly into the lingering darkness, stopping Vales' ramble.

My eyes fluttered open, staring at the roof of the stoned castle in the Slave's Quarters. I turned from my back to my side, my eyes meeting that of Vale a few bodies away.

Only a single streak of moonlight illuminated our bodies through the open window allowing us to see each other.

A hand rested over my heart as I stared at her blankly, ignoring the anxious look in her eyes.

I was way too gone in my thoughts. Moments I had lived throughout the day kept replaying on repeat.

"He-" I began, a breath escaping at the word.

I thought back to what had occurred between the master and me. "He went along with it."

Her eyes widened, blinking rapidly.

"He said yes?" She huffed in disbelief.

I hummed a quiet yes.

I was just as baffled as she was but I had no desire to wake up the other sleeping slaves. It was at least an hour past midnight and everyone else had gone to sleep but Vale and me.

"He was genuine then? True to his word?" She called over in a whisper.

I flipped over to my back, taking the study of the roof again.

My thoughts slipped back to what had occurred whilst my fingers traced the inside of my palm remembering how he shook my hand.

He had agreed to become a friend despite all conceivable logic. Even going as far as to seal our trust with a secret. He had no obligation to do that either and yet he did.

I was still confused about what had occurred. How easy it had been to talk to him after that shake of a hand. It was like a promise that I was safe. That I was free to speak.

Logically, it was foolish to feel that way by a mere handshake and a few words spoken which I had no idea if they were true or a mere well thought out lie.

He could have just conjured a secret to tell me and yet, despite knowing the possibility something about the blatant honesty in his eyes reassured me all he said was true. Either that or he was the master of deceit.

Everything had seemed to be working according to plan and then...

Then he walked away abruptly. My eyebrows arched in the dark.

"Shade?"

"It's the first day Vale, I can't be sure." I replied with a soft sigh.

I twisted my head slightly in her direction though my eyes kept to the ceiling, "You should rest now. Dawns almost here."

I knew she was about to say something more but this was neither the time or the place, and I wanted to be in my thoughts for a while.

"But-"

"Sleep well, Vale."

She paused at this, letting out a frustrated huff and then muttered something incoherent beneath her breath. I heard a light shuffling which indicated she had turned over.

I waited for her movements to stop before I let my mind wander.

I still couldn't believe that I could be this lucky. That the plan I had never thought would work played out so smoothly.

He was quite...intriguing that I must admit. Certainly, different from any master I had seen.

A master who wasn't afraid to lose his title to a keffer no less.

I shut my eyes trying to retrieve logic. I had to play it safe. I had no idea if he was truly honest despite our seal of friendship.

He said he was committed to the study, nothing else.

I would never know how true his friendship was until he revealed his deepest secret whatever that may be. Something about the peculiarity of his eyes led me to believe he had one. One that was great too.

I let out a loose breath, blinking rapidly in the darkness as if that would calm my pounding heart.

Despite it all, I had made progress and that should be considered.

Whether this friendship was a sham or not was yet to be seen, however, I would not let such an opportunity flee me. I would get all the information from him as I could so Vale and I could escape.

Yes. That was all that mattered.

I needed to know about the maze. The shadows that lurked in them, and about the Night Wolf.

And the Night Wolf's most trusted master, and now my 'friend' was the only way I could get all three.

I turned over to my side staring at the darkness of the cold wall. A cold wind breezed past the open window and I shivered. I missed AMA in this instant.

On chilly nights like these, there would be tea heating on the fire. She would be detangling the hornet's nest I called hair whilst telling us stories of Beta Samuel. Something told me he had been just as kind as her when he had been alive.

I made a silent prayer in her honor. I hoped she was coping well with us gone.

With a lofty sigh, I shut my eyes.

Tomorrow begins the first step in my plan for freedom.

————————————-

I brushed the dusty shelves with caution noting that this section held some of the most ancient books in the library, books I was assured the other masters would rather I handle with care.

Speaking of masters, I glanced around the illuminated library.

No, I was still alone.

I found it strange I had only met one master. Even though the library was undeniably large, I had thought I would have spotted quite a few by now.

I let out a loose sigh, my gaze shifting to the open window that streamed the sunlight. I would have to get up there again. I had spotted some ink and paper and I'm sure it would be easy to draw the maze.

But not now, I couldn't risk being caught by any of the masters. Not that I had seen any except my 'friend'.

I pursed my lips at the title.

"Friend," I stated, tasting the word. It was still weird to me that I, a keffer slave had a master for a slave.

I clenched my jaw at the thought, hand tightening around my cleaning cloth.

No.

I deserved to say that word without feeling like an imposter. I had risked my very life for it. I would not back down from this. I cracked my neck, letting out a deep breath.

"Friend," I repeated, this time with more urgency and authority.

"Is that what I shall be called now? Is it a title?"

I spun around almost immediately my hand holding onto the shelf for balance, the other flying to my heart that pounded harshly when I met his stale bluish-green peculiar orbs.

He stood posed, wearing all black as usual, his ash hair sleekly pulled back, the red streak gleaming lightly in the firelight, as he tilted his head slightly.

"Have I startled you? It seems that will be a usual occurrence."

"Huh?" I huffed, still rattled at the abrupt intrusion. I tried to calm my nerves but that seemed to be very difficult. I didn't know why my body was acting this way.

"You called for a Friend. I was under the impression I had been seen but this is the fourth time I seemed to have caught you unaware."

"The fourth time?" I chuckled nervously, whilst for some reason, I wiped my dusty hand behind the back of my skirt hoping he wouldn't notice the action.

"Yesterday, the first time we met, and.." he paused for a moment, before clearing his throat, taking his eyes off me for a second.

"It seems it's only three."

I awkwardly grinned at this, not really listening to him. It was like my body was a million more times aware of every little thing. Truth is, I did not know how to act in the presence of a master turned friend.

I still had that instinct to kneel, but I was fighting against my body. Reassuring myself I would not get punished for speaking.

"I am told I am easy to scare," I replied with another nervous chuckle.

"Because you have no wolf."

My gaze flashed to him at this, throat running dry at the blatant remark.

"Yes," I replied softly. "I am a Keffer."

Silence consumed us for a bit, my eyes falling downcast whilst he seemed to study me. I awkwardly moved back to my dusting, trying to push back the hurt feelings forming within me.

"You cannot sense a lot of things as a keffer," he continued, and I shut my eyes momentarily. They flashed open as he continued to speak and I kept them glued to the book case I was cleaning.

"Without a wolf, you cannot sense danger. You cannot heal from minor wounds as quickly as Omegas do. Endurance I would think is questionable. Tell me, how have you survived for so long?"

My fingers were shaking slightly at his words, but I let out a posed breath slightly turning and glancing at him momentarily,

"Whew, that is quite the question," I replied with a faltering grin

He did not reply, though I could feel his eyes burn the side of my head awaiting my answer.

"I uh..." I trailed off trying to bury the panic, "As I said I was saved by AMA."

"AMA?" he echoed.

"A-A pack warrior." I rephrased with a slight stutter, "She took me in and kept me safe."

"You said she found you in a forest, what were you doing there?"

"I have no memories of that day or the days before," I rambled quickly, my fingers zooming in on a speck of dust that seemed difficult to clean as my heart raced faster with every question.

"Nothing? Not even glimpses in your dreams?"

Flashbacks of the voice in the forest, of fires burning and ash falling all around me, filled my head. I bit my lips, scrubbing harder, my fingers quaking slightly.

"None."

"And you've never searched for your beginnings?" he prodded on. I heard him take a step closer, "Have you no interest in your history?"

I blinked rapidly at the speck of dust.

"Have you never desired to know why you are so peculiar? Why your skin is so dark and why do you have no wolf."

"I'm a keffer, master, there is no other explanation," I replied dryly, my jaw ticking.

"You were found alone in a forest covered in a pile of ash."

"As peculiar as it may sound, abandonment is not that strange for a keffer." I gritted out. Grinding my teeth together.

"And yet a warrior took you in?"

"I was lucky."

"Luck?" He echoed, a slight scoff in his tone, "Indeed, you are quite lucky for a keffer." He mocked.

"Is this an interrogation?" I suddenly snapped, turning around fully, anger laced in my tone. My eyes met his squarely, a fire weaving in them. My fists clenched tightly around the cloth.

He raised an eyebrow at what I assumed was the defiance in my eyes. A hint of surprise mirrored in them. The longer we stared at each other the quicker common sense returned to me and my gaze quickly dropped from his to the floor, bewildered at what I had done.

"I uh..." my fingers shook slightly, as I placed my now unclenched fists behind my back, "Forgive me master, I- your questions are quite direct." I began slowly raising my eyes back to him gauging his reaction.

I had to rectify this.

"I understand you only agreed to this... friendship for your study but if I am to truly be free and willing.... I'm afraid I will need some room to trust."

When he remained quiet his eyes still holding mine, I continued.

"I-I say this because I understand the importance of accuracy in your study. I do not feel free in my responses. As your friend, I..I owe you the truth."

I waited for his reply anxiously but he only seemed to further study me for a lingering moment. One that made me more nervous and made my heart pound. Perhaps I had made a mistake. Perhaps this friendship could not be compared to the one Vale and I had.

He was a master-

"What do you wish to speak about?" He suddenly asked.

My gaze raised back to meet his.

"What will make you free?"

I was paralyzed for a moment, swallowing softly, "I-It could be anything really. Perhaps casual conversation?" I offered.

His eyebrows arched at this as if the term was foreign to him.

"And what is that?"

I faltered an amused chuckle for a minute, "You know," I pressed, "meaningless rambles like, how's the weather?" I prodded on, "it cools the mood."

He seemed to remain confused, "it's a cloudless day."

I studied his face for a moment, reading the honesty in his eyes. He was being sincere when he said he didn't have any friends it seemed.

Neither had he had one before.

I turned slightly to the window where the rays of sun gleamed only lighting up the highest part of the library.

"Indeed, it is." I continued, turning to him as I studied him once again, "perhaps we should begin with, how your day was?"

"Why would you want to know that?"

"I would like to know how you spent your day. What made you happy, what intrigued you, what made you sad..." I trailed off.

His eyes narrowed on me, "And why would you wish to know that? How is that of any use to you?"

I let out a loose breath.

He was new at this whole friendship thing it seemed, right to the very beginning.

"It's what friends do. You said you always wanted a friend, right? Is it not because you wanted to share even the little moments with someone else?" I asked.

He paused at this, his eyes slowly trailing up to the window, then he spoke rather uniformly,

"The day has barely begun; I have not done many things but attend to matters of the Court as I have been doing since yesterday."

"And what happened in the Court?" I prodded with a grin, returning to dust the shelves for a bit.

He remained silent for a moment and when I glanced at him, he was staring at me intently. My whole body became aware.

Perhaps I had overstepped.

"Y-You don't have to say anything if I should not hear. I know there are matters of the court that I should not listen to neither would I under-stand-"

"Matters from the port," he cut, his stale gaze stuck in mine, his eyes narrowing for a moment, "Boring issues about trade."

My body froze for a moment at the mention of it.

The Harbor.

"Y-you mean the trade done with Men?" I asked a slight shake in my tone despite trying very hard to control it.

"Yes," he sighed, moving the length of the shelves standing a few feet away from me, as he stared upwards at a line of books-

"They have advanced medicines, fabrics, and gold they trade with us. In return, we offer herbs from our ancient forests, horses, and silk. Many we do not need but trade must go on to broker peace."

"I have only heard of the port; I've never seen the sea. Not that I remember," I replied, softly.

"The sea wasn't meant for wolves. Waves are tedious and unforgiving. That is why many escape rogues and slaves die in its torment." He grunted not seeming to particularly care.

"Good thing I'm not a wolf then."

His eyes snapped to me, holding my gaze.

"Because I would love to see the sea one day. They say it's as blue as the sky. I fear as long as I am here in this court, my days of seeing the sky are numbered," I quickly replied.

His eyes remained glued to me, only narrowing slightly, "is that because you are keffer in the Night Court, or because you are in the home of the Night Wolf and you fear the tales of the Ever Night?"

"B-both," I shrugged after a thought. "Is there much of a difference? They all lead to death."

He hummed at this, "Death comes to all but there are certainly better ways to die."

"And which death would you propose I choose?" I chuckled rather darkly, glancing at him for a moment.

"Death by the hands of the night wolf or any guard under his order will be quick and painless if he chooses to be merciful, at least then you'll have hope," he replied, "The Ever Night on the other hand is an endless Night of his cruelest parts. There is no mercy in those days."

He seemed lost for a moment at this. He then turned away a tick in his clenched jaw.

I pursed my lips, eyebrows arching for a moment as a thought crossed my mind,

"Tell me of Criston the Cruel."

•|•|•

Merry Christmas! Hope you guys had a wonderful day!

Enjoying the story? Please leave a comment and vote and I'll be sure to reply.

Chapter [15.1] Criston the Cruel and Chapter [16.1] The Diamond Raven are now available on Patreon!

A sneak peek of Chapter [15.1] Criston the Cruel is down below. •|•|•

[15.1] CRISTON THE CRUEL

[Kayos]

I paused at this question, my gaze lingering over a random book I had not paid much attention to until now.

"T-that is if you know the story," she quickly rephrased, clearing her throat.

My mind had already wandered away. Back to the dark place it loved so much. It was comforting but staying in that place for too long allowed the darkness to consume me. Many times, though out the years I had contemplated staying there. Losing myself in it's endless.

It would certainly be easier as my great-grandfather once did. Something deep inside me craved for that release.

There was only one person who had kept me from drowning peacefully and losing my soul in the shadows.

Mother and her ever-optimistic words.

But as the years drawl by, even her soothing words do not carry as much weight as they used to whilst the darkness grows more alluring by the day.

"Master?"

"I know the story quite well," I replied, taking out the book.

I had not read it for so long, because parts of it I knew were not true.

I may have once believed the history written of the cruelness of Criston, cruel even beyond the natural darkness that the Night Wolf was born with, but as the years dwindle, I know the truth for what it truly was.

He simply gave up. Simply remained in the dark place.

Where there was no feeling, no despair no thoughts that reminded him of loneliness. Why should he be faulted for wishing to remain in a place where there was no torment as compared to reality where nothing but utmost despair rained?

I could feel her eyes study the side of my face as silence fell between us. I let out a loose breath, still despising the feel of that obsidian gaze that seemed to be ever slowly, mastering how to pull back that curtain.

But she was not ready for the truth. She desired the story that was told in songs and legends. That was what she would hear.

"Criston the Cruel," I began flipping through the pages. I reached the dark drawing of my great grandfather handing it over to her.

She quickly wiped her hands taking the book with both hands, eyes slightly wide at the gesture as she cradled it with utmost care. It was an old book after all. One I had not opened in over eight years.

"Was the 6th Night Wolf after Alexander the Prime," I explained, as her large gaze darted across the image. Criston was drawn in shades of black and white, shadows dancing around him, his eyes two embers to which her fingers shakily trailed.

"He was not gifted a mate by Selene as punishment for his cruelty and for forty years he searched Valcane for a maiden that did not exist. " I paused, a dryness in my throat

"For forty years his cruelty grew until it consumed every corner of Valcane in a never-ending night that lasted 15 years. There was no stopping his cruelty, many tried and many failed," I continued flipping the page over to another depiction.

Here the image showed the torment that reigned in the years of the Ever Night. It showed the shadows that roamed freely, slaughtering and killing.

"But i-t says here he was killed," she commented, eyes trailing over the words under the image.

My gaze narrowed on her, caught slightly off guard, "You read?"

She blinked at the page for a moment her eyes softly drawing up to mine gain, "Yes. A-AMA taught me how."

Her gaze shifted back to the drawing and I studied how intently she examined it. She had soft features that echoed in the firelight highlighting her blatant curiosity.

"He was killed," I confirmed, "by the other Arc Wolves."

I flipped over the page showing her the depiction. A silver sword dipped with the blood of 3 Arcs was what was strong enough to kill him, and blessed by Selene herself.

"It took them fifteen years for even Arcs to kill him. He was powerful." She muttered under her breath as her eyes glazed the picture.

"He was consumed by darkness. There is power in that."

Her eyes flashed to me at those words holding my gaze more boldly than she had ever before a certain curiosity in her eyes, "Why was he always sad?"

My eyebrows arched at this peculiar question, "what makes you think we was sad? He had all the power in the world."

"Yes, he was powerful and yes, he had the world at his finger tips and yet in every picture," she continued flipping back through the pages, "it almost seemed as if it was the world that cruel to him and not the other way around."

I was frozen by her statement.

Her eyes narrowed on a drawing, bringing the book closer to her face, a faltering yet confused grin on her face for a fleeting moment.

"There are- " she paused, shaking her head for a moment, bringing the book up for another examination as if she couldn't believe what she was seeing.

"In this picture," she began, her eyes trailing to mine slowly, a single finger against the image, "I-it almost looks like-like there are actual tears in his eyes."

I snatched the book from her as if it was a need, my heart pounding harshly within me as I stared at the picture. I had never noticed this before.

Despite the death and darkness around him there seemed to be an echo of sadness in his glossy eyes.

"I-it almost looks like he's trapped in the darkness, rather than controlling it," she continued, eyebrows drawing together.

I froze at this, a coldness filling my body for a moment. I slammed the book closed as the feeling grew.

The abrupt sound startled her, and I could feel her eyes enlarge as she stared at the side of my face.

I shut my eyes trying to calm the sudden abrupt anger that seemed to grow within me, slowly opening them.

"I would not know why the artists chose to depict him like that. He was certainly free." I grunted turning back to her.

She pursed her lips, her fingers tightening around her rag cloth, "Well, perhaps he was sad because he didn't have a mate?"

My eyes kept on her, "I assure you his cruelty began long before he was of age."

"How cruel could he have been before that? He was what? 17 summers?"

"He was dark as all Night Wolves are."

"Then he wasn't cruel, he was simply as he was designed."

My breathing hardened at this, taking a step forward and towering over her, "You understand you're defending a mass murderer?"

"No... " She gulped slowly taking a step back, "I'm simply trying to see the bigger picture."

"There is no bigger picture."

She pursed her lips again as her gaze wondered away from mine. "I-I just think maybe he wouldn't have turned out so bad if he was given what he craved for most."

My breath became trapped within me as she spoke.

She chuckled nervously shaking her head, "A mate," she added, "Not that I truly understand it to be honest," she prodded on.

"I don't understand how not having that one thing could cause so much destruction," her eyes snapped to mine, "of course that is if that was truly the reason for his cruelty."

My jaw ticked trying to stop the strange feeling over taking my body at this moment the more she spoke.

"I mean," she began wringing the cloth as she spoke, her mind seemingly far off, "Could he not have merely mated someone else? Could that not have cured him?"

"That is yet to be seen."

She paused for a moment, true confusion in her eyes, "I don't understand why wolves obsess so much for it. Love exists in many forms not just love at first sight," she squabbled with a slight eye roll, "Men live just fine with learning to fall in love. Is having a mate truly that important?" she scoffed.

"It. Is. DIRELY. Important." I growled back, causing her eyes to flash to mine, stepping back in alarm.

I could hear her heart pound fast, wide gaze on me. Her fingers had curled around the wooden shelf for support.

I took a step back knowing I had been intense, gaze finally trailing off of her as I swallowed softly, licking my lips.

"It means the absolute world," I continued quietly, "that is why he destroyed Valcane, his home so easily. For what is power and wealth, without no one to truly share it with?"

A moment of silence passed between us before I added clearing my throat, "At least that is what I would have imagined if that was truly the cause of his cruelty."

She seemed to take this in momentarily, nodding.

"I guess I sort of get it," she began, "The world is miserable, I don't know where I would be without AMA and my sister."

"You have a sister?" I asked, eyebrows arching. My gaze darted to a shadow that immediately hid around the book case, squirming back into the darkness against my intense glare.

Alchest didn't reveal everything about her it seemed.

She paused at this, eyes widening for a moment, "An adopted sister. She too was abandoned and AMA took her in. She's of rogue descent," she pursed her lips at this, silence raining once more.

"Without her-" she began, "I don't think I would have coped in this place for too long. We have each other and that's what makes it easier."

She smiled for a bit as if reliving memories and for a moment I wished I had memories that brought a smile such as that to my face. I didn't believe I could however.

Smile that is. I hadn't for a long while.

"She listens when I need an ear, she warns me when my curiosity leads too far, Selene knows I wander too far," she chuckled, "She wakes me up from my nightmares and she looks out for me-"

"Your nightmares?" I echoed.

"Nasty things," she chuckled slightly, turning back to dusting. Her smile faltered for a bit, "Relentless too," she whispered.

"Why? What do your nightmares show so relentlessly?"

"It's just a blurry dream of fire and ash, burning forests and what not," she hummed with a slight shudder, "it's always so cold as if I'm not surrounded by flames."

"Perhaps it's a memory. You said you were found in a pile of ash."

"Perhaps, or it is just a nightmare," she added, pursing her lips as she kept on dusting.

"Is there nothing more you see?"

She did not reply though she paused for. Moment, then shook her head, "No, I wake up."

"Perhaps you should sleep for a bit longer then-"

Her gaze slowly reached mine at this.

"How will you ever know who you truly are if you never try?"

Her eyes dropped back to her dusting, "I don't think I wish to. The past is often dark."

"The past also has secrets, secrets that could unlock your future."

And mine too I wished to add. And possibly save Valcane from another Ever Night.

She paused once again at this, "Perhaps I'll try, one of these days."

I nodded at this. That was all I needed.

From the corner of my eye, I caught the shadows moving once more. Alchest had a few more things to tell me it seemed.

Without further ado, I abruptly took my leave.

•|•|• Wishing y'all a prosperous New Year! Thanks for reading! Please drop a comment and vote! Chapter [16.1] The Diamond Raven and Chapter [17.1] The Other Mate is already out on Patreon! Links in bio!

Here's a preview of chapter [16.1] The Diamond Raven available on Patreon! •|•|•

[16.1] THE DIAMOND RAVEN

● |•|•"Who knows of your gift child? Have you told another soul?"•|•|•

[Shade Shadows]

"Then again, who wants a few extra hours of their nightmares?" I chuckled, glancing over at him.

My eyebrows drew in when I noticed he wasn't where I thought he was standing only paces away.

Turning, I paused my dusting for a bit, searching for the master. How quickly could he have moved? He was here not a second ago.

"Master?" I called out.

I tried to see if he had moved to another row or just moved out of sight, craning my neck to take a peak whilst nervously clenching the dusty cloth. I searched for the brooding master but he remained out of sight, not bothering to answer my calls.

Could he have just left without even as much as a goodbye?

"Master?!" I called out again for the last time.

When only an echo and silence responded, I concluded that I had indeed been abandoned.

"Just like that," I muttered beneath my breath turning back to my dusting. He had no manners at all.

Relieving my thoughts from him, I kept dusting, recalling all he said to me.

He talked of the Harbor and trade done with men.

I pursed my lips trying to think of a way to solve my problem.

I had to learn where the items traded were packed and who took them to the port. Heck, I needed to know the direction of the port, I had no idea how to get there.

Letting out a loose sigh, I packed a few more books but I was lost in my thoughts, thinking of ways to end this torture. My days were numbered in this court, even if they had been slightly extended by the master.

This escape was going to be more complicated than I thought.

At least when I was back in the Night Moon pack I had a map.

Though I still had it, the routes were certainly different. And the map was limited to the packs I had to pass before reaching the seas from the Night Moon pack.

It would have taken us less time to get to the port there than it did from the Night Court. My rough estimate would be at least 3 more days added to the already week-long journey. Give or take.

Of course, if we had wolves we could shift into, the time estimated could easily be cut in half but sadly, Vale and I had no such luxury. I had no wolf and if Vale shifted her scent could be tracked faster than if she remained human.

If only we had another map, that would be helpful.

A loud caw got me spinning around, catching the sight of a bird flying through the high window.

I watched as the raven flew right by me, perching on one of the master's study desks in the library.

It hopped to the edge of the table, studying me with its beady eyes, head crooked to the side.

I let out a relieved sigh, leaning against the shelves and studying the peculiar bird for a moment.

"And....you've returned," I grunted, letting out a loose breath.

The bird only blinked back at me, studying me with as much intensity as I did it.

"Here I am trying to find a map to escape and you come back so willingly," I scoffed still trying to understand this bird.

"If you're trying to thank me, you don't have to stay. I accepted your gratitude already."

It simply adjusted its perch, moving to the side, before looking back at me with those black eyes.

Why was I talking to it like it could reply?I shut my eyes for a moment, shaking my head and chuckling at the humor of it all.

Well, on the bright side, at least I had someone to talk to. Or something to talk to. Who would care if I was slowly losing my mind in private?

Taking a breath out, I took note of my surroundings.

"Where am I going to find a map?" I mumbled to myself, eyes trailing back to the Raven, who tilted its head, staring back at me.

I suddenly froze when something clicked.

"Wait-" I began standing upright.

The raven cawed as my gaze trailed my surroundings. I took a step back from the bookshelves, spinning around, taking in the full sight of everything.

My gaze snapped to the raven with a wide smile, "I'm in a library," I hinted.

The bird blinked.

"I'm in a library." I repeated with a chuckle, "The library. Valcanes oldest. Where else can I find a map of Valcane other than in a library?! There must be a map somewhere around here," I grinned moving closer to the raven as I spoke.

"I mastered the map of Night Moon Pack by heart, I just have to figure out the territory on a map of Valcane and from there, I can tell what route to use to get to the port!"

I gleamed at this now only a foot away from the bird and it watched me carefully not bothering to fly away despite our proximity.

"Yes! Yes! Yes!" I threw a fist in the air. Finally, something was coming together.

"Okay, okay," I tried to calm my excitement turning back to the Raven, "I'll just have to find a map right?"

My gaze trailed to the vast library

-"And how hard can that possibly.... be?" I trailed off gulping at the width of the library. I side glanced at the raven and it blinked again.

Taking out a breath, I went to a random section of the library.

"Here goes nothing." I breathed.

———————————-

"Nothing, nothing -nothing" I grunted, slamming a book shut.

I was sweating, glancing about for my next prey but my fingers were already shaking and my arms hurt from grabbing stacks of books.

I crumpled against the shelves letting out a deep breath. I had flipped through as many books as I could find but there were no maps of the valcane or even the Night Wolf territory.

To make things worse, I couldn't get the filing system that had been put into place. There were no clear sections. You could be reading factual history books one moment to books about myths and legends the next.

Opening another random book I flipped through the pages.

"Oh for the love of Selene!" I shut my eyes, slamming the book closed. I looked up at the raven, "it was about mates."

I rolled my eyes, siding to the floor, and wiping the light sheet of sweat across my brow.

I was never going to find a map at this rate. And I had to get back to cleaning before ea master walked by.

There were too many books and they were all randomly spaced.

The vastness of the library was much too great. I hadn't even moved from the first row and I was sure I would have to leave soon.

I looked up at the perched raven, "You wouldn't happen to know which one in these gazillion books has a map of Valcane?" I huffed.

The bird blinked, and I scoffed, rolling my head forward in my folded arms with a soft sigh. I buried my face into it, trying hard not to crumble within. Despair seemed to slowly creep in despite my best efforts.

What was I thinking? Nothing came easy for keffer. Just when I found a solution another problem reared its ugly head.

"I wish one of us knew," I whispered.

The bird cawed. And I grunted, nodding at nothing in particular.

It cawed, again and again, causing me to look up at it. It was almost as if it waited for our eyes to meet before taking flight, my head whipping in its direction.

I watched as it sped past, getting lost within the rows.

I got to my feet, not understanding why I felt like I should follow it. Did it know the way? I paused for a second, unable to divide.

Another claw caused blindly walk in its direction, unsure of what I was doing, or how sane I was at the moment.

Perhaps it was desperation, perhaps it was hope.

"Raven?" I whispered. My voice was low, reminding myself there could be other masters lurking about.

I heard the ravens caw up ahead once more. Straining my ears, I listened for each one.

I knew it was crazy following a bird. For all, I knew it was circling the place till it finally flew out the window.

It had stayed perched on the table for a few hours now, it had to go home sometime right?

When silence loomed I stopped in the middle of a row, glancing around again, resisting the urge to regain my sanity,

"Raven?"

A moment passed and I almost scolded myself for being so gullible when I heard its faint caw once more in the distance prompting me to hurry in its direction.

"What am I doing? It's a bird for the love of Selene." I muttered to myself, walking through a narrow pass shelved on each side.

Breaking through the opening, I entered another center.

Here I spotted the raven flying above, circling a few times before it lowered.

My gaze followed its every flap, perching on what looked like a table. It was too dark to see in this center.

I grabbed a torch from one of the sides, placing it on a nearby hanger, my eyes widening at what I saw.

It was a large table sprawled with numerous papers and scrolls. I approached, gaze trailing the papers, unable to believe my eyes when I saw what they were filled in by-

Maps.

Hundreds of them, just laying about.

My jaw dropped, scanning the table where the Raven perched. Grabbing one medium-sized piece of paper with a section of Valcane on it, my fingers trembled in disbelief.

I quickly cleared a section of the heap of papers, finding a piece of the largest map at the bottom of a massive paper where the whole continent of Valcane was drawn out, the sea and even the land of men from what I could tell.

I glanced at the raven and it looked back up at me with its beady black eyes. Slowly and carefully, I picked it up.

It didn't caw or fuss almost as if it trusted me. I brought it up to my face, my heart pounding within me.

"Y-You can understand me Raven, can't you?" I whispered.

It only blinked.

My gaze narrowed on it, "I know you can, or you wouldn't have found this and guided me to you."

It only blinked again.

I pursed my lips, doubting myself for a moment when it suddenly cawed loudly, ruffling its feathers.

A wide smile grew on me.

"You can." I reasoned.

Deep down inside me, I knew there was something special about it. The peculiar mark on its forehead. A white-spotted Diamond.

That was unnatural, unusual.

Like me.

I brought it back to the table and it hopped off. Its eyes trailed the map as if in satisfaction.

"You're a peculiar Raven aren't you?" I asked softly.

It hopped forward on the papers, seemingly studying it.

"Raven.." I trailed off mostly to myself as I watched it curiously.

"It's not right to call you by your title." I thought back to how I disliked it when people called me Keffer.

"If you truly wish to stick beside me, you will need a name."

It turned to me at this and I held a breath in. It looked right at me, its wings folded neatly behind it. Head tilted to the side as if awaiting my decision.

"Uh.." I panicked for a moment, unsure of what to say. I had never named anything living before. My eyes trailed to its peculiar Diamond-shaped spot.

"Diane?"

It instantly cawed twice at this name. Almost like it wanted it.

"First try and you like it?" I chuckled, surprised. It cawed again, this time taking flight.

I watched as it circled high above before flying down, perching on my shoulder.

I froze in surprise. The warmth of the creature heated my shoulder and left cheek.

"Diane it is." I grinned.

My eyes trailed back to the maps, "okay, let's see what you've found Diane."

•|•|•

I hope you enjoyedthe double update just because I couldn't post on saturday! Leave a comment to let me know your thoughts!

Chapter [17.1] The Other Mate is available on Patreon!

Preview of chapter [17.1] THE OTHER MATE is down below!

•|•|•

[17.1] THE OTHER MATE

• |•|•"The Ever Night has ended but another Night Wolf reigns. It is only a matter of time before fate decides to weave with the same strings."•|•|•

[Kayos]

I moved out of my sanctuary, the doors closing behind me as I treaded the length of the dark hallways.

A sound caused me to pause near an intersection, spotting Alchest as he crawled out of the shadows. He moved toward me in the empty hallway, crawling up my shoulder and whispering his secrets in a low hiss.

I remained passive as he informed me of everything he had learned, my expression hardening with every unlikeable news he had gathered, till the very last.

I growled at what he had said, my jaw ticking. Alchest scampered away sensing my growing irritation. My wolf gripping the edge, eyes shining those deadly embers.

She would always find a way to get under my skin it seemed.

A rage forming deep within my wolf I stormed off in the direction of her quarters, guards scurry out of my way, their eyes glued to the floor in fear of meeting my gaze.

I pushed the double doors open,

"Why has the date been moved?" I growled, trying to keep my tone from sounding more deadlier than I intended.

The five maids surrounding my mother immediately stood, bowing and scampering off in no less than ten seconds.

Mother held a mirror in her hands, calmly studying her reflection, looking back at me through it, "ah the rumor has finally reached you."

"Why have you changed the date?" I gritted my patience a single flame in the midst of a hurricane.

She turned back to puckering her lips, examining her reflection, "The date has not been changed, I merely spread the rumor. You can calm down now Kayos."

My eyebrows drew in slightly at the statement, my wolf calmer, irritation booming instead, "Why?"

"To bring you here, why else?" She sighed, placing the hand mirror down and getting to her feet as she turned toward me.

"I told a maid, who told a guard, who told another and the rest is history," she sighed with a shrug, "I knew your demons or shadows or whatever you call them would pick it up sooner or later and report back."

"You went through all that trouble?" I huffed with a slight eye roll. My mother was the queen of drama.

"It worked didn't it?" She retorted, "and I wouldn't have to have gone through all that trouble if you simply replied to my summons." Her gaze narrowed on me, "I've sent many letters and you've answered to none. I've called upon you and you haven't been here in nearly three weeks."

I let out a sigh, walking passed her to the open window, "I've needed some time alone."

"Time alone? When are ever not alone?" She echoed, and I could feel her gaze on me. When I didn't reply she let out a sigh of her own.

"I am aware that you've been trapped in your sanctuary for a few days now which would have worried me but the sun has been in the sky for a week now so I know you're not in a grave mood."

My eyes trailed from her to the window, my gaze falling first on the courtyard below then trailing upwards slowly to the tower of my sanctuary, staring at it for a moment as she talked.

"It was your father's favorite place too. I will never truly know why." She mused, "but as long as it helps calm you, I find no fault in it."

I hummed at this, absent-minded as I spotted a raven flying out of the high window, getting lost in the bright sky. My eyebrows arched at this for a moment, again the light feel of magic reaching my senses.

"Are you listening Kayos?"

My attention snapped back to reality, though I didn't look back at her, "speak mother," I sighed, "I'm listening."

I turned to her, placing my hands behind my back as my gaze traced back to her.

Her concerned eyes cleared slowly, a soft look in them.

By far that was the expression I hated the most. When she had that look on, she would say something to make me believe she understood however I felt. I know she only hoped to raise my spirit but I don't recall a moment it ever had.

"I know you grow agitated the closer the date of your mating ceremony draws." She began, holding the same look in her eyes.

"Yes," I muttered, my throat dry. I was not fond of the date, it was no secret.

The date felt like a bright sun looming over me, burning my eyes. I longed for a dark cloud instead.

"And I know you wish for more time. The time I can not give."

My eyes studied hers as she spoke. I knew all of this. I did not understand why she was repeating it once again as if it would change anything.

"I am aware."

She let out a loose breath walking towards me, the closer she drew the more uncomfortable I felt. Not because she was a threat in any way, but simply because I knew she would try her best to bring me comfort.

Something that worked when I was a young pup, but her efforts were now wasted and I had no feelings of comfort drawn from her anymore. All I felt was her pity and her disappointment. Those eyes that held so many promises, shattered hopes and wants.

She stopped a foot away from me searching my eyes. The only other being who could.

However, I could feel her fear in them, no matter how hard she tried to hide it.

"This was the agreement made. Time has come and gone and now you must be arranged to be mated on the eve of your 25th. I wished you more time, truly," she urged, her hand caressing my face, "but it is necessary to avoid an Ever Night."

Her fingers slipped away from my face, as she turned away. She seems to be holding in a breath, or tears, one or the other, it did not take away from the shake in her voice.

My jaw tightened, though I didn't bother to reply to her remarks. Even my mother feared an Ever Night.

Still, I couldn't blame her. It was simply what I am, and even as I stood, I longed for that dark place. To waste into its nothingness before the date of my mating.

Only one thing made me want to wake up another day. It was the mystery of the Keffer. Shade. The girl whose very skin mirrored my soul. Whose existence held a shallow promise I was determined to keep.

"We can not fail the treaty." Mother continued.

I knew of the agreement.

After Criston the Cruel, every Night Wolf that had not been mated by his 25th birthday would be arranged to be mated.

Normal wolves usually found their mates days or months after their eighteenth birthday. If one had to wait for two to three years it was considered long and unlucky yet not completely unheard of.

If one had to wait for 4-5 years it was considered a punishment by Selene, for one's wrongdoings.

If a wolf who was not a keffer had not found his mate in six years or more, they were considered unworthy by Selene, but since they had a wolf, still had some sort of redemption, therefore they still amassed respect.

A keffer had no such luxury. They were cursed from birth and despised by the moon.

I had been searching for seven years.

Seven years could still be held as merely unworthy if I had been a normal wolf, but I was not.

I was a Night Wolf.

They did not wish for another Ever Night. With an arranged companion they hoped my loneliness would be subdued.

It had worked for my grandfather, and they hoped it would work for me.

I studied her as she walked toward her chair, "I know you're disappointed."

She froze at this and I continued. I felt no emotion except the expansion of the dark whole in my chest.

"That I am not successful as Father had been with finding you.."

She remained silent for a moment, before taking a seat. Her soft gaze trailed back to mine.

"I am not disappointed in you. How could I as if you are the one who weaves the strands of fate- no. If there is any emotion I feel, it's anger towards Selene." She hummed, pausing for a moment, her gaze snapping to mine. "Screw her."

I grunted at this, a soft smile appearing on her face and I nodded at the crude statement.

"Vivian," mother spoke.

My eyes remained glued to hers, not familiar with the sudden mention of the name.

"It is the name of your chosen mate."

My chest constricted again when she said it.

"Vivian," I repeated, tasting the stale word.

She nodded, her eyes trailing off me, speaking carefully with a more serious tone, "She is the first daughter of Alpha Cain, one of the thirteen. Leader of-"

"Greenwood Pack. I am the king mother. I know who Cain is."

She nodded after a short hum but continued to explain as if my statement was irrelevant.

"He remains Alpha of his pack because his first son, who turned eighteen summers 4 years ago, has yet to find his mate. Vivian has yet to find her mate, at twenty summers. She will be the perfect mate for you." she stated.

"You approve of her already? You have not even set eyes on her."

She paused at this, "True, it's been years since I last saw her," she chuckled softly as if reminiscing, "Last I did she was 12 summers old but if remember correctly, she was a beautiful child. Grey cloudy eyes and hair as gold as the sun."

"I do not recall her."

"You never did pay attention to anything that did not catch your interest," she defended, "but she was just a girl then. As a woman, I'm sure she will be able to draw more than just your attention."

"And she agrees to abandon her hopes of finding her true mate? She agrees to marry the dark Prince?" I mocked.

Her gaze narrowed on me at this statement, "Her father says she's quite eager. I believe that means she's ready."

My gaze hardened, "Her father only desires more power."

"And that is what he deserves after the ceremony," Mother quipped, "that is his prize for a sacrifice so great."

My jaw ticked.

"The bride will be here in 3 weeks, and the council of courts will start arriving soon after."

"That I am aware."

"Good." She stated.

"Is this all you wished to say?"

"It was a reminder Kayos, and I had to make sure you were still as brooding as ever," she chuckled, "it warms me to see my son."

I grunted at this but nodded knowing she would only tarry my release if I continued the conversation. Without another word, I walked toward the door.

"Kayos"

I froze, with a sigh, turning around again, "Yes?"

"Don't be a stranger." she breathed, her soft eyes falling on me.

I paused at this statement, before walking out the door.

•~•Thanks for reading! Please leave a comment and tap the star! Read chapters [18.1] A ROGUES FRIEND to chapters [22.1] DIANE (Five chapters ahead!) now available for early access on my Patreon! A sneak peak of chapter [18.1] A ROGUES FRIEND is down below. Link to Patreok in bio!•~•

[18.1] A ROGUES FRIEND

•|•|•"Do you think life is fair, pup? Walk amongst the slaves. Listen to the crack of the whip against their naked backs, their sharp wails as their blood splatters against the edge of the silver blade. You will know then."•|•|•

[Vale]

I scrubbed hard at the stain that refused to budge, furiously grunting at it, knuckles turning white.

She wouldn't even let me get a word in! Such a hot-headed girl!

I ferociously wrung the mop, going back to scrubbing, and grinding my teeth together. My guess is we're sore hit I was used to the pain now.

Selene, she never listens! What happened to doing this together? But no- Shade's got everything handled. Shades got it all under control.

I scoffed, scowling as I mopped ignoring my aching arms.

She would land herself into a pile of trouble, that's right! Trouble. And then what will I do? How will I help her then? Why can't she just let me in-

"Vale—"

"What?!" I growled, my wolf showing for a brief moment as my eyes snapped to a wide-eyed Eve.

The requisites of my actions immediately gripped me, as my body ran cold, afraid of the consequences of talking out of line.

It was only Eve but had it been anybody else, I would have regretted this moment for the rest of my life.

She froze with a soapy bucket of water cradled in thin arms, a smudge of dirt against her bland cheeks, staring back at me with those big eyes of hers. She pursed her full lips as she shuffled backward a bit.

Her gaze dropped to the floor and guilt raced through me, shame for barking at her.

Compared to Shade, I wasn't the bravest. I was considered soft-spoken by most but compared to Eve, I simply had never met anyone nicer.

I felt awful for yelling at her.

She was much like me in many ways, gentle and kept mostly to herself whenever she wasn't being sent around by Haven or Idah.

I paused, letting out a soft sigh as I rested on my heels, pushing a thin strand of my hair backward.

"I'm sorry, Eve. I didn't mean to yell-"

"I-It's okay." She hummed, offering me a small smile as she peaked from her eyelashes.

I often admired the length of them. Eve was prettier than most. Red rosy hair and plump lips, it was simply ill fate that she was here with us. It still bothered me she was- and I couldn't for the life I understand why she slaved.

She had no rogues scent about her like most slaves. She did not carry a dead look in her eyes as if she had been rejected and yet here she was, scrubbing these floors amongst us.

I managed to smile back at her, and she sat beside me, scrubbing.

Watching her for a moment, I returned to work.

A pair of guards marched by and my eyes darted to them whilst my heartbeat increased slightly as metal clanged against the floors leaving large dirty bootprints.

When I realized they were just on regular patrol, I sighed, moving to mop their dirt.

When I was done, I continued scrubbing and soon enough I was back in my thoughts.

A lot of things plagued me with worry these days. I could barely get enough sleep.

Perhaps my life would be easier if a certain someone just listened to me for once.

She was going to get herself killed, I was sure of it. She never listened to me or told me anything!

Never.

"Shade, don't go into the woods. You know the pack kids play there often."

There she goes, racing into the woods. Something about being around wildflowers.

"Shade, please don't provoke Gabrielle. He may still be a pup but he'll be Alpha one day."

Very next moment, slandering his name.

"Shade, don't go to the tower."

There she goes! Up the damn tower!

"Shade, don't trust the master!"

There she goes trusting the masters! Stubborn girl!

Selene! It was a clear miracle she was still alive.

I pursed my lips, scrubbing harder. Shade and I were two sides of a coin.

Whilst I thought logically, Shade—well she thought like a slave addicted to the thought of freedom.

Every slave dreams of freedom but I understand where I am now. There is no hope for us here in the heart of the Night Court. Selene! If only she could realize how lucky she was to still be breathing whilst trapped in these walls, perhaps she would understand the dangers of her unrest.

One wrong move and we could be killed, or even worse, imprisoned for the hunt.

I shuddered at the thought.

I have always admired my sisters' courage and ambition, but she was too careless.

Unable to see what I could, to sense the danger around her as I could. Perhaps it was because she had no wolf to guide her as mine does. But that was all the more reason to listen to me!

By Selene! How do I plunder sense into her?

I could trust nobody but she and she would do well to remember the same.

"But she never will." I scoffed aloud, scrubbing harder, grinding my teeth as I moved my arms.

"Y-You're worried about Shade aren't you?" Eve whispered, glancing over at me.

My fingers froze against the brush whilst My heart began a hard pound within me.

It was because she called her by name, Shade. I didn't think any slave knew my sister by her name, they called her by her title.

Keffer.

How did she know who I was worried about?

My gaze never left Eve, my heart still pounding harshly without me.

She glanced over at me as she shimmied softly closer to me, scrubbing before peeking back at me, speaking shyly, "I know you two are close," she began peering at me, "I-I hear you talking at night sometimes."

My eyebrows arched at the statement.

"I'm sorry, I-I don't mean to eavesdrop, but it's hard for me to fall asleep sometimes." She pursed her lips for a moment, before wringing her mop and dipping it back into the bucket.

"I-I don't know what you're talking about." I stuttered momentarily.

She glanced at me for a moment, before returning to scrubbing, "perhaps you should continue scrubbing before the next patrol."

I glanced around, noting that we were the only two slaves cleaning the hallway.

I swallowed momentarily, going back to scrubbing beside her.

"I-I won't tell." She stuttered once more whilst I slowly scrubbed, eyes on her.

"I don't think it's fair that the others seclude her. We're all slaves here, all unwanted." Her eyes dropped to the floor, biting her bottom lip as she scrubbed.

I watched her for a second. My heart thudded, as I studied her innocent expression. There was something trustworthy about her. Something that bid my wolf to be of ease about her.

"Shade," I stated.

She paused, looking at me, "is my sister."

She blinked at this. Her eyes dropped to the floor for a minute before trailing back up at me, "then it can't be easy for you to sit back and watch how they treat her." She finally stated, "it certainly isn't easy for her too."

A pang of guilt rang through me. Sure it had been Shades' idea to pretend like we didn't know each other but that didn't make me feel any better.

Shade had always been the protective one, even when I was 6 months older. She would take the brunt of the bullying by the pack kids as a sister, and even now in the Night Court when she was in much more danger than I could ever be, she was still protecting me.

My gaze trailed to the bucket, as I wrung my cloth, "No, it isn't."

Silence loomed between us for a moment.

"But I-I think she'll be okay."

My gaze snapped up to Eve.

She smiled at me softly, "She strikes me as quite brave."

I chuckled at the statement, "She does, doesn't she?" I hummed.

Eve nodded, "is she?"

I paused, eyeing her for a moment, "bravest I know."

She smiled at me, before moving back to scrubbing.

I found myself smiling, eyes set on the side of her face as she mopped. I had been in the Night Court for nearly a month, and it felt like a prison.

I had never really talked to anyone else for long. No meaningful conversations other than the rushed ones I had with my sister.

Even in the Nightmoon pack, I had been secluded, but at least then I had AMA too.

It was nice to talk to someone else for a change, even if it was in hushed voices against bruised knees and aching arms covered in filth.

"And you?" I whispered as she hummed in reply, not looking back. "W-What's your story?"

She froze at this, the light in her eyes slowly draining.

I frowned, watching her expression, "You don't have to—"

"It is alright to ask. We're all slaves here. I have nothing to hide," she replied.

Her eyes flashed to mine, offering me a small smile.

"Slaves, yes." I confirmed, "I am a slave because my parents were rogues. Shade is a slave because she was born without a wolf despite our blood running through her veins. Half of the slaves here were either rejected, rogues or like me- but-"

"I have no scent or air about me that speaks otherwise." she finished, still with a sweet smile.

Her gaze fell to her hands, fingers feeling her palms as she closed them. "And my hands are soft."

She sighed, wringing her mop, glancing at me for a moment.

"My mother was a promiscuous soul in her youth-" she began with a sigh, a strand of her rosy hair falling forward as she mopped. I squinted slightly as a stray of sunlight streamed through the open window we had reached.

Eve glowed naturally in its light. I found myself envious of even this slight moment. She was frail as me, if not softer, and yet she still stood as if a goddess.

A gentle breeze blew in from the window as Eve continued to speak.

"She had me before she found her mate."

I let out a loose breath at this. An Illegitimate.

"Gamma Levi allowed me to stay with my mother till my eighteenth summer. When the time clocked, she bought a bit of time for me in hopes that I would find my mate but I reached my nineteenth last summer. No mate to claim me. I was then trialed and slaved." she finished.

Illegitimates were not too different from Keffers as they were mostly abandoned. But, they had wolves which was a grace if any.

They were known to be a disgrace, for even if they were not born inside the bond created by serene, the parent had no decency to create inside a bond agreed upon. I was surprised she was allowed to live by her mother's side for so long. I've heard of illegitimates with worse fates.

Then again, we were in the Night Court. Surely, there wasn't a fate alive worse than this if not death itself.

Her gaze shifted to the left, eyes set on the open window where we could barely see the large tower peeking from the shadows of the Night Court, a single bird flying out of the highest window.

"I wish I chose freedom," she whispered as she watched it. "I may have become a rogue but I would have run far enough to not worry about if the sun was going to rise or not."

Her gaze darted to mine, blushing softly as she blinked quickly, "I-I did not mean that."

I watched her carefully, "it's okay." I whispered in a hushed tone, repeating her words of comfort, "We're all slaves here."

Her gaze melted in mine, searching- searching for what I seemed to have been searching for not minutes ago. When she found what she had been looking for in my eyes, she let out a soft breath.

"So why didn't you?" I whispered once more.

"Leave?" she asked and I nodded.

"My wolf isn't very strong-" she paused, her eyebrows arching, "I'm not very strong."

Her eyes flashed to mine, "mother thought it best to be a slave to the Coalwen Pack than to be hunted forever as a rogue. She thought it was best to stay near, that I would live the rest of my life slaved t the pack but then the letter came and..." she trailed off.

"And now you slave in the Night Court with the rest of us."

Her eyes met mine and she nodded.

"Life isn't- it isn't fair." She murmured lowly, eyes downcast.

I was about to reply when both our gazes snapped at the sound of clanking, going back to mopping as the guards took their rounds again.

I stared at boot prints on the floor, relieved they were only two pairs.

My eyes trailed to the tower. Letting out a loose sigh.

No, life isn't fair at all.

•|•|•Hey guys! Thanks for reading! Please leave me a comment and vote to let me know you're enjoying the chapter! Read 5 chapters ahead on my patron! All links are in my bio! Below is a sneak chapter of [19.1] FOOLS AMONGST FOOLS now available on Patreon!•|•|•

[19.1] FOOLS AMONGST FOOLS

|•|•"Freedom is but an illusion pup, for everything has a prison. Even the widest field has an end and the wildest sea finds the land."•|•|•

[SHADE SHADOWS]

Diane cawed momentarily as I flipped through the maps.

"So- many," I managed a low gasp as I studied each one, walking around the table. My eyes were glued to the sight before me, my heart thudding within me as my gaze skimmed the detailed drawings.

There were maps of all kinds.

Detailed maps of Night Wolf territory, separate Detailed-maps of the other three territories. Old maps that detailed Valcane in the time of Alexander the Prime, the paper old and crusty, almost crumbling in my grip.

I handled these with the utmost care. The last thing I wanted to do was anger a master by ripping them. The thought of losing my head for something so stupid made me even more careful with the ancient maps.

I had to leave everything as if it was untouched.

There were current Valcanian maps, trade routes, and roads. It would be easier to just take one of these many maps but getting caught stealing was the last thing I needed. I would just have to sketch it out as best and as quickly as I could.

I could already spot paper but the ink had long dried out as if it had been quite a while since someone even touched it. Come to think of it, most of these maps were dust collected.

I lifted one map gently, dust coming up in short puffs. I coughed and then immediately covered my mouth. I didn't want any lingering masters hidden away in one of these rows to know I was here.

I stared at the maps that spread out over the seas. My gaze traveled the width of the seas to the land after it. My fingers trailed the outline of the land.

"The land of men," I whispered.

Freedom. Just a sea away.

My throat run dry, as I stared at it. So close and yet so far away.

Grabbing a piece of paper, I set the map down, sketching each point, comparing it with the map I had hidden away in my memories to figure out which direction Vale and I would have to take if indeed we managed to maneuver past the maze and the forest of the Night Wolf.

My fingers moved quickly across the page as I sketched. I wasn't a very good artist, but all that was required was a good memory and a resemblance of places that my hand sketched.

I worked quickly trying to put in as many details as I could whilst glancing momentarily at the setting sun that peaked through the high window. My heart tattered through me as my fingers skimmed across the page, fear of being caught gripping me.

Diane suddenly launched from my shoulder, and I froze watching as the bird took flight and pelted through the high window, getting lost in the fading bit of sunset, leaving me alone.

I let out a loose sigh, bidding my heart to relax when a sudden harsh knock was heard against the door. My body went cold, my heart hammering within me. The knock repeated, and my heart pounded. I grabbed a torch, my shaky fingers carefully rolling the sketched map and hiding it within my folds.

When the sounds refused to cease I carefully walked toward their steady thuds.

I had to pass through a lot of rows and shelves. I was afraid if it wasn't for the steady knocking against the door, I may have never been able to find my way back so soon. The library was vast and each route seemed similar. It was like a maze within a maze.

I approached the crimson door, slowly opening it, about ready to meet another master, though I wondered why one would find the need to knock.

Madam Catherine stood before me, her dull eyes nodding an expression I had never seen behind them. Perhaps worry? I wasn't too sure. The emotion made no sense. She had no reason to worry for a keffer. Perhaps there was something else that bothered her.

But her expression seemed to clear the moment our eyes met. I immediately bowed, keeping my gaze low, "Madam."

"Three days and you still breathe." She let out a loose breath.

I blinked at the floor but said nothing. It wasn't required of me to reply.

"Let us not stretch your luck, keffer." She replied, her voice becoming more monotone, "it is nearly evening and Luciferous needs you in the kitchens now."

"Yes madam."

She let out a loose breath and a moment of silence followed. I do not know where I found the bravery to peek. Perhaps I had let that bad habit brush off me when I risked a glance.

She was staring into the library behind me as if sniffing the air once more like I noticed she had first done when I had opened the door.

"You will return tomorrow. In the evenings, however, you will be required to work in the kitchen. You are the help after all."

"Yes madam."

She hummed at this response, "Follow."

I closed the door behind me, marching after her. Sure my arms were already tired from lifting books all day and dusting in high places but I was a slave and I would work until the day I dropped. As long as I could still move, there was no such thing as tired.

I moved behind Madam Catherine, my head bowed low as we moved past several guards and finally down a flight of stairs. Moving through grander hallways where slaves moped for hours and here, I searched for signs of my sister, but she was not among these slaves.

Going down hallways and stairs we finally made it to the kitchen where Luciferous was barking orders like he always did when it was near dining hours.

"Lucy darling." Madam Catherine called.

His fiery gaze latched onto Madam Catherine who gave him a sweet smile to which he scoffed, his gaze throwing down to me, "what are you waiting for keffer?" He growled, "furnace, now!"

"Yes, master!" I screeched, speeding past him and into the familiar territories. He seemed to be angrier than when I had left.

I let out a loose breath, as I walked into the furnace room, the heat the first to reach me and the smell of coal. Barnabas turned, shirtless, sweat glistening down his back, a shovel in hand. He stuffed it into a pile of coal leaning against it.

"The brave one returns," he smirked, and my gaze toppled to the floor. I was unsure of who he told of my endeavors but reason reminded me if he had told Luciferous or Madam Catherine I would have been punished already.

"Catch."

My gaze snapped to him just in time as a shovel was thrown in my direction. I moved away just as it skidded past, my eyes wide. My gaze slowly trailed from the shovel to Barnaba in shock.

"You were supposed to catch it, Keffer." He grumbled.

I don't think I could have caught that. But I was quick to pick it up, as he stepped aside, grabbing his shovel.

"Quickly now, before Luciferous loses his head." He huffed, shoveling some more coal into the furnace.

I was careful as I stood beside Barnabas, shoveling beside him.

"The fat man has been a living nightmare since yesterday," he grunted, as he shoveled another pile of coal, "cooking nonstop, experimenting with foods and such."

My gaze studied the side of Barnabas' face partly illuminated by the dancing fire.

"W-why?" I managed a hoarse whisper. I expected him to growl at me as usual, but he merely explained as he shoveled.

"Council of courts is coming in a few weeks I'm told. He wishes to prepare the very best meals for them. He isn't known as the best chef in the four territories for no reason." He huffed.

"Council of courts rarely commune. It will be his greatest audience and hence we will suffer in utmost misery until he makes that perfect fucking menu."

I threw another pile of coal in there until the fire blazed so brightly I could feel the ends of my puffy hair coil.

Barnabas laid the shovel down, taking a seat, and so did I.

Silence loomed between us and I tried my best to ignore the feel of his stare as I watched the flames dance before me.

"You plan to escape this place."

My heart froze within me at the stale statement. My heart rammed within me.

"N-no." I blurted and turned around to see him. Eyes wide. My gaze immediately dropped, "of course not. T-that would be treason—"

"You're a shit liar," he scoffed with an eye roll, "illusions of freedom are an echo in your very eye. I know a restless spirit when I see one."

I pursed my lips, fear gripping my very bones. I did not confirm it, my eyes stuck on Barnabas as he leaned forward, eyes searching mine.

"Freedom is a fool's game and a slave's downfall." He growled, "you would be wise to erase those illusions unless you wish to end with your soul in the hands of a shadow, put in the hunt, or worse, in the claws of the Night Wolf."

I let out a short breath as the corner of his lips lifted, the smell of ale heavy on his breath though his bright eyes seemed to read my very intents.

"From the tower, you've seen the maze haven't you?" he grinned knowingly, "You've seen the forest too, and if you've heard the stories thus you know it is utter foolishness to seek an escape."

"The stories of monsters." I managed to breathe in one escaped breath.

"Monsters?" he grinned, laying back in his seat, "monsters only feast on your flesh girl. These are shadows, demons, and dark ones! Whichever you wish to name. Present since the first day the sun rose, old and ancient. Your flesh ripping off your bones at their hands is a hearted rainbow compared to the rest of what they will do to you," he spat.

His gaze trailed away from me to the dancing flames.

"Keffers are indeed foolish," he mumbled.

I stared at him for a moment, a certain fire sparking within me, "And I-I suppose you would propose I wait for my death here, in a place where the sun rarely shines? W-What is it to die there, than here? It is death in the end isn't it?"

His gaze snapped to mine, and I held my breath though for some reason my bravery refused to waver. Holding his gaze as best as I could.

"It is the way you die that counts." he finally grunted back.

My gaze traveled to the ceiling, tears filling my eyes, "this is the second time today, someone speaks of my death." I pursed my lips, "I am truly cursed." I realized, mostly to myself though it was loud enough for him to hear.

"I reckon death is near to a keffer. You have heard of it a million times, you are weak if such a thing still fazes you."

"A million and one," I replied, "the number of times I've heard it."

His eyes remained to study me for a moment.

"I know I will die. I do not care how. I just wish to die free."

"And that is your foolishness." He quipped with a low huff..

"If it is the foolish that are free, then perhaps I am," I retorted before I could control myself

His gaze hardened in mine, and my heart pounded, my fingers tight against my dress as I tried to not show my fear.

The corner of his lips lifted once more, nodding for a moment, "I am known as the drunken fool that works the furnace," he huffed, getting to his feet. He shoveled a heap of coal in as I watched.

"I am free and I am a fool." He continued with a shrug.

My fingers gripped around the shovel. Had I been stupid to speak against him?

"Fools have nothing but other fools amongst them." He paused, turning around as he leaned against his shovel, "if you make it past the maze, the shadows, the forest, and the wolf," he grumbled, taking out a bottle of ale he had tucked in his pocket.

He unloosed the top, shaking the contents in the bottle, "alive," he added, his gaze melting in mine, narrowing for a moment, "then I will take you as far as Yulis. I'm sure if you can survive an escape, You will be able to find a way to the port from the city."

My heart pounded at this, eyebrows arched. He was offering his help? How did he know where I wanted to go?

"It is the port you wish to go, is it not? To be free across the sea." He chuckled, chugging down the bottle of alcohol, "it is the only place you can be truly free unless you wish to be hunted as rogues for the rest of your days."

"If - and only if I was planning an escape," I managed to gurgle, my heart pounding within me, "w-why are you keen on helping me?" I whispered.

He paused at this, shrugging as took a seat, leaning against the wall, taking a cool rug he covered his face in, "perhaps it is because I am a fool."

I watched him for a moment, when he suddenly peeked from the cloth, lifting it slightly, "Dig keffer, the fire burns low."

•|•|•Please leave a comment and vote! A sneak peak of Chapter [20.1] A KEFFERS DREAM is down below! •|•|•

[20.1] A KEFFERS DREAM

"Even the faintest whispers are carried by the wind. Listen, for the wind has many secrets."

•|•|•

[SHADE SHADOWS]

The slaves whispered amongst themselves as I walked in. As usual, eyes ventured my way accompanied by light scoffs.

My gaze traveled to my sisters whose eyes rested on me momentarily sending me a discreet nod, before returning to the conversation whispered amongst the group of slaves.

I made my way to my secluded area knowing I would remain unbothered.

Sitting by the ledge of the window where the cold wind blew in, under the gentle moonlight, Glancing around, I carefully took out the map. My eyes trailed over it, my feeble fingers trembling, before tucking it back into my sleeve.

I was lucky today.

From finding the map to Barnabas' mysterious turnaround. I had no reason to trust the drunk, he could turn us in for all I know and get a reward.

It was simply not wise to rely on him.

Sure, it would be easier to travel to Yulis with a castle worker successfully covering the stench of a rogue's scent, but it remained quite plain that he could not be trusted. In this equation, I could only trust my sister and she could only trust me.

I could not risk or rely our freedom on anyone else.

Nevertheless, Barnabas was a good source of information and if indeed he wanted to help, I could get some more information from him. He was a worker that ventured freely out of the Night Court. He knew other ways I was sure.

I simply had to be careful. I could not confess all my plans.

Even if I was a fool for freedom I could not be that foolish.

"Slaves!" a guard suddenly barked causing all of us to look at the two guards standing in the doorway.

"Blow out your candles! The Night was meant for sleep," he growled.

My gaze traveled from the guard barking orders, to the silent one standing behind him. Blue eyes stared back at me and my eyebrows arched.

I had seen those eyes before, somewhere.

The candles went out and so did my vision of those eyes, darkness encircling us.

It took a while for me to maneuver around the now-settled wolves, bumping into a few who growled back at me in a string of colorful curses.

Had I had a wolf, vision in the night would have been easier for me. Instead, I was as blind as a bat until I got to my reed mat.

I laid across the rough surface staring at the stone roof. Blinking for a moment. Memories from the day drained through me, of Diane-that mysterious bird, and something even more mysterious.

Of the master who was not afraid to be friends with a Keffer.

My eyebrows arched in the darkness. He was very coarse and— blunt I dare say. He was certainly arrogant and had no feelings of selflessness. No- not altruistic in the least. However, there was something --kind in his eyes?

No- I almost scoffed aloud--kindness wasn't the word.

My lips pursed in the darkness. Something innocent? I shook my head, turning around restlessly on the reed mat.

No- there was something dark in his eyes, but that darkness only hid another emotion that was at his core-

I could not put my finger on it.

It was something curious, something of innocence but not innocent. I rolled my eyes in the darkness. I would damage my head if I kept thinking like this.

I rolled onto my back, staring back at the roof. His words were so blunt, it was certainly annoying. Perhaps what annoyed me most was the truth in them.

Many times I had thought of my history. Of my parents, who they were. If they had been Keffers too. But AMA said it is quite unlikely.

Keffers are born randomly. Even an Arc could have a keffer for a son. I scoffed at this.

Wouldn't that be something?

I let the silence consume me for a moment, my eyes closing.

Sometimes I pictured them in my mind. In my head, my father's skin was as dark as mine. And my mother's wolf had fur the shade of shadows, and they loved me- my fingers shook slightly as I let out a shaky breath.

Despite all the stories I heard of abandonment. I dreamed they wanted me. Perhaps, I only wished it so, but I feel no hate towards them. Living or dead, they are my parents. As their daughter was it wrong I hoped they cherished me?

Perhaps I should live a minute more in my nightmares. Maybe I would see them, even once...

It is a fair price to pay.

I yawned softly in the darkness my eyelids closing shut.

A price I would certainly pay, gratefully.

—————Screams and the sound of Horses neighing like haunting echoes through the branches of the trees in the darkened forest sounded. The sounds of their steady hooves drew closer and closer with each thud against the leaf-covered ground.

I could hardly see with the heavy fog in the air, the moon was barely visible against the blackened sky.

I coughed, dropping forward, my hands covered in ash. It was only then I realized this was no fog, it was smoke.

Thick and merciless, choking like a lasso on the neck.My eyes were watery and my knees stung from my fall.

"Up! This is no time to fall!" a desperate breathless voice urged above me, grabbing my arm and causing me to stumble forward to my little feet once more.

I could not see the woman's face beside me, draped in a veil, a shadow across her face as we pushed forward. Her hands clasped mine tightly as we run through the trees' smoke trailing behind us.

The howl of wolves began to ring behind us and I dared a peek seeing nothing but shadows and shapes racing towards us in the mask of thick smoke, ashes falling from the sky-

"Do not look behind! Eyes ahead, flower!" She cautioned, gripping me tighter.

I feared my legs would give out and yet there was a pounding in my head full of fear giving me the adrenaline to push forward.

Low bushes grazed the back of my legs and the roots of trees tripped me from time to time but we pushed on until a large wolf suddenly bounded before us, blocking our way.

We froze in the midst of the burning forest, petrified at the sight of it.

The wolf's fur was gray ash, bigger than the average wolf, his teeth snarling at us.

The woman placed a hand in front of me protectively, pushing me behind her where I was hidden by her wide skirt.

"Stay behind me," she whispered lowly as we moved backward into the smoke, eyes never leaving the beast who stalked toward us like prey.

The crunch of leaves beneath his paws was heavy and fear paralyzed me.

"You cannot have her!" the woman was fierce in her statement, but the response was fiercer.

I turned away just as the beast pounced, fearing this was my death, but nothing came, instead the sound of growls filled the air.

I looked and the woman was no longer beside me. Two wolves fought with claws and teeth viciously in the surrounding ash, one gray, the other the color of the earth.

The battle was mighty, the brown wolf was smaller but it was not weak and the gray wolf was bigger and deadlier, but the skill driven by the brown was its downfall.

Blood spilled into the earth as the gray wolf breathed its last.

I run over to the brown wolf as it twisted back into its form, a naked heap on the ground.

Tears filled my eyes when I realized the woman had blood seeping from a wound she tried to hide from me, her body weak and the shadow still on her face, her skin the echo of mine-

She was the winner but it had come with a price. I wept over her body as life faded from her, her fingers bloody and ashy reaching for my skin, pulling my jaw up to face hers, "Go my little flower," she gasped--

"Go find your alpha."

I did not wish to leave her, but with her command, she breathed her last.

The sound of wolves and hooves of horses only drew closer and now even the sound of voices. My heart grieved within me as I ran, beating faster with each howl, closer and deadlier than the first-

"Shade!"

I glanced behind me as I run-

"Shade, wake up!"

I gasped, as I sat upright, darkness filling my eyes. Vale let out a loose breath, sitting back on her heels, as she knelt beside me. I could only blink as she pushed a loose strand of her thin blond hair behind her ear, gaze looking me over-

"Another nightmare." She stated.

It was then I found a breath, shaking my head, pulling my knees up to my chest.

"It's the first you've had in nearly two weeks," she murmured.

My eyebrows arched, trying to remember my dream, "it was different this time—stranger," I managed to say, gaze lifting to her.

Her eyes searched mine for a moment, eyebrows arching, before they suddenly cleared, "you will have to say another time, we can not stay here." She huffed getting to her feet.

"It's morning."

My gaze immediately traveled to the window where the darkness loomed. My heart fell,

"a dark day."

Vale nodded, "you're lucky it was too dark for madam to see you still asleep. The others went to the bathhouse. We should do the same before a guard finds us."

I nodded at this as she gave me a hand up. We took our jackets and headed to the pump.

"There you are keffer!" Haven gleamed when she spotted me, "I was afraid you were dead and I would have to pump."

The girls chuckled at her remark as I made my way into their midst, beginning my usual routine. Working off my arms before I even started a day's work.

The lever seemed heavier today, and I was slower. Perhaps it was because my head was wrapped in thoughts of my dreams, of the strange woman I believed was my mother if my dreams were truly memories of my history.

It was her voice I heard in my nightmares. Yes, I was sure. And if my dreams were truly memories then she was not alive, and hence sadness dawned, and for the first time I relished a dark day so that even Vale could not see the tears that threatened to spill from my eyes as I pumped.

I could only pray that the master was wrong and that my dreams were only dreams and nothing more.

When most of the buckets were done, and only Vale and I remained, I pumped for her mindlessly- and she stood beside me lighting the endless night with a torch in her hand.

"Shade I can do it-"

"You can not keep staying behind," I breathed, glancing at the bathhouse, "they will know what we are if you keep this up," I warned.

"How else will I talk with you? Where else?" She huffed, "you do not say a word anywhere else," she argued.

"We can not talk every day, you know that," I whispered back, pumping more water into her bucket.

"True, but you wish to not say a word at all."

"I am alright, and I'm working on the plan. That is all you need to know. If anything else arises, I will inform you," I stressed, finally looking at her.

"I do not believe you."

I let out a loose breath, gaze trailing to the bucket which I was filling, "believe this. I have found a map for us, a route to take up after we find a way to escape the forest."

She took a step closer, eyes wide, her voice low, "Are you mad Shade? You still wish to venture into the Night Wolf's forest?"

"It is the only way." I reminded her.

"Look at your feet and your hands." She urged.

My eyebrows arched at the absurd statement, looking at her instead as she spoke-

"Go on then, look," she urged once more.

I glanced at them and then back at her.

"Do you know why they do not slap chains around our hands and feet whilst we stand in the Night Court? Because they know that even the most insane of our kind could not possibly try to escape."

I rolled my eyes at this, my gaze snapping up instead, eyes meeting that of the guard that was perched a distance away, his blue gaze lingering in mine.

"He's been missing," I stated.

"Who- what-?" Vale asked confused before following my gaze to the guard. Her eyes quickly found the ground, staring at me, "do not hold eye contact, shade" she hissed.

At her warning, my gaze fell back to the pump-

"He hasn't been there these past 2 days." I urged."it's been another."

"They have shifts and how does that concern us? Are you changing the subject?" Vale gasped, placing her hands on her hips.

Her bucket overflowed with water and I took a sneak peek at the guard again and noticed his eyes never left mine. What Vale failed to see is that it was important we understood the shift cycle if we planned to escape. We had to find the perfect time to begin.

I studied the guard. He was the guard that looked away when I was being bullied, not that I expected him to care, and the very guard that had come to our quarters yesterday.

"Shifts are hourly, aren't they?"

"Perhaps he fell ill then. Shade, you can not change the topic," Vale retorted.

My gaze snapped to her. "It's the forest. It's the only way if we wish to get out of here," I whispered lowly. "The only way."

Her gaze met mine, studying me intently for a moment, "We have to find another."

"There is no other Vale!" I grunted-

"At least promise me you'll try to look for another!" she stressed, her hand gripping my arm, "there must be another way."

I glanced at the action for a moment, then glanced at her nodding, "if you promise me to think about this one first."

Her hand dropped, pursing her lips, "fine."

I nodded, turning back to the pump, "You should go now, your bucket is full." I stated.

She stared at me for a moment before glancing down at the bucket. She perched the torch nearby and picked it up, a debate in her eyes as if she desired to speak more before deciding against it to my relief.

She squeezed my arm and escaped in the direction of the bathhouse.

I let out a loose breath at this as I watched her for a bit, placing my bucket beneath the pump. Pumping my gaze shifted back to the guard.

He was still staring intently at me against the firelight. I swung my torch away, grabbed my full bucket, and made my way to the bathhouse.

•|•|•Enjoying the story? Read Advanced Chapter 21 to 24 on Patreon! Please vote and leave a comment if you're enjoying the story! Want to ask an in depth question or start a discussion on MTTNW. Join my discord community we're I'm always available for questions/discussions. Link in bio!•|•|•

[21.1] A DYING HOPE

"For if the world was to end. It would surely end by Night."

[KAYOS]

My eyes opened slowly, and yet it was as if they were still closed. No light to reveal if it was day, but I needed no light to know that.

Darkness of the blackest kind filled the throne room, and the throne itself felt as cold as ice beneath me, my fingers stiff around the arm of the iron throne. I had spent a night on the throne as I had done so many times before. My body felt stiff, but I relished the pain.

I could feel shadows around me, whispering things that made me shut my eyes once more, reaching out for the darkness around me.

Despair is what I felt, and despair was what poisoned the air, what manifested as the darkness around me and cursed the sun from shining, and yet I had to confess there was a certain peace in this despair.

I took in a deep breath, relinquishing the air from between my lips, and the shadows around me fought for that breath of life.

A shadow crept up my arm, and I gingerly turned as Alchest perched by the high of my throne.

"What is it you wish to say?" I asked lazily, feeling the shadow move to right above my shoulder, where he perched once more.

"Ressst, massster," he hissed softly.

I hummed at this, closing my eyes for a bit. I turned my head forward to where I knew the doors that opened to the throne room faced, though there was nothing I could see in the darkness, typically because there was nothing to see but darkness.

"I rested a full night and now I have brought the night with me to the day." I replied in a low whisper, "perhaps it should stay for another, and another....and another."

My wolf growled within me showing its frustration. I gritted my teeth trying to reel him in as I have done many times, my eyes heating beneath my skin and I knew they were glowing their deadly embers.

My wolf argued within me. A taunt of mockery. Of weakness.

"I can not stop it. It will happen." I urged, gritting my teeth.

My wolf growled within me and a streak of lightning flashed in the night sky illuminating the empty throne room for a flash of a second, shadows scampering to the corner.

I groaned out loud as I felt him wish to tear me apart, throwing myself forward, my fingers stiff against the arm of the throne.

"You think I wish this?" I gritted, my teeth clenched, "To mate with another? We have no hope-"

My wolf would simply see no reason. Only heating the battle within me. I jutted forward, gripping the throne tighter, determined to grip him in, but his anger could not be quenched this time, and I moved off the throne, hunched over, my body heavy for my feet.

"Massssster," Alchest hissed, as I grunted, trying to stop my transformation in time.

"Stay!" I growled back at him, stopping his approach. He scampered backward, whilst I stumbled into the middle of the throne room.

If I turned in this castle, chaos would reign. I was not a pup that would merely damage a room anymore, the spikes on my back were deadlier, my wolf larger and his anger and thirst for blood unquenchable.

Darkness gathered from all corners of the throne and I fell to my knees as my wolf fought to be loose. The doors of the throne room remained shut and I could only hear heartbeats a few halls away, scampering in the opposite direction, moving farther.

No one wished to be near me whilst the Night inside me formed.

The darkness gathered in the middle of the room as I grunted and howled in agony, the shadows reaching up to the stoned roof, a beam of shadow in the center of the throne room.

With a last agonizing push, I managed to stumble through the shadow, my feet crunching against the leaves of the forest, and I staggered against a tree. The darkest night formed above me, manifesting as I transformed.

Lightning flashed and the storm began to pour as the Night raged on. I was a wolf the image of night, wearing the very stroke of midnight as my fur. My spikes quivered in the roaring wind, heartbeats scampering every which way as the animals began their race to freedom.

Shadows moved with me as I hunted through the forest, the storm beating down my back, cold giving only more power beneath my paws.

It was easy to kill. Easier than ever in this form. Perhaps too easy.

I was faster than any animal in this forest. I was the predator to predators.

I hunted the bear for only it could somewhat appease my hunger. I was quick and the shadows were my allies. Nothing could escape me, and the rain that beat down my back only refreshed me. The fog soon loomed with the forest as I found my prey.

There wasn't much of a fight to remember, even when I heard a second growl of the beasts mate and it the next fall.

My memories often sunk into the dark place when my wolf was laced with anger and hunger.

Images came in glimpses, and I understood I was losing the will to return.

I could stay in the endless, allow my wolf to lead, lone and feral, and with him an Ever Night.

I would never have to worry about despair again.

It was what he deserved after all, freedom after my failures.

The world was farther than it had been a second ago, and I felt my hold on it loosen between my fingers. I did so willingly as I watched the world through a narrowing window in the endless.

Glimpses of the world before it could fully fade.

Bloodstained against my midnight fur, spikes quivering in the wind, the smell of death in the air as my teeth ripped into the hard flesh, muzzled shadows hiding from the death in my fangs. Yet eager to live in a world with no sunlight forever.

Glimpses only, fading slowly.

It was calmer here.

The sounds of the forest around me became less audible and replacing it was the silence of the endless.

Glimpses. Foggy trees. The storm, Corpses of eaten bears, the darkness that hung in the sky,

Glimpses

A last look at my home. The Night Court, ancient and bold against the ruling wind of the storm, lightning flashing. My mother would miss me but she has lost and survived before.

Glimpses.

The tower....

I blinked, noting a small glow through its singular window, against the beating of the rain.

It was hope then? The keffer- the trial.

A dying hope but nevertheless, hope.

I reached out for it, unsure, and I grunted, throwing myself through the sliver of a window in the endless, finding my naked body in the river of blood between carcasses left by my wolf.

I gasped for air, breathing harshly against the wind. The storm still raged above me, rain running through my blood-stained hair and bear fur that clung to my skin.

Dragging myself out of the pit of bones, blood, fur, and mud, I staggered to my feet. Barefooted against fallen branches and wild bushes I limped forward in the darkness, a shadow scampering out of sight.

I paused, gaze following it, and watched as Alchest perched against a low branch, right above a dark robe that hung loosely from a branch.

My eyes narrowed on the creature, "I commanded you to stay."

I scoffed, grabbing the coat.

My body was still weak as I draped the coat over me, my bloody scratched hands healing as they felt the trunk of the tree for support. My gaze lifted past the tree, the Night Court barely visible in the heavy fog.

In the mirror of my eyes the echo of that single flame in the highest tower.

The shadows gathered behind me and I turned, limping through the shadow.

Lay weeping,Begging to the moon,

For a heart to rest his soul

My head rolled back in the darkness, leaning softly against a wooden shelf, hidden discreetly in the darkness. Seated on the floor, only the dark robe draped around me to shield my blood-stained body, I sat on the floor of the darkness listening to the soft singing.

The Keffer moved only a few shelves behind me, and though I could not see her, her scent, her heartbeat, and her voice were all around me, warmth seeping into my skin in the torch-lit library.

She moved with heavy books in her arms, humming as she dusted. I could hear every wipe of the cloth in her hands, every breath that brushed against her lips, but I knew she did not know of my existence.

Without her wolf, she could not sense me barely a few feet away.

It was in her favor and mine. I did not wish to explain why I was drenched, water dripping from the curls that clung to my face. Blood stains on every inch of my body, the taste of death on my lips.

If she was scared whenever I first spoke, I could not imagine what would happen if she was to see me in this state.

No- her ignorance was certainly best.

I scoffed lowly when I realized I had stopped wasting in the endless and now, and instead, I was thinking of how unlucky and lucky the keffer only a few feet away from me was.

Her humming continued, and I sensed her move to the next row. She came close once, had she not turned she would have seen me. Part of me wished she had. She was the only one who was able to see me- see me truly.

I shut my eyes, letting out a loose breath as her soft hums filled me. I should not be this wanting. She was a trial I was sure, a trial I would fail if I let her slip too close.

My eyebrows arched when the soft hum stopped and instead soft grunts were replaced. I turned slightly watching as she pushed the ladder toward the window.

She began to talk and for a second I thought she had seen me, but she did not look in my direction. Not even once.

I staggered to my feet, as Alchest crossed the shadows perching on my shoulders.

Peeking past the shelves I watched the curious girl, speak again to what seemed like the shadows. My eyebrows arched, until I heard another heart-beat, my gaze narrowing to the shadows beside her.

"I have to see it, Diane, tell me the fog has cleared," she breathed anxiously and my eyebrows arched as something fluttered above her perching on the window sill.

It was a raven, with a strange aura, cawing loudly back at her, hoping by the ledge. I stood beside the shadows of the shelves camouflaged slightly, the firelight only lightly illuminating me as I studied the keffer curiously.

"Truly?" she asked with a wide grin moving up the ladder. She peered out of the window, sitting by the ledge beside the strange bird.

She took a paper from a hidden space underneath her skirt, looking out into the vastness of Night Court.

I knew what she could see from that height. I had gazed upon it myself.

The court, the maze, the forest, and the land beyond that occupied my territory.

I watched as her face fell, glancing down at the bird beside her that refused to take flight, looking down at the view.

"The storm and the fog are gone but it is still too dark to see." her tone sounded disappointed as she let out a loose breath.

I watched as she stared at the view for a few more moments before a small smile spread across her face, "Nevertheless it is beautiful. Even with so much darkness."

The bird cawed as if in approval. And she grinned down at it. Her gaze traded to the paper in her hand, "we will draw another time. Perhaps the sun will return tomorrow."

With that, she slowly climbed down the ladder and I stepped back into the shadows, as the bird flew over the length of my sanctuary.

My gaze narrowed on it, turning slightly to Alchest, a short pause between a breath.

"Bring him to me."

"Yessss master."

•|•|•Enjoying the story? Read Advanced Chapter 22 to 24 on Patreon! Please vote and leave a comment if you're enjoying the story! Want to ask an in depth question or start a discussion on MTTNW. Join my discord community we're I'm always available for questions/discussions. Link in bio!•|•|•

[22.1] DIANE

• |•|•"Don't you know that the forests died with the faerie folk? True Magic is not in these lands."•|•|•

[KAYOS]

The bird cawed loudly in its cage, and my eyes gleamed a sparkled ember as I watched it from the shadows of my study.

The light trails of magic coming off it in shimmering waves intrigued me for I had not seen something quite like it. So easy to miss and yet so irregular.

I studied the bird for a moment, before leaning forward into the candle-light. Inspecting it closely I confirmed a few things about the abnormalities of the bird. It was larger than a normal raven, it seemed to watch me as well, and its heart was racing the closer I got.

The bird blinked in my direction, growing quiet, and paused as if frozen at the mere sight of me.

It wasn't unusual for animals to behave this way toward me, I knew.

Each animal was born with an instinct. It was simply natural that they knew when a predator was in their midst.

It is why whenever my wolf forms, the birds take flight, the deer runs, and the bear gallops as fast as it can into its dark cave.

It is only a shame it does not understand that the darkness is my home too.

My gaze trailed the bird. It had a diamond-shaped mark on its forehead, watching as its feathers shivered under my heavy stare, dark beady eyes never leaving mine.

They say darkness is felt in the wind.

I opened its cage and it remained at the center of the far back, even as the door was left open wide for it.

A bird in terror should have taken flight unless it somehow understood that escape was futile.

Alchest gripped the bars, moving across each hissing at the bird perched in the center, before slipping off to a shadow at the corner of the table.

My hands slipped in, fingers wrapping around its silky body and it shivered once more under my touch but remained still and quiet though the very tips of my fingers could feel the steady pounding of its small heart.

Fast as a drum.

Getting up, I walked to the window that slowly swung open courtesy of Alchest. I placed the bird on the ledge stepping back, hands clasped behind my back as I stood before it.

The bird blinked in my direction, head bowed low, a shiver in its feathers.

"You have two options, Raven." I began, "You may reveal yourself now, in my presence, and disclose why you fly so freely in the borders of my sanctuary," I breathed.

"Or you can simply escape-" I suggested, my gaze drifting to the open window behind it, where the taste of freedom manifested as a gentle breeze that blew through its feather and into the darkness of the dark day behind it.

"— Knowing that every time the sun refuses to rise, or every time it sets, whenever you fly in utter darkness or may find rest in a presence of a lingering shadow no matter how small. Your life will be cut short, abruptly, painfully- " the words were blunt and stale across my tongue, "and your soul trapped within the claws of a demon, never to set flight again."

My gaze dropped to the bird, lips pressed in a cold thin line.

"It is your choice."

A moment of silence passed between us.

The bird seemed to be staring at me. Its head bowed lowly, as it hoped from one leg onto the other, another shiver crossing its spine, and then— it transformed.

So abruptly, if I had wasted a moment to blink, I would have missed the better of it.

In its place stood the smallest humanoid creature I had ever seen. Perhaps the size of my palm.

A round face puffed and red. A green hat, and dark clothing against its pale skin accompanied by large green eyes, a shimmer of silver hair peaking from its hat, where sharpened ears peaked. Accompanied by pointy green shoes.

The little funny looking being pursed its lips, refusing to meet my eyes, as it slowly took off its hat, gripping it to its front, head bowed, and large green eyes staring at the floor.

Alchest perched on my shoulder as we stared at the creature.

"A faerie," I stated in a stale realization.

It glanced up at me at this, shy as its cheeks run as red as tomatoes, shuffling on its two feet as if it were still a bird. It was skinny, standing by the edge of the ledge, yet still daring to titter forward.

"The books say your kind perished in the old war, with the elves," I stated, eyes never leaving the figure, "but Father always said you were somewhere out there if you looked hard enough." I mumbled to myself, "Faeries were his favorite stories."

I tilted my head slightly as I took in the queer creature who snuck glances at me, and when it was caught it would stare at the floor so hard it seemed it wished to be eaten by it.

The grip on its tiny hat was tight, lips shivering.

I shut my eyes, remembering the stories, "And a faerie does not speak unless it is caught and named." I grunted with irritation.

The first thing to learn about the Fae is their affinity for names.

My eyes reopened and the faerie's gaze immediately snapped back to the floor.

"What will I name you then?" I let out a loose breath.

"Diane!" It blurted out quickly, eyes wide as it stared at me. Its voice was a high-pitched squeak, loud and abrupt.

My gaze narrowed on it, and it immediately shut its mouth, eyes wide but seemingly frozen in mine, unable to look away.

It was frozen in place as if time itself had stopped. I could not even hear its breath. Save for the racing of its heartbeat, I would have thought it had died of shock.

It was such a fearful creature.

"Diane." I repeated, "That is a female's name."

I looked him up and down. "You are male."

"R-Regardless, it is my name! I-I own it! Yes, sir, I own it," It stuttered a reassurance to itself, "And I will n-not give it back! No sir! It is my name and I adore it! It was given to me and I-I, I will not return it! Not for all the honey in the world and heaven beyond! I will fight to the death for it good sir, it was given, yes given! and will certainly not be returned!" It screeched, seemingly about to blow its head off, before freezing again when its large eyes met mine.

It darted to Alchest when he hissed in response to its unwelcome outburst.

"Y-your majesty." It squeaked. Bowing its head lowly once again. Little fingers gripping its hat tighter.

My eyebrows drew together.

"You know who I am." I realized. "What I am."

It shivered at my words, raising a shoulder in a short shrug, little hands still gripping its hat tightly, whilst its silver hair echoed in the glowing candlelight.

Even without a wolf. This creature knew of me.

"Y-you are very well known amongst the faerie folk, your majesty. You are the Night Wolf- prince of shadows,—a-and- and demons," he squeaked, peering up at me for a second, he blinked back down.

"My brothers speak highly of you, they say your wolf is as tall as the Silverbane Tree and has spikes deadlier than those silver-tipped arrows but I think it is pure hogs-wash. Those sprites are keen on scaring me- " he frowned as if lost in his narrative, eyebrows drawing in together, "lying flat nose chumps!" He grunted, "Earth, they even say darkness is whipped around you like a cloak. I'm standing here, aren't I? And I see no darkness save the dark around us, pfft! Staring into your eyes would send a faerie straight down to the gutters of hell, that is pure-" His gaze shifted to mine once more before quickly looking down and breathing heavily.

"P-Perhaps they were right about that part-" he mumbled softly, biting at his lips. His heart was racing and I could hear it quite clearly from here.

"You still live, your kind." I stated, "Hidden in the forests."

"N-not your forest your majesty," he squeaked, then nervously chuckled, "Earth! No fae would dare live there. Oh not there! T-too much death," his gaze traveled to mine, smile wiping off his face in a second as he swallowed, "w-we live in forests." He finally confirmed, pursing his lips once more.

"Hidden after the old war. It is too dangerous for our kind you see. We live by the oldest laws."

"And yet, you fly in my sanctuary, high and free." I mocked. "You are certainly brave in your venture into my most private."

I tilted my head studying the creature.

His lips pursed, peering at me from his long eyelashes, "F-forgive me, your highness," he bowed lowly, "You see, I have no choice. I-I must be near my master."

My gaze narrowed on him, curiosity plaguing me, a sliver of disbelief in my tone "The master who names you- the Keffer?" I realized.

The little fae gasped, eyes wide, hurt in his eyes, "Shade! My master's name is Shade!" He screeched, no fear in his wide eyes as he looked up at me.

I found it weird, to say the least.

I was not sure if I would rather take his head off for screaming in my face, however, the picture of a headless faerie was not an image I wanted to see. It was something my father would have frowned upon too.

And truthfully, such A tiny body with no head seemed wrong- even for me.

And if the Keffer was indeed his master, perhaps killing a friend's pet was not something I should do.

"How does a keffer master a faerie?" I asked, "It can only be done unless that faerie has a debt to pay." I remembered my father's tales quite well, and the books I had read.

My gaze fell heavy on the tiny being, "what did she do for you, that you owe a lifetime?"

He pursed his lips, glancing at me, shaking his head slowly, "I-I can not reveal it. It is a secret I fear I must take to the grave. It is an old law."

I studied the little being that shuddered beneath my gaze, fingers tight around its hat. Alchest dropped from my shoulder, threatening the tiny being with his hisses and the claws of shadows.

Scared as it was the faerie remained firm, "Hiss at me all you want you, big bully! I am vowed to silence. My soul isn't worth much, but you can take it if that is the price," he grunted, closing his eyes, "they will sing songs of me in fairy halls. Of my bravery, that I, Diane, the first fairy to stand against the prince of shadows! It will be a legacy to behold-"

But I was not listening to his senseless rambles, it was fruitless to torture him into submission. Faeries might be annoying creatures, evidently, but they were known to be amongst the most loyal creatures and bearers of good luck. They remained cheery even through torture which made them unbearable rays of sunshine.

Takes away the fun in torture if you asked me.

Faeries took their laws as if it was chained to their very necks.

I paused, a thought growing, "so the keffer does have secrets," I breathed beneath my breath, a dying hope drawing me in.

A secret that was strong enough that even a faerie took a vow of silence.

"I wish they do not sing with the old melodies. It is pure balderdash; they can not sing a song with a new tune. Ugh! I will turn in my grave and pluck my ears out if they do. But Diane the Brave has a nice ring to it! Surely someone somewhere will write a new song. But Fate is not one to rely on- no- I should make my own whilst I'm still alive! Yes! But how will they hear it if I am to die soon? Ah, yes! The wind will carry it home. Where was I then? Ah- the melody—"

"Do you need a moment?" I growled, causing him to jump.

He paused, blinking at me, "be-before you suck my soul dry you mean? Rip the flesh of my b-bones?"

I rolled my eyes, getting up-

"Is that a yes, your majesty?"

"Alchest,"

The shadow snapped towards me, and we headed towards the door, when I froze, a dark shiver suddenly rattling through me. I turned immediately to the faerie who looked up at me with wide eyes.

"Have you told her who I am?" I asked blankly.

"S-Shade?" He echoed, his heart racing.

I did not respond but he shook his head profusely, "We are not allowed to speak or transform to others beyond our kind. I should not have spoken a word- but you did threaten my life in ways only the prince of darkness could, I believe I will be forgiven-"

"A seal of silence then?" I cut. One that protected the face from the outside world.

Is this how they have survived hidden for centuries even unto me and my shadows?

"Y-yes your majesty."

I nodded walking out the door but not before he screeched after me, just before the door shut.

"Shall I write my eulogy?! If I trust it to my brothers it will end up being poppycock-"

I shivered, as the door closed though I could still hear his ramblings through the wood.

Alchest hissed lowly.

Secrets-he said.

My jaw ticked, walking back through the dark halls. A streak of lightning illuminated my way.

•|•|•Sorry for the late updates! Had plenty to do over the weekend. (see my latest announcement)Please enjoy the chapter! Read 4 chapters ahead on Patreon! Please leave a comment and vote.A sneak peak of Chapter [23.1] A MASTERS PLAY is down below! •|•|•

[23.1] A MASTERS PLAY

● |•|•"And what is the price of a Soul? Tell me pup, what can equate a sacrifice so great if not only the price of another soul?"•|•|•

[Master Greygory]

Before the Evernight, there were signs.

Signs written down and recorded through time.

Before me, I see them. Stronger than before. More than mere changes of the wind in the air these last few months, but the whispery echoes I hear within these walls at night-—they can not be of this realm.

Shadows are not meant to be heard, and yet their voices resound, almost inaudible but so close I could swear I hear the victorious banter. Stronger than ever through the storms of this morning.

"Master Gregory."

I turned slightly as the door opened watching as a King's guard saluted. His eyes remained straight ahead, the scent of his wolf submissive beneath mine.

"Speak."

"The King summons you, my lord."

My gaze shifted away from the soldier, sending him away with a wave, "acknowledged. I will serve."

He saluted once more, closing the door behind him as he left.

I glanced down at the small paper parchment between my fingers, my gaze darting up and out into the darkness of the window open before me.

Only little lights could be seen in the far distance. Random lads with lanterns maneuvering below in the dark day.

The dark day had just stormed and thundered for hours as the echoes of the Night Wolf's haunting howls filled the empty sky, hunting in his forest.

It was only a few hours ago that lightning had roared as if weapons thrown by the gods themselves, striking down trees that now littered the court-yard.

The guards and soldiers moved with lanterns in the now-still darkness, cleaning up the aftermath of the shift.

So much destruction and it was only becoming worse.

The darkness was growing, the storms were stronger, and the Lightning more furious.

The day of the mating could not come sooner.

His loneliness would incage us all in an Ever Night if he chooses to yield to the endless.

And past that.

Past the worries that littered the Night court came notes by bird, letters about the darkness spreading. His rage was now so close to Yulis that it could be seen in all its fury from outside the city gates. Daunting and haunting.

The people feared soon the city would be enraptured in it. Yulis would be the first city to fall.

I glanced down at the parchment in my hand again, finally crumbling it up.

Borrowed time.

That was what this was.

Something was coming, something I couldn't quite understand. And it carried the scent of war, the taste of tears, and the feel of a deathless kind of dread that chilled my very bones.

My wolf could feel it even stronger than I was.

The coming of woe.

Ancient forests dying. Bodies disappearing, Elders with visions of wars far from that of resources. All this was proof.

I moved to the candle alighting the note until it burnt to ash.

Selene save us.

Clenching my jaw, my gaze traveled off the small stains of ash across my desk. I blew out the singular candle, surrounding myself in darkness.

"Selene save us all," I muttered.

With that, I turned to leave.

Minutes later, I came to a stand a few feet away from the familiar large oak door.

My gaze shifted to the king's guard who guarded the door. The boy's frame was strong, his build as only that of a warrior of Beta bloodlines could yield.

"Has he spoken since his turning?"

Elias shook his head. A tightness in his jaw when he spoke uniformly. "Not a word, Master. He returned after the storm, very calm with a bird trapped in a cage." he explained, "he then left and returned a few moments later, seemingly in deep thought."

My eyebrows arched at the absurd statement.

2 things were inherently wrong with that statement.

Firstly, Birds were delicate creatures. Beings as hard and dark as the Night Wolf would not waste a moment to capture a single bird, nor would a bird fly too close to the Nightwolf.

Birds were like all other creatures, humanoid or beastly. They knew that they prey to the Night Wolf, and they knew when to take flight.

Secondly... Calm?

—that was not a word spoken about the Night Wolf after a Storming Dark Day.

The Night Wolf was normally at his worst after a turning.

Brooding and angry were the only words fitted to describe being in his presence after a shift.

"Was the bird harmed? Injured perhaps?"

"Afraid. But I saw nothing wrong physically." Elias replied, his eyebrows creasing slightly.

I nodded at this, wheels turning in my head. "Thank you, Elias."

"Master Gregory," henodded, before looking forward and out, remaining in his military stance.

I turned away from him approaching the door. Letting a loose breath I recaptured composure, knocking firmly against the door.

I didn't need his verbal response to know his invitation. A low hum that echoed to my wolf, was enough for that.

I opened the door, walking into the vastness of the King's study. His third favorite place after the Library and the Hall of Thrones.

The Night Wolf sat on the large throne-like chair behind his desk, an open birdless cage near the window, his frame hidden by shadows all except his face where a small candle burned, illuminating his most dangerous features.

Eyes that shifted to mine as I entered.

Standing before him, I awaited his words.

He leaned back in his chair, not bothering for a greeting. There has never been a greeting offered. Always straight to the point.

"I received word."

Ah, a word from his shadow demons.

"From my investigations. Vaeln is not stupid to worry about his forests."

I listened carefully.

"They are truly dying, rapidly and the scents that surround them are non I can recognize."

He sees things through his shadows. But he also smells them. Perhaps he's seen them now. The room smells of oak and redwood.

Redwood is only found in the Light Wolf territory.

If so, Then he shadowed this morning, after his turning. Yes, he must have shadowed to the Light Wolf Territory. This is where he went after Elias saw him leave.

"Certainly not even Firdon is capable of this much damage."

"Do you think that perhaps the humans are truly behind this?" I asked, careful with my words, tucking my hands behind me. "I would not have thought them that brave, your majesty."

His gaze shifted off me with an approving grunt. "I know scents of men. They're plain and horrid. No- those scents are... Different." he seemed lost for a moment.

My eyebrows arched at this. He seemed lost in thought.

One thing the Night Wolf isn't is unfocused.

"Your majesty-"

"What do you know about the faerie folk, Gregory?" he suddenly asked.

The abrupt change from issues of a potential war with a dangerous unknown enemy to that of an extinct race only remembered by dying myths surprised me.

"F-Faeries, your majesty?" I repeated, unsure if I heard correctly.

His gaze snapped to mine. "The small sprites and Woodfolk. Do you not know the stories of the Fae, Gregory?"

I quicklynodded, collecting myself and clearing my throat. "Indeed your majesty, I know of the tales of the small folk. Most are only stories, stories of magical folk that kept the ancient forests alive, pure and green."

When he didn't reply, his eyes steady on me, as if waiting for more, I continued I felt rather out of place, unsure of when I became a story teacher instead of the Royal Advisor.

"The books say that they died out after the old war. When the Elves diminished."

"The books.." The Night Wolf trailed off, "What if the Faerie Folk still live?"

I raised an eyebrow at this, ready to chuckle but the dryness in the air stopped me from making that brutal mistake.

"Had they survived, they would be no threat. They were known for peace. Additionally, I think they would be too small to kill a dozen packs of rogues and somehow dispose of their bodies. Since Faeries are the spirits of the forest, they were meant to heal and not poison them."

"Gregory, I am well aware Faeries are not the enemy." He grunted, looking away, "I am familiar with their scents now."

I froze at that statement, watching as the NightWolf stood up, pacing in the darkness. Confusion spread through me.

"Now?" I echoed.

Had he seen a faerie? That could not be possible. T-they were extinct.

Gone for more than five hundred years- Surely, he could not have seen one?

My mouth remained agape at the revelation, unable to fathom what was being spoken but the Night Wolf seemed to be in a world of his own.

"What would enslave a faerie to a wolf or man?" he asked.

My eyebrows arched at the statement. Swallowing blankly as I thought through. I was much too taken by the revelation but through the chaos I arrived at the answer.

"A faerie....slave to a mere being?" I echoed, "Perhaps anything that would cause a great debt For even wolf to wolf, or man to wolf, enslavement by choice should be as a price of something nearly un-repayable. A life-saving deed perhaps," I hypothesized.

Silence loomed between us, the Night Wolf slowly turning and glancing at me for a moment. I thought he would expand more on this question. But he went cold, his gaze switching back to the singular candle.

"Send word to Vaeln. Let him know I have done my investigations. We shall speak when he arrives at the council of courts."

I am at a loss for words. Many things I wish to ask. But I know a voice of finality when I hear it.

A wise man knows there is a time for everything. A time to listen and a time to speak.

The Night Wolf has discovered something. Something I need to discover also. Alone.

I bowed low, "I will take my leave as your highness pleases."

With that, I turned and walked out the door.

Nodding to Elias, I loved through the dark hallways, thoughts swirled inside my head.

Something had occupied the mind of the Night wolf. Nothing takes his mind away from matters as important as the looming danger grazing Valcane.

He spoke of scents that killed the ancient forests. Forests that carve out every being. Forests are where we hunt and survive. Where are wolves roam free and howl at the moon?

For what would our wolves be without the trees around us and the animals that serve us?

And yet, he seemed to care less about a matter so important. For if it is true that the Faeries still live, and he knows their scents are not the reason for the deaths of rogues and the ancient forests then why does he ask questions of these beings?

How a faerie can slave to a wolf?

Ideas and hypotheses slid in and out of my mind. Faeries were once known to be kind quiet creatures. How did he catch one? My mind slipped to the cage. They were known to take shapes- could it?

My eyes slightly widened at a particular thought stopping in my footsteps.

Surely his cruelness was not as evil as to slave a faerie?

For what reason would he wish to do this? For if the forests are truly dying, then there is no need for torture.

A faerie will give his life to save a singular tree. They are spirits of the forest, aren't they?

No- there was something else. Logic told me this was something else. The purpose was telling me to look deeper.

Something else also occupied his mind.

Could it be the Keffer?

I nodded to a couple of matching guards, moving across hallways whilst I delved into narrower stairs to my study.

Only candles illuminated my way in the coldness of the dark day.

The keffer.

He did not mention her, not once.

However, was it not she who had been on his mind just yesterday? Could it be a mere coincidence that it is only after her arrival that he is suddenly calm after a shift?

I pushed the doors to my study open, freezing in the doorway of it.

There was a person here. Someone hiding in the shadows.

A scent caught my wolf, painfully familiar but different.

I grunted at the emptiness before me, closing the door quietly behind me. I knew this person. I knew the pain and anger in he was holding in his presence. Nearly 3 days in the endless would drive anyone insane. Unless the Night Wolf.

"You never t-told me the price I would have to pay to pledge." A shattered voice spoke.

I let out a breath, shaking my head. I could not tell him. It was not the way. Each man must see for himself.

"I told you it would cost you everything to learn the truth. That was warning enough." I replied.

Turnjng around calmly, my gaze fell upon the hunchedshadow that hid near the window.

A dry sigh was heard accompanied by a low whimper, "Look at me Uncle!" it broke and broke and broke until there was nothing, "I -I am empty. I am nothing. My soul has been ripped from me. Mercilessly."

I blinked in the darkness, understanding the pain hidden in the shadow.

Walking calmly toward the figure, I laid a hand on his shoulder, the clank of his metal uniform ringing as he slouched forward.

"You still have the soul you were born with. It was only the other was what was taken from you."

I moved from him, lighting a candle and placing it on the desk until the room was lightly illuminated.

I turned back to my nephew, his pale blue eyes watching me with a gone look I had once mirrored once a time before.

"Y-You've taken her from me, uncle" he spoke, his voice a broken wimper. "She can not be felt. I can not Feel her."

"The connection." I stated, my case falling, "The feeling that your other soul is out there is gone?"

He shook in the light of candle, body a slight quiver.

"You've pledged your soul to the purpose. The purpose of the Mage Wolf. You have no loyalty but to her. To your other soul whoever or where ever she may be can not exist anymore. Your loyalty is now pledged to the Purpose."

He looked at me in horror. A horror I understood. A horror I knew would one day turn to clarity as it had for me.

"You stand there and lie?!" he yelled, his voice quivering in unshed tears, "you pledged and still have your soul! Why was mine taken?" he growled.

I watched him in amusement. I understood his vision. He saw what I wanted to be seen. What I had to create around me so I could protect the order.

"You see me smile." I began carefully, "You see me hold my other half, kiss her hand, and think I have a bond with another soul? None of us have bonds, Liston. None of us are whole until we meet our Purpose. Till we fulfill it."

He looked at me in confusion, "Aunt Drisha-"

"A pledge," I spoke.

I put a finger to my lips drawing him closer to the candle, "Only speak near the light. Shadows linger in the darkness." I warned lowly.

He looked at me, a broken face only a few inches away from me. Grief in his eyes, and fear.

"I-It was horrible-" he stuttered, "the endless..." he trailed off.

I nodded, knowing even after many years I had nightmares of that place- "But here you stand."

His eyes searched mine, shifting in glitching waves.

I knew what he was searching for. I searched for the same thing once upon a time in different eyes.

Truth.

Truth is what he found, for truth was all there was.

He let out a breath. One I knew held shock but yet some kind of relief, a slow small step to acceptance.

"Aunt Drisha, Y-You-"

"Not truly bonded." I whispered, "bonded to each other out of service to the Purpose. We would not want to raise suspicion if we neared 35 and remained unclaimed." I chuckled.

He studied my face, his own expression stoic.

"You do not have to worry about that quite yet. You are still young, and other pledges will need to be hidden in bonded service." I explained.

My hands rested on his shoulders, "I will not lie and say you have not sacrificed much. In honesty, you have sacrificed all for the truth. And with the truth, you are free. You know the secrets, you know what must be done."

He searched my eyes but after a moment nodded slowly.

I patted his cheek, drawing him in for a hug,.

He could not hold on. His body was much too shaken.

"It is a slow process to acceptance." I breathed slowly, "But it will be acceptance, once you understand the importance of the purpose."

I pulled away from him and he stepped back, still in a short daze.

I glanced at him. "Have you seen her yet?"

His gaze slowly trailed back to me, nodding, "Twice. Last night and this morning."

"What do you think of her?"

He paused, blinking softly, "B-Before I could see nothing special-"

"And now?" I asked eagerly.

I knew It was different for him. He was a new pledge. Blessed with a gift by Selene to see clearer than the average as all who pledge are.

My gift is old, his is stronger and newer.

He seemed to go off in a lofty daze.

"Her gaze is wise.." he trailed off, "she is peaceful, but full of mischief. Scared but stubborn. She has secrets she whispers in hushed tones to her friend. Secrets she fears others may hear. She is vigilant and keen on detail. I-I think She sees me, just as I see her." he breathed out

I nodded at this, taking all his words carefully.

"You understand your role?" I asked.

He nodded, "The Elder was clear."

Humming to this, I moved back to my seat.

"Then it is best you begin. The Elder has lived long, but time will always be precious."

With a nod, his gaze slowly fell from me, a tick in his jaw before claiming his leave.

I watched him go, the door closing behind him.

I stared at the oak for a moment, a chill passing through my bones.

A dear price he paid. A dear price I paid.

A price so precious for a play so righteous.

•|•|•I hope you enjoyed the chapter! Please leave a comment below and vote! Do you have any questions you would like an in-depth response to/ just to banter about the book? Join my discord channel where I associate actively. All links are in my bio! Here's a sneak peek of the chapter [24.1] A KINGS GUARD.Read ahead on patreon!

•|•|•

Word count- 3224

[24.1] THE KINGS GUARD

The fates have designed your way, and Selene brought you forth from the earth and gave you life. As an Alpha you will live to rule, as a slave, you will live to serve, for always till fate and time reunite you in the fields from which Selene first brought you forth.

[Shade Shadows]

Sweat littered my forehead in shiny sheets as I stepped off the ladder to examine my work. I had cleared one full row of shelves of books from top to bottom. The row spanned nearly half of the vast room, and my arms ached from the mere load.

I felt like I had worked 24 hours straight. But of course, time seemed to be held in suspense as there was no sun in the sky to tell me how long I had worked.

It felt like I was stuck in a timeless loop that was dipped in a pitch-black world.

No stars to litter the sky, and no bright moon either. If it weren't for the lanterns lit up by the soldier in the court, it would be impossible to even see the ground from this height.

Not that there was something to see. Trees had fallen from the storm and the soldiers and guards were hurriedly trying to clear the grounds.

Strangely, however, no matter how much I despised dark days I couldn't help but admit there was a certain calmness in them.

A safety perhaps.

Knowing that here in the darkness is where I thrived. That I blended into the shadows and for a moment I may not even exist.

That these feelings deep within me may just be dreams of realities I whip in this vast imagination of mine. That one day I would wake up from this nightmare and open my eyes to a beautiful garden filled with people who saw me as their equals.

Like all this, everything to this point in my life was nothing but a bad dream.

My back slid down the shelves till I sat on the ground, my dusting cloth sprawled before me, head in my hands as I yawned.

I was tired and my back ached from lifting books all day. Coupled with the darkness and seclusion, it felt like I would lose my mind.

I tried reading but even that seemed to wear me down after a few pages.

I closed my eyes longing for something more in this vast library. So vast I felt so alone.

I was beginning to doubt any other masters existed within these walls, at least not at this particular moment.

I hadn't seen a single one after my unusual master. The so-called King favorite. I longed to see someone, reassure me I wasn't alone in the vast darkness...Where time was void.

Even Diane had flown away this morning and hadn't returned in a few hours.

This had been a disappointment. I thought it was a peculiar bird but perhaps it had gone now.

My hands touched the floor stopping on something wet. I brought my fingers up to the light, realizing it was some reddish-brown mud. My eyebrows arched, noticing some scarce bits here and there, by the shelf, and even a handprint against it.

My eyebrows arched at this. How could wet mud have gotten into the library? Was it I that tracked it in?

A steady thud drew me from thoughts.

Cleaning my fingers off the cloth, I walked towards the large doors, faster than I normally would because I was dying to see someone else, even if it meant I would have to bow a thousand times and be called a Keffer and all and any manner of names that would fit.

I opened the door, immediately lowering my head at the sight of the armor, knowing this was one of the guards.Silence loomed as I awaited orders.

"Shade-"

The voice came out more like a question, his tone was deep and silvery. My eyebrows arched at the direct name call, my gaze slowly lifting and emerging into familiar blue eyes.

It was the King's guard. The guard I saw last night and the same guard I saw just this morning. The one who was missing all this time and was back, the one by the pump.

"Is it not?"

I nodded, slowly, unsure of what to say. Knowing guards were normally tough on slaves I decided not to test anything, lowering my head again, "It is, Sir."

Silence loomed between us and I stared at my toes, unsure of why we were just standing there. Was I in trouble? Had he overheard Vale and me discussing our escape-

"A pretty name." he finally grunted, causing my eyebrows to arch at the absurd remark, my gaze snapping up to meet his but he had already turned, walking off.

I took this as my cue to follow, closing the door behind me, I treaded in silence behind the guard.

There was something strange about him. Why would he say a kind word to me? I would not dare call it a compliment.

That would be too good to be true.

I already know this guard. He watched the other slaves bully me. I already know him by the look in his eyes when he looked away. It is the look that I see every day.

I am of no importance- lesser than none.

Why then did he seem kind today? Why was there a different look in his eyes? Why did I notice his eyes only yesterday?

"Liston," he spoke glancing back at me for a moment as his armor clanked with every heavy step

I glanced at his back as we walked down the halls. Unsure of what he was saying.

"That is my name if you wish to know." he hummed.

I was only further confused. Why would he give me his name?

I knew not what to say so I merely hummed. Unsure of this conversation. Unsure if I was comfortable talking to a guard this way. I uttered a singular word.

"Okay."

I noticed his pace gradually slowed, allowing me to easily catch up. I was a bit feeble this day: I had woken up late and not had my breakfast, neither was lunch served for slaves unless supper. 2 meals a day.

"I wish to apologize."

I froze at these words. Words such as those are never supposed to leave the mouths of selfish guards.

I gazed at him through hooded eyebrows pacing only slightly behind him, lest it looked like I had thought myself an equal to him.

"I should have stopped the other slaves from letting you pump water into all their buckets."

I blinked at this, my throat running dry.

Part of me thought I was still in the library, dreaming and I would wake up and keep cleaning.

For in what world would a guard apologize to a slave- A keffer no less?

"I do not deserve your apologies, Sir. It is not your job."

He grunted at this, "No.." he paused, "It's mere decency to be kind. And I am a decent man am I not?" his gaze shifted to mine and I caught it unaware-

Certain humor danced in them as he spoke. Pleasant humor not one of spite, but I could not register this in real-time.

Instead, I stumbled over my words, "Of course, sir. Quite noble."

He nodded at this turning away, the soft smile that had grazed his lips pursing into a thinner line- silence filled between us for only another second before he spoke once more.

"My vision of the world was just- blurry. I see better now-" he states, glancing at me, "I see my errors."

I held his gaze before they shifted back down, my pace slowing further behind him when I heard the clanking of another round of guards.

They passed us by, and I kept my head low.

I glanced at the King's Guard, not truly convinced as we moved down the stairs to where more guards passed.

We did not say another word and I was delivered into the hells of Lucifer- ous kitchen. A hot furnace waiting for my touch.

Barnabas was keen to throw me a shovel.

I caught it this time.

I could not stop thinking of the weird encounter with Liston. The King's guard. I wished to think that the world could be so kind once in a while- that it would throw me a bone.

But I had been a Keffer all my life. All good things passed that of AMA and Vale we're evil things disguised in a beautiful lie.

Shall I not tell the tale of Gabriel the Alpha's son? Was it not him I found wounded in a field when we were nothing but pups?

Trapped in a bush of odsgrave thorns, "the wolf's prison".

Was it not I that freed him? What did that do for me?

He was kind for a moment, a moment when no one was looking, and then for a lifetime in the eyes of everyone, I became the Keffer that I am today.

Shall I make the same mistake and believe a King's guard, out of the blue would decide to be kind to me?

I shook my head as I lay on the weed mat, darkness lingering outside.

I was aware of the stories whispered amongst the slaves- of how they do things to get extra bread, wine, and treats from the guards.

Is that what this is?

Am I a trophy bargained about between guard's lips? Perhaps a trophy is of high esteem.

An ugly bet of some sort.

I shook my head, pulling myself closer. I shall trust no one but Vale.

Friendship with a master, Leaning on Barnabas, and accepting Liston would all be foolish. I nodded in the darkness.

And I was desperate...

Not foolish.

When the sun kissed my cheek in the morning, a smile voluntarily crossed my face.

There was nothing to stop the good feeling that whispered through my body. This time, I pumped for the slaves and rested in my own joyous world.

The Kings Guard, the one named Liston, was not at his post this morning.

Hence it was not his shift I figured.

I only thought of it for a moment before brushing the thoughts of him away. He could have been drunk last night that he thought to make conversation with a Keffer.

It was a mistake he was surely embarrassed about this morning had it been as a result of a horrid bet amongst guards.

Stooping so low.

My throat run dry, but I kept my spirits alive, bidding Vale to join the others and not stay behind this time.

It was getting far too suspicious.

With defiance still in her eyes, she moved toward the bathhouse and I kept pumping, my gaze trailing to the library tower, knowing I would soon be trapped within its walls.

Would I be visited this time by the master? He had not come yesterday since his abrupt leave.

I scoffed at the thought. Who leaves without saying goodbye? Only a man who has had no company about him. The Master was such a man.

And why did I wish for it? For a farewell. What did he owe me? Of a friendship, I had initiated all on my own?

I wiped my brow off the sweat, staring at the library's high tower for a moment.

He owed me nothing, I reassured myself. Absolutely nothing.

My gaze darted back to reality when a blurry flutter spun by me, perching on the pump, beady eyes blinking as I looked at my diamond-shaped raven in surprise.

"Diane." I breathed. A small smile erupted on my face, my high spirits returning, "Hello."

She cawed back and I grinned.

This was a good sign. I was not going to be alone this morning.

Getting my bucket, I moved toward the bathhouse.

Cleaning the Library as vast as this sometimes took my breath away, but perhaps not as much as looking down at the maze and the gardens from this height.

Diane was perched beside me as I sketched the maze. My third time trying. It was certainly harder than it looked. I could not get the lines correctly and my failure of this could leave Vale and I trapped in a haunted maze of shadows.

I crumpled the paper, with a sigh, watching it drop to the floor where three others lay couples near it.

Shutting my eyes, I opted to take a short break and allow the slight rays of the sun to kiss my face.

From this height, it seemed to be shining for me and only me. I lifted a hand toward it so it felt as if I could touch the sunlight, a small smile on my face as the rays twisted passed.

After a few moments, I opened my eyes to Diane's soft caws. Glancing at the bird, I smiled at it, my fingers shifting through its silky black feathers.

I sighed, looking back up at the view. Up here it felt calmer, but if I wasn't going to draw a proper map I might as well get productive.

Stepping down the ladder, I continued dusting

Grabbing a handful of books I trod between rows toward my usual table, thrifting through the books as I walked humming to myself while checking the titles.

I looked upwards as I reached the table, stopping abruptly in my tracks when I spotted the figure of the master seated by it, causally flipping through a set of books I had earlier disposed of.

Because of this abrupt movement, and the surprise of it all, the top book in my arms toppled to the floor, with a large splat drawing his attention to me ...

Gaze beautifully trailing slowly down to the book.

"I see I've startled you, yet again," he spoke blankly.

•|•|•Thanks for reading! If you're enjoying the story please vote and leave a comment . Join my discord group! Read 3 chapters ahead on Patreon!•|•|•

[25.1] BOUNDERIES

● |•|•

"Why do you think they hide in the dark pup? Is It not a safety they seek, lest their own failure be revealed in the sun? Then they call the darkness evil, because because in it lies pieces of themselves they thought to conceal."

•|•|•

[KAYOS]

And Indeed I Had.

My eyes shifted from the fallen book, capturing hers. Her heart hammered quickly within her as our gazes locked, but no sooner had I spoken, she broke contact and bent to pick it up.

"I wasn't- I wasn't expecting you. Not this soon," she replied breathily with a seemingly nervous smile. She glanced at me momentarily, whilst her fingers stretched toward the book.

I stared at her efforts for a moment, registering her weakness. It was something that could not be ignored.

Every time I saw her, it was laid bare before me. A taunting reminder that although the sight of the Keffer calmed my spirits, though her scent was dabolically sweet, though my wolf yearned for her touch, and though the mere thought of her had pulled me from drifting into the valleys of the endless, she was merely the rope thrown to me.

To survive I would have to find the one that held the rope down for me.

And the Keffer...

Two more books toppled over as she bent down to pick the first with a hard splat. The stack of books in her arms was far too heavy it seemed. Her gaze darted amongst the books, whilst her arms still full, adjusted and tried to recapture the fallen.

Was certainly not her.

I stood to my feet, the scrape of the chair loud in the quietness of my sanctuary and I could hear her breath hitch at my movement.

At least she was aware.

Standing before her, her heart beat faster, her gaze lifting to my feet and then drawing upwards to my eyes.

The stare was short. Seconds uncountable and yet, I marveled.

Perhaps it was because she, the wolfless girl, had stared at me with an emotion that had never been looked my way before. So rare that even I could not put a name to it.

A certain intrigue?- one she was able to mask as her gaze darted back to the floor.

I bent down, picking up the books, only a few inches away from her.

Her scent had always been a welcoming lure no matter how far I was from her, whether I was standing a row away hidden in the shadows, a few feet away as we spoke, or even now, where a mere space separated us.

But at our Proximity, a stifling want, a yearning to be wrapped in her scent grew unbearable the closer I got.

Especially when her eyes were watching me attentively, as my fingers curled around the hard books, placing them on top of her pile. Her gaze shifted as mine did, and it locked once more.

I was so sure she would look away. For though she had gotten braver with her eye contact, she could only hold it for a few seconds.

But this time, she lingered, her head tilting to the side, just

Staring-

My heart rammed within me whenever so slightly, her lips curled upwards. Her head tilted to the side as if studying me.

My gaze immediately shifted away first. I did not want her to study. Would she not see the darkness hidden beneath me? Would she run when she knew I was the very wolf she feared so faithfully?

I stood up to my feet, and the air between us shifted, almost as if she too had been taken from a trance, a sense of embarrassment filling the space around us.

She hurriedly thanked me and scrambled to to her feet. I watched her for a moment.

I had come today only for answers. Yes... Answers only and nothing else. It was the yearning for these answers that had saved me from slipping away last night. Her mysteries that had kept me in this reality.

"You are right-" I began, her fingers realigning the books seemingly trying to make busy. She barely looked at me, opting to keep busy instead.

"You do scare easily as a Keffer, I fear there's nothing I can do about it. It's the consequence of being wolfless."

Her fingers stiffened, eyes raising only slightly and then she pursed her lips, walking passed me and leaving the air before me begging for her scent.

My eyebrows arched at the blank response, and I could sense a shift in the air, from a mild embarrassment to something of anger or irritation.

My gaze flocked to the sound of a bird flying past, perching on the table. I watched the raven, and it stared back at me, almost as if it were shooting daggers at me.

An angry aura commuting from the little faerie.

Ignoring it, my gaze drifted back to the Keffer, watching her offload the books onto the table. It was quite likely that she had not heard me. Wolves had an impeccable hearing, and she- well. She had no wolf.

"Did you not hear me?"

"Oh, I assure you I heard every. Single. Word." she muttered back, a splat of a book, hard on the surface of the wood after every pause.

My eyebrows gathered at this, both intrigued and amused, surprised even.

"Anger," I stated in realization, studying her back for a moment.

She froze at this for a slight moment but didn't turn around, continuing her stacking and dusting.

My gaze drifted to Diane, slightly uncomfortable with the way the bird seemed to be staring me down.

A fiery little thing wasn't it?

My gaze darted to the shadows where I spotted Alchest watching attentively.

"You're angry with me." I rephrased looking back at her.

My eyebrows drew in confusion. I was best familiar with Fear, but I was aware that other emotions existed.

I had seen love before. I had seen happiness, if but from a distance away, or amongst my mated cousins, or feeling the essence of joy from the aura of a castle worker, working the courtyard whilst I watched perched from the highest tower.

No emotion but fear was ever directed directly towards me. Not since I had met the keffer. Perhaps my mother had shown me a few, I can't recall many, but anger towards me was not one of them.

Not from a subject, perhaps from my cousins, but their emotions were barely accountable.

My subject's knees knocked in fear at my judgments. If ever I had felt their anger it would be either masked as unhappiness after a judgment that did not fall to their liking or after a mix of relief and only after walls and doors separated them from me, though privy to their knowledge, I could sense their auras even as they traveled out of Night Court down the road to Yulis.

"Is there a reason that you're ang-"

"I know I'm a Keffer, master," her tone came out sharp, and spiteful cutting me off entirely.

It was bold, and took me off guard, raising an eyebrow at the action as she continued to speak.

If this had been anybody else I do not believe they would have lived to speak again, not a second after-

but for her- I only yearned to listen.

My wolf felt no anger at her disrespect. Surprise? Yes, but instead much like me, he was still, watching and studying her, desperate to understand the reason for her anger.

"True-" I acknowledged.

This only seemed to anger her more as her aura darkened.

"I do not need to be always reminded of what I am, master, I assure you, every waking day I am reminded quite thoroughly, amongst the slaves, amongst the guards, amongst the maids and the workmen, and every single soul I have had the most pleasure of meeting in my lifetime up till this moment and now-" she let out a loose breath.

Her tone got quiet, her aura defeated.

"I know that I am weak but Friends Don't.." she gaspeed reaching for the words, "they don't remind each other of their weakness. Neither do they mock it."

"I do not mock you." I countered defensively. Speaking a fact was not mocking.

"Which is why you choose to keep calling me Keffer, even after knowing my true name?"

She turned to me, her arms empty, now only with her dusting cloth. Her gaze reached mine for a second, before falling below my chin.

"Master." she finished with a short nod, walking passed me.

I stood there for a moment, gaze only shifting to the raven's beady stare which snapped a caw at me and then flew after its master.

I paused, slightly overwhelmed by her words.

Perhaps I should not tolerate that attitude. I have been immensely considerate.

But she was right.

I was not her King, no- I was something entirely foreign. A friend. And to her, friends do not speak of weaknesses nor do they mock them. And friends call each other by name.

Shade. It was her name.

I had always known it. I do not know why I preferred not to say it out loud. Perhaps because I didn't want it to become common against my lips. Or familiar.

I should not grow a bond unbreakable with her if she is but a trial. Naming her, speaking her name may drown me in her ocean. I was unsure if I would want to be saved after.

Names had power. I knew better than anyone.

But it had to be done if I was to win her trust. I had to play the game Selene's wayand the selfish wench would never make it so easy.

I trailed after her slowly, and though she was already out of sight, finding her scent was easiest thing in the world. I found her taking down more books in a row, her face was expressionless and there was a tightness in her jaw.

I stared at her for a moment, ignoring the usual lure of her scent, or the urge of my wolf to talk to her.

I stared longingly and I fear it was long enough to keep her image nailed within me. Not that I wished for it.

"I do not think you are weak," I began.

She did not reply, and I felt uncomfortable.

Is this how Mother felt when I ignored her? My lips felt dry.

I was not gentle, that I was aware. I knew nothing about comfort, which is why I felt lost as I tried to justify myself.

Finding words was never this hard for me. Perhaps it was because the words I always spoke were ones of stale blunt commands.

Here- it required comfort.

Whatever that was, I had no knowledge of it.

I cleared my throat, my gaze shifting to the Raven who watched me attentively.

"I confess I do think you have a weakness, as many do, but- I believe you are certainly brave," I confessed.

It was something I had pondered on for a while. In truth? For a time I was not entirely sure if it was bravery or simply an unforeseen advantage of being wolfless- to be able to look into my eyes without a trace of fear for the being that I am.

But as I pondered, I remembered even men fail to reach my gaze. And when they do they do not last 2 seconds. And even Diane, a faerie, was unable to meet my eyes.

I also realized a life of a keffer is not a life that comes easy if they are thought to be beneath even that of a slave.

There are many ways to establish fear, with or without a wolf.

For a girl taught every day of her insignificance, she was able to look a master in the eye and demand equality in the name of friendship, and now, she dared lose her temper to teach me her dstain for her title. For the words I named her with.

"If you do think of yourself weak, Shade, I am embarrassed about the darkness you wear."

"And what do you have against my darkness?" she gritted, her eyes shifting to me, then to the floor, her tone quiet, "it would be best to state it now."

I could see the shake in her fingers. I was unsure if it was because she was nervous or angry.

I could see her hands tighten against the spine of the book in her hands.

"Against?" I echoed, confused at the accusation, "is there anything finer?"

The stormy look in her eyes dissolved into a look mirroring my own, surprise and confusion. I could barely pay attention to her face as my gaze skimmed every piece of exposed skin.

I could not help it. I was a being of darkness and to me, She was perfect.

Physically, everything about her was perfection. Physically, I know it would be stupid of me to ever touch her farther than a handshake for than had been a risk to. I could never trust my mind to keep to the task.

I could bask in her scent and yearn for it, a distance away, 2 feet away, and even an inch away- but should I ever make the mistake of touching her--

My fingers tingled. That handshake would be the last I would ever do. For if they were ever allowed to wander- I would allow myself to be blinded. And utterly waste in that moment.

I took myself out of the trance, eyes darting back to hers, taken aback by her intense thoughtful stare. I had been caught lusting. I was embarrassed as I cleared my throat looking away.

"Darkness is strong and beautiful. Many fear it because they do not understand it. And it was meant to be that way. Some things are only meant for those that understand it. I- know it well. And if you wear it so.." I fumbled for the word, unable to say it,

beautifully-

"perfectly, I would have thought you would have its strength too." I studied the books for a moment, silence looming between us.

When nothing else was spoken, I was curious and so I dared look in her direction. She was still staring at me, and for a moment I wondered if I had misspoke-or perhaps I had said something to upset her further-

"Do you have a mate, my lord?"

"What?" the question took me off guard, and my heart started its rampant beat, my Lord.

Her gaze faded slightly as if trying to find the answer by herself in mine.

She walked slowly toward me, but all I could feel was blood rushing to my brain.

"You are very.. Direct." she began, taking a calming breath out, "a-and I think it's because you seem to have lived a life of isolation or b-because as a master and the Night Wolfs favorite, the others may fear you too?" she asked, rather than stated, her tone nervous for a moment.

Her gaze shifted away from me, "I just think despite being brass, you have other peculiar sides of beauty only one close to you sees. She is certainly privileged." she smiled softly, before walking passed and disappearing into the darkness.

I blinked at this. A certain feeling growing within me.

"I have a side of beauty?" I repeated softly into the empty space around me.

"I believe she said peculiar- a peculiar side of beauty your majesty," a voice squelched. My gaze flashed to the shifted faerie seated on the bookshelf. A cheeky smile on his face, legs swinging off the ledge.

My eyes narrowed on him.

"C-Context is extremely important," he gulped, legs frozen in mid air, though his voice remained a light mock.

"Shift back into your little birdy form before you get eaten, Diane." I growled.

He gaped, "you wouldn't!"

I flashed my fangs and that was enough to make him shift turning into a raven, flying after it's master.

I watched the bird go, with a slight eye roll, staring into the darkness once more.

"Beautiful." I murmured. Before following after the keffer.

•|•|•Read 3 chapters ahead on Patreon!Hope you enjoyed the chapter! More to come .•|•|•

[26.1] ALEXANDER THE PRIME

"We live in a world of reflection where balance thrives. To the left, it is right. To love there is hate, and to darkness there is always light."

•|•|•

[SHADE SHADOWS]

"And how was your day, master?" I asked as I stacked the books on the table.

A smile was stained on my face involuntarily. My spirits had dampened after his crass comment but re-lit after the redemption of the one that followed.

Perhaps I was foolish to be happy simply because of a compliment. The thought paused me.

No- I shouldn't be too high upon horses to believe a master would actually offer such a thing to the likes of a Keffer. I admit it sent something warm deep down my insides to hear of my difference being spoken in a different light.

One that seemed positive.

I hoped, though hope was dangerous, that it was how he truly saw me. It was refreshing to hear it be spoken so highly, not as a peculiarity or a deformity, not as a curse but a thing of-Perfection.

My smile returned, and I glanced at the master that had shown up, standing a few feet behind me.

He had an expression on his face I couldn't quite tell, but when our eyes locked, like before when I was caged in them as he helped me pick the books, I marveled at the shades of them.

I still did not know the exact color of them.

And every time our eyes met, the more often, it seemed the previous fear that I had, that any word I would say could be held against me had dissolved.

Instead, I had grown a curiosity, one that was fueled by each side the master showed me.

I knew he was a blunt man, who had no reason to care for the feelings of others, and yet he accepted to be my friend. Even now, when I couldn't control the anger that had crossed me when he reminded me of my title, I had recoiled, believing I would certainly be punished for speaking to him like that-

However, he remained silent. And then....

He listened.

He called me by name this time, and despite his brass nature, he fished for the right words to say-

Truly, it could have been uttered a lot better, but I understood the effort the moment he spoke it.

"I know the day has just begun, but you did not visit yesterday," I informed, glancing at him, as I fixed the book.

"Was it alright? It was a dark day filled with storms and lightning, I don't imagine there were many places to go."

When I looked back at him, his previous expression had-been displaced, his gaze shifting off me as he walked around the table, taking a seat.

"No, there was not much." He replied rather quietly.

I registered this, my eyebrows arching. I did not know why I was interested to know what caused that reaction in him.

"Are you alright?" I asked, my head tilting to the side.

His gaze snapped to me, "What sort of question is that? Am I hurt some-where?" He grunted, touching his face for a moment, "Bleeding? It should be highly unlikely. My wolf takes great care of these things-"

I couldn't help but chuckle, causing his eyebrows to arch momentarily, watching me in what seemed like confusion and wonder.

I assumed he did not like being laughed at so I stopped, pursing my lips though I couldn't contain the amusement in my eyes.

"No. Of course not." I grinned.

My gaze shifted to face, marveling for a moment, the red littering his black hair in long streaks, being about those eyes I couldn't quite place on the color spectrum.

Quietness roamed between us, "You just seem, out of place.." I finished.

He blinked for a moment, then searched my eyes, a realization crossing over him.

"You were asking how I was feeling." He stated.

I nodded, now a bit confused as I watched his expression, "Have you never been asked before?" I joked.

When his eyes darkened slightly and I watched a whisper of loneliness fill them, I felt them fill mine. A touch of a feeling that seemed to echo against my skin. He looked away, for a moment, swallowing lightly.

"I don't recall a moment."

The air was heavy between us, as I watched him. I couldn't understand why he seemed so isolated. Was this the price that came with being favored by a man like the Night Wolf? Was he feared to that extent that even men he held in reverence were feared too?

But why did it seem like the master before me's isolation run deep? Like it was created from the moment he was born.

Never had a friend before. Not even his youth.

I pursed my lips looking away, trying to lighten the mood. This was difficult for him I tried to sympathize.

"Well, you will soon get tired of it. I make it a point to make sure all my friends are well." I grinned, offering him a smile, to which he looked on in curiosity.

It was then I realized I had never seen him smile. Not even once. How peculiar.

An urge formed within me. A solemn promise.

Perhaps our friendship was not built on a sturdy foundation. There were certain parts I didn't trust myself.

But I know the truth when I see it. It was written behind the heaviness in his eyes, his loneliness was apparent.

So, for however long it lasts, this friendship we formed, I will, I will get him his lips to rise in warmth, even if it is ever so slightly. At least it would leave a footprint in one empty hallway of his life.

It must count for something.

"Well, will you sit and watch me work, or, perhaps," I pushed a stack of books his way, a small grin on my face.

In truth I was unsure how he would react to this. He could simply refuse and I would not hold it against him. He was a master, and this was my Job.

A slave's job.

His gaze dropped to the books, his fingers gleaming in silver wealthy rings, grasping the edges, "I will walk with you."

The statement was blunt, but it made my heart shiver as I watched him get up, pulling the stack of books closer toward him.

With me.

Not before me as a master leads his slave, but beside me, like a friend.

My gaze followed him upwards and I soon remembered that he was certainly a master.

I needed no wolf to acknowledge this. He had an authoritative stance, and towered high above me and half of the men I had ever seen in my life. His shoulders were wide, and his eyes blank at first glance, but I have seen them more than once and I know they hold more-

SoMuchMore.

I nod at this gesture, getting a few books up, and he trailed around the table, walking beside me as we slipped through the rows.

"Was he angry then?" I asked.

He glanced at me, seemingly confused and I continued to explain.

"The Night Wolf, yesterday? Madam says we should fear the dark days, but they are much more harmless than on the dark days it storms and thunders," I explained.

I noticed he was quiet, but I kept on.

"Did he call you to his presence? Is it not scary in those moments before him?"

"He was not in the castle for most of the dark day." He calmly stated.

"The howls.." I paused for a moment, before glancing at him, trying to ignore the fact I felt quite small beside him, "he was in the forest-" I muttered, realization crossing my features.

I had heard them in the distance as I stared out the window to the dark forest past the maze

"When he shifts it storms," I muttered mostly to myself.

That was it.

If Vale and I were to use the maze and then the forest to avoid the night wolf, we would have to pick a day when it did not storm.

"Yes." He replied. Once again, his answers were stale and stiff.

"Always?" I asked again. I had to be sure.

"Not always," he huffed, "when he was younger, he could shift without the dark day or the storms. But these things are connected to him. To his emotions."

I nodded at this, listening carefully. "The angrier he grew, the more out of control it got." I realized.

I could feel his gaze on me, as we turned into the row I had dusted, I paused, turning to him, "it is Because he can't find his mate?"

He let out a loose breath, eyes swimming in emotion. He nodded, and I pursed my lips, stacking the books.

"Do you think he is close? To be coming like his great grandfather?"

The master remained silent, causing me to turn. His hold on the books seemed to have tightened, his gaze trailing to me.

"I think they are days when he doesn't want to look at the sun or the moon."

I watched as he placed the books on the shelves I would have needed to drag the ladder to place.

"I am quite aware of all the songs they sing about the night wolf," I hummed, as he stacked, "and I am not foolish enough to think they are not true- I just believe if the moon could give him what he wishes, perhaps he would not be so cruel- why does the goddess hate him so much?"

He grunted at the question, and for a moment I truly thought he seemed irritated.

"I have no explanation for her destain of my kind, keffers.....perhaps his has one." I pushed.

Seconds passed before he spoke.

"The first Wolf, the Prime wolf, and first Alpha, Alexander the Prime was given 3 gifts. Fire, Ice, and Light." He explained.

"Light to lead, Fire to protect, and Ice to judge."

He glanced at me as I said this and my gaze fell, my cheeks warming up, "AMA taught me."

He nodded, looking away, "But like the Night Wolf, He was not given a mate." He continued, "But it was not a punishment. Selene thought it best that if he should retain the power to judge her creations for eternity, he should do so without distraction or influence, and for a time, for a couple of centuries, she was correct."

He placed each book perfectly, spines out and ready to be spotted. His fingers trailed a few of the first books, taking it out and placing it behind the others, before turning back to me. He took a few books off my stack to pack-and I listened attentively.

"But she created a human heart for him and if even gods themselves can not stand to be alone what made him different? He spoke of this to her, but she would not listen. The realms had only prospered the way she had created them. She thought creating anything more would be destruction. There was perfect balance. Nothing else was needed. So in desperation, he sought other ways-"

"The Shadow realm."

"The endless." He corrected, "a place filled with endless everything. Endless wants, endless emptiness, endless powers. Endless chaos. It came to him, whispered a solution- a host for it, in exchange for a mate."

My eyebrows arched, "what is the endless?"

"It is hard to describe." He paused, his gaze seemed to go off into nothingness, "It is everything and nothing at all. It is a mirror of worlds by which shadows and shades are born. It's a place and a being, a god in its own right-"

"And did it- did it give him a mate?" I managed to utter. I was taken in the story and though I knew the answer, something about hearing it from his lips seemed more genuine.

"It gave him chaos and night." He stated, "It corrupted him, and the gifts Selene gave him. Everything requires balance you see. Good and evil.." he trailed off, "Because of this she was forced to design him a balance. Something pure to counter his darkness."

I watched him as he finished stacking- he turned to face me, gaze drifting into mine, "His mate was called the Mage Wolf. A being designed entirely by light. She brought balance to the world, balance to his darkness."

I stared down at the floor, remembering the stories, "The mage wolf? But don't they sing songs of her destruction? Don't they speak of how she brought down the Empire? They call it the mages curse."

He nodded, "They say to create her, Selene took the Primes' immortality, a gift that allowed peace to reign under his rule for centuries. It was not twenty years later that the Prime Wolf died. They say all life had been taken from him. She was a mistake, is what history claims. For if she had never existed, our world would have been in harmony as Selene intended in the beginning. Death began in the lines of the Arcs after that. Her children, each born of Selene's gift, except the oldest, born of night."

"And that is why Selene despises the Night Wolf? Because he was created in the endless and the beginning of all destruction for her creation?" I asked.

He nodded, tilting his head to the side as he took a step forward, towering over me, he seemed to be too close as I looked into his eyes, holding my ground, though I was tempted to step back.

"She would rather not create a mate for that side of the prime wolf. If she had her way she would."

"But Criston the Cruel.."

"Balance," he breathed, his gaze shifted in mine, "even darkness itself yearns for it. It can not be denied for if it does, chaos is unleashed, but that does not mean she can not make it extremely difficult."

I let out a breath, trying to follow him. Difficult? What did he mean by that?

I had so many questions but none of them could be voiced clearly.

I couldn't think with our proximity, my brain was under fire. Perhaps it was his eyes that held me still, I do not know, but I could feel his warmth from here. My tone came out breathy-

"I-"

Diane flew right between us, our gaze landing on the bird as it perched.

My heart was thumping harshly, and it was only now that I registered it had been nonexistent a few moments ago.

"It's a peculiar thing isn't it?" The master asked.

I glanced at him, noting his eyes were now set on the bird and I nodded, moving away from him. I took a stand near the Raven.

"Her name is Diane." I grinned, my fingers shifting through her feathers.

"Diane.." he repeated a certain mischief and a layer of amusement in his eyes as he turned toward us, "He seems attached to you."

I nodded at this, "I am in awe as well."

"It is not easy to gain the loyalty of a free bird, and yet, I've noticed he follows you wherever you go. Loyalty like that always comes as a price paid," his gaze dropped to me, a question in his eyes, "why does he seem bound to you?"

My fingers crippled and my heart thudded, as I glanced at the bird, knowing I could not say why. I promised AMA. She told me never to reveal it.

I did not wish to lie to a friend. But even Vale didn't know. I could not simply dispose of all my secrets, especially to a master.

I managed a nervous chuckle, "bound? You make it seem like I force her to be here. You would be mistaken, Diane here is quite free-" I grinned, my fingers shifting through her feathers, "I think she simply likes me."

He did not respond, and his gaze remained stationed in mine and for a moment, I thought he could read my soul.

I turned away, gazing at the bird and trying to breathe slower.

A blast of a horn in the distance caught both of our attention, my eyebrows arching, "w-what is that?"

He stared out into the direction of the blast, a rigid look dawning his face.

"Trouble." He muttered.

I tried to listen for another sound, but nothing came, "it sounded like a horn-" I began turning to face him but there was nothing there.

I looked around for him, "m-master?" I called into the darkness

Nothing else echoed back.

My gaze shifted to Diane, my face falling, "he left without saying goodbye didn't he?"

Diane cawed in reply.

[27.1] VAELN

● |•|•"The sea is no place for a wolf."•|•|•

[KAYOS]

Vaeln was here.

2 weeks before he was intended. His scent was strong as I pushed the doors of my study open, my eyes falling on the Light Wolf, a hardness in my jaw I couldn't quite get rid of. Vaeln was a menace if I ever had one. He was the reason for the noise he had blasted throughout the court with a bloody horn.

He sat across my desk, staring at me with an amused smirk.

The longer I looked at him the more irritated I got.

"Will you not speak-"

"What are you doing here?" I growled, gaze hardening.

His lazy smirk dawned into a chuckle.

"Sit Kayos. Standing there makes me feel so goddamn uncomfortable." He grinned, turning in his seat for a moment, "Offer me a drink or something. A decade-aged wine is what I would prefer."

I stared at the obnoxious Arc, trying to stop my anger from reeling its ugly head.

"I was unaware it was my duty to make you feel ...comfortable." I gritted through my teeth.

"I am your guest. Therefore it is." He shrugged, eyes skimming my desk.

"Ah," he grinned, reaching for a Jug, "Tell me this is wine."

"You are not a guest, Vaeln, do not be deceived," I growled, prowling further into my study.

"Water," he gagged, sniffing the contents before setting the jug down, glancing over at me, "As plain as you are, I suppose."

"You- are the farthest thing from a guest in my court. You have barged into my home, unannounced, unwanted, unwelcome, and unaccepted and now you sit before me-" I looked at his casual state, "and you dare to speak?"

"Now how else am I supposed to bloody respond if speaking is forbidden?" He scoffed, gaze narrowing on me, "It sounds like a bloody paradox if I've ever heard of one."

I ignored this, "You may very well be considered an enemy. Breaking the treaty once more, showing up before your selected time, creating havoc and unnecessary unrest in my court-"

"It was the blast of a horn, Kayos- I did not shoot a canon through your walls,"

"If you do not realize it yet," I cut, "I am not amused at your intrusion, Vaeln, I truly hope you have a valiant reason to redeem yourself-" I grunted, my head tilting slightly, my wolf a lingering threat of red in my eye.

He paused at this, searching my eyes for a moment.

The door suddenly swung open behind me, and the lure of a soft flowery scent caught me, and I inwardly groaned.

In walked Mother, a wide smile on her face.

"Vaeln!" she gleamed, passing by me, "I can not believe it! Goddess, It is you."

The Arc stood to his feet, "Grand Luna, Aleya," he grinned as Mother trapped him in her arms.

I stepped away, irritated at her intrusion.

"In the flesh." She beamed holding him at arm's length, looking him over.

I stared blankly at the action as she studied him, "I haven't seen you in nearly two years- oh and you've grown so much, so much more handsome." She gleamed, brushing his newly trimmed beard.

"I would have visited Aleya, but as you know, for the sake of peace, the treaty had to be respected." He grinned.

"A treaty you have just shattered, twice," I grunted.

"Nonsense, the treaty was meant to protect the four territories, not to make them enemies," Mother huffed, glancing between the two of us.

"Ah, if only we all looked at it that way," Vaeln joked, gaze straying to me.

I rolled my eyes at this, as Vaeln watched her with more compliments. I stood frustrated, waiting for their moments to end.

"I- trust you have been properly welcomed." Mother began

Vaelns gaze trailed to mine, "Certainly, Kayos has been a ray of sunshine," he grinned, "he even offered me wine."

Mother's gaze met mine, raising a surprised eyebrow at this and I shook my head.

She turned back to Vaeln.

"I was not expecting you for two weeks- where's Gail?" she suddenly asked, now searching the room for his mate.

Vaeln calmed her down, guiding her to sit beside him, " Gail's not here, Luna."

"You left her behind?" Mother asked, slapping his arm, "You dare come to visit and deny me the chance of seeing the Arc Luna of the Light Court?"

Vaeln chuckled at this, "She isn't here yet, but she will be coming," Vaeln eased, patting her arm.

His gaze met mine, "I had to be sure it was safe here. The last time I came to visit someone was direly unkind. I would not want her to live through the embarrassment again."

"Last time?" Mother, echoed, her gaze snapped to me, disappointment dawning in her eyes as she seemed to read between the lines- but I was done with Vaelns schematics.

The light wolf was my direct opposite.

Whilst I repelled everyone away, he seemed to have the uncanny power to charm everyone that ever set eyes on him.

Even my mother. He was by far, her favorite of all my cousins. I had little knowledge of what love was. I knew my mother cared for me. It was no secret she cared for Vaeln as if he was another son too. Perhaps a son she would have rather had.

One blessed by Selene and not Cursed by her.

Either way, I was immune to Vaelns charms.

Perhaps that's where his power failed him.

"He means when he camped at the edge of our borders a few days ago, breaking the treaty. I would hardly call that a visit," I informed, walking around my desk, "neither will this be considered as one. If you will not tell me why you're blasting horns in my Court, I will get you settled in as soon as possible. The dungeons have not seen any light since they were built. Perhaps you would do them a kindness. And of course, as soon as your little mate shows up, she can accompany you too. "

"Kayos!" Mother gasped, her eyes stern.

My gaze reached to hers, "They will be released at the appropriate time Mother. Two weeks."

She gasped at this, her hand tightening around Vaelns arm. "You can not be serious-"

"—It's alright, Aleya ." Vaeln calmed, leaning forward for a moment, patting her arm tenderly before his eyes trailed back to mine, more serious than it had been. "Do not fear Kayos. I do have a valiant reason for showing up the way I have." He started.

I remained stoic, waiting for his response.

His gaze shifted to mothers before landing back in mine, "I have come because- the situation has gotten far worse than I ever thought. Then we both could ever have imagined."

"Situation?" Mother echoed, glancing between us.

My gaze trailed to hers, enlightening her. "He has concerns."

"Concerns?" Vaeln scoffed, "You confirmed there were things to fear-"

"Things that could be discussed in two weeks," I growled back.

"Well, I will have you know that these so-called concerns have drifted into something much more dire. They are concerns that finally have faces.." he trailed off, catching my attention.

"I- I do not follow.." Mother stated, her curious gaze trading between us, whilst I stared at Vaeln with more intrigue.

Faces-

He was telling me he had seen whatever it was that was killing the ancient forests, and killing the rogues. That he knew what scent polluted the trees. A scent not even my shadows could pinpoint.

"Faces?" I echoed.

"Faces that will make your insides turn. " he stated glancing at Mother before looking at me with a hesitant pause, a certain emotion crossing his face, "well, perhaps not you. Since you are part of the darkness, perhaps it will not host the same effect."

"I- do not follow!" Mother repeated, this time harsher, "Will someone tell me what these faces and concerns are?" she huffed, seemingly frustrated, her cheeks reddening as her fingers sifted through her gown.

My gaze snapped to hers, but Vaeln was the one to explain, "The forests are dying, Aleya."

"What do you mean the forests are dying? Are they being cut or-or burned down?" she huffed, "what wolf would be stupid enough to do such a thing?"

"No, no-no, Aleya. I fear it is far worse," Vaeln corrected, "they are simply wasting to bark in a matter of days. As I speak now, half of my western forest has been turned into a wasteland. There are no leaves, no grass, the trees are dead, and a fog lies heavily between the dead stumps. There is a whisper in the air, a scent unlike any I had ever smelt before-"

"Wasting?" Mother echoed, her voice a loose gasp, "The Western forest? That is the largest in Valcane!" Her eyes widened glancing between the two of us, "A-And you say half of it is gone?" she started, a certain look of surprise and bewilderment in her eyes.

"Nearly," Vaeln replied solemnly.

I must say, even I was surprised. Half of a forest as large as that in a matter of days.

Vaelns gaze met mine as if knowing what it was I was thinking, before looking back at Mother, nodding.

"You understand why I am here, now?"

Her gaze fished in his, "the forest- " she gulped, her gaze shifting for a bit as if trying to wrap her head around the news, "were there any rogues found? Those trees are known to be infested with rogue packs."

Vaelns gaze met mine again, nodding once more, "There were first reports of bodies of rogues found dead, rotting within the trees, however, when I sent for an official report, not a single one was found."

Mother was at a loss for words for a moment, before she spoke, "No bodies?" She blinked for a moment, "You said you found, faces for your concerns."

Vaeln nodded, pausing for a moment, "It is the true reason why I am here. I did not know what these scents were..until now."

I watched him carefully.

"This ...face we found. I feel only Kayos can understand it."

My gaze reached to his, watching as he spoke-

I could feel mothers eyes on me at his revelation.

"The problem I fear came from far beyond the borders of Valcane-" Vaeln continued.

"Beyond?"

He glanced at Mother, "These faces are forged in the lands of men."

"Men?" It was my turn to interrupt, eyes narrowing on him, "I know these scents, and I know the scents of men. They are not the same."

This was a fact I knew true.

"I did not say they were men," Vaeln scoffed, sitting back in his seat, "I said they came from the land of men-" he reached into his pocket, taking out a singular small piece of drenched wood.

The bark smelt different. It was damp. I didn't need to touch it to figure this out. Its scent alone spoke many things, including the fact that it came from a tree that was not planted in Valcane and was most likely a piece from a boat.

"A ship," he stated, "was found wrecked a mile away from one of our ports. They were no bodies on the ship, we think they might have died at sea-" he started, "however two things were recovered from the wreckage." he got to his feet, "one is more of a monster than a mere thing." he drawled, "I brought it here."

"What?" Mother began, looking up at Vaeln.

I, however, was curious, my head tilting to the side for a moment. My tone is slow and easy-

"You brought a monster from the sea, here?" I asked.

"Does that upset you?" he raised an eyebrow, smirking.

I could have smiled but I remained stoic, "Where is it?"

[28.1] MONSTER ACROSS THE SEA

● |•|•

"What do you know of the endless pup?"

•|•|•

[Kayos]

A dark tent-covered cage sat in the Hall room beneath the castle. There was no light in any crevices except the candles that were carried by six of Vaelns men, who guarded the cage on all four sides, standing as still as statues.

My ears stretched noting that whatever creature that was trapped here was so silent, it could not be breathing. It must be dead, for it had no heartbeat either.

Master Gregory stood a little ways behind us, and Mother stood beside me, whilst Vaeln approached the cage. It was large I registered, judging by the size of the cage, big enough for a Full-grown wolf to roam freely.

- An Alpha wolf to be exact.

My ears sharpened at the sound of a hiss and grunt from the depths of the covered cage. It was alive.

No heartbeat, no breath- but alive. Either it could mask these things or it simply was something diabolical.

Scratching sounds followed, rough and hard against the silver bars.

"I will warn you," Vaeln huffed, before turning to one of the guards and nodding his head, "it is hideous."

The guards moved forward, each grabbing an end and drawing the tent off with a quick tug. I watched, noticing that the hisses, grunts, growls, and scratches of the creature had suddenly ceased, as if now aware that the tent that covered it was being lifted.

As the tent came off, my senses sharpened and I fished for a heartbeat once again, and that could be hidden within the shadows of the cage- I had to be sure...

there was none.

My gaze narrowed within the shadows, noting this creature was of darkness, so much so, I could only see its shape.

I realized it was simply because there was no color to see, this creature had wrapped itself in darkness, making it blend seamlessly, but I could still see its edges, sharp, humanoid but somehow wild and large-

"I can not see it, I can not see anything-" Mother began.

Her eyesight was not as good as one of an Arc.

Vaeln moved closer, his hands forming a ball of light, which he sent floating high above the cage and the creature screeched as the light dimmed slightly, but bright enough to see its hideous facade.

Mother gasped behind me, clutching a hand over her heart. I was enamored with the sight of it. I stared for a moment then edged on toward the cage curiously.

I could also hear a spike in Gregory's heartbeat with every step I drew closer.

"Sure, perhaps that is close enough."

I paid his statement no heed walking right up to the bars.

Something was calling out to me from the darkness.

"It is most sensitive to light. We found it hovered in the darkest corners of the wrecked ship, below deck," Vaeln explained, as I studied the creature through the bars.

The creature was humanoid but larger than any ordinary wolf.

Its skin was dry like ash, dark as night, its eyes, red as blood and in them I could see the most familiar element.

One I carried within me this very moment- Chaos.

It sauntered hunched on its shoulders, on all fours as if truly more animal than humanoid. It barred its fangs at me-

My head tilted slightly, taking in its most exquisite features, the most feral hate in its eyes, eyes that never left mine.

"It is from the endless..." I stated.

"Yes." Vaeln nodded.

I could feel his eyes steady on me as I circled the cage studying the creature. Its eyes turned with me.

"I could feel it from the moment I set eyes on it." Vaeln continued.

"What?" Mother echoed, her worried gaze shifted from the creature to me, "From the endless? Did you create this Kayos?" She asked, her voice echoing in disgust, and fear.

I did not pay it much mind.

"I do not have the power to create a being this close to mimic life, Mother- it is not within my power." I stated, studying the figure of the creature, the sharp fangs it sprouted, sharper than most wolves, differently molded too, "At least it has never been done, and if it has, I have no knowledge of it."

"I know that to be true," Vaeln spoke, my gaze shooting to him for a moment-

"Is that disappointment I hear?" I scoffed.

Vaeln rolled his eyes.

"No- I am not here to accuse you of summoning this thing from the bowels of the endless," He continued, "I know you have nothing to do with it. I know your shadows- this one is not one of them. But you are the only being in this realm connected to that godforsaken place, the endless.." he huffed, the only being that truly understands it. You are the only one who could explain to us what this is."

I paused for a moment, silence looming among us. Mother opted to speak but I raised a hand silencing her-

A minute passed and I looked at Vaeln- "you see that it does not breathe?"

Vaeln paused at this for a moment, then nodded, "It has no heartbeat either."

"Which simply means it is not alive," I stated.

"Then it is a shadow? Like the ones you summon?" Mother asked.

I shook my head, "This creature can not de-form, for if it could, these bars could not have held it," I muttered, looking at the large silver cage.

My shadows changed forms, forming and deforming. This was certainly not one of them.

"My shadows do not have fangs, neither do they have limbs formed like rotting flesh and they do not have eyes that mimic ours, and some can even pass freely through solid walls. None of which this creature is capable."

Silence loomed once more and I moved to the farthest corner of the cage, the eyes of the creature following me, death spelled in its gaze.

I used one of my claws to cut my palm open, and the moment my blood spilled, the cage rattled immensely. A loud growl erupted as the creature lunged in my direction, my mother gasping behind me.

Vaeln stared wide-eyed as the creature clawed to reach me through the bars-standing on its two feet and stretching out....but I was unnerved, but quite intrigued, my bleeding palm just a breath out of reach watching the psychotic behavior of the creature before me.

I noticed its pointed ears, tall and powerful physic, slender but agile, yearning for my blood until the wound was closed by my wolf.

My palm lowered as its growls subsided.

"It feeds on blood," I stated, shaking my head, my gaze dropping to the stain of blood on my palm, wiping it off.

"Blood?" Vaeln echoed.

"Yes. Which is- quite unfortunate." I mumbled, rolling my eyes for a moment.

It seems there would be no peace in this territory for a good while. I would not be able to focus on the one thing I wished to focus on now more than ever.

It was just like Selene to do this.

To hand me this thing- I glanced at it with irritation.

This thing occupies me so I may delay in my quest to find my mate. My thoughts trailed to my sanctuary- Shade- this would keep me from her for a while...

"Will you leave the sentence hanging like grapefruit?!" Vaeln huffed, snapping his fingers, forcing my gaze to snap at him in annoyance

"Goodness, where did you go?" Mother huffed, folding her arms in disbelief-

My gaze snapped between the two of them. Then trailed to Master Gregory who seemed to be staring thoughtfully-

Vaeln rolled his eyes, "What do you mean by "it is quite unfortunate?" He huffed in desperation.

I turned to the cage with an annoyed grunt, "If this being did come from the shadow realm, it would care not about flesh and blood. It would hunt souls. For that's what the endless desires." I stated, "But it hunts for blood, which means it desires life."

I glanced amongst the three of them and they stared on as if unable to comprehend my simple lines.

I took out a calming breath, "The being before us is not from the endless, but created of it."

They stared at me blankly, and I shook my head, "someone is wielding Adzar, and raising the dead."

"Adzar? That is forbidden! It was long, long gone, long forgotten." Mother stated.

"The Elves kept that magic far from mortal hands, protected it with their life. The old secrets died with them," Gregory added, "It is well known."

"Yes, we've all read the stories .... yet here the creature is. " I started watching the red eyes glimmer in the cage.

I turned to it for a moment, studying its eyes. It seemed to be watching us too. Listening-

"it would explain why the forests are dying, Adzar burns life to keep the dead alive-" Gregory stated.

I let this linger for a moment, "It burns in light, does it not?"

I don't look at Vaeln but he answers, "Yes and I believe Fire will also do the trick. The creature burns in sunlight, hence why we had to carry the darkest tent over it."

I glanced at the tent, "Then it also hunts at night."

I turned away from the cage, my gaze trailing around the group, noting Gregory stared at the creature with a mix of intrigue and fear although his stoic look revealed nothing to the public.

I paused, remembering something-and I turned to Vaeln, "You said you retrieved two things...."

His gaze shifted to mine and nodded.

"What is the other?"

Vaeln paused for a moment, then turned slightly to the right, nodding to a guard. He saluted and left for a moment.

"We found her near the wreckage." He began, "seemed to be the only survivor, but she refuses to speak- I do not believe she can speak."

My gaze sparkled in intrigue, "she?"

The doors opened and I turned to look.

Ah...

A human.

[29.1] THE HUMAN

"The stories are real Dula. The nightmares father used to tell. The beasts are coming. The villages have disappeared. There is darkness in the air. Do you not feel it?"

•|•|•

[KAYOS]

The human girl trembles before us. Her hair is thin, long, and stringy, a fade-off from the color of the earth. Her scent is strong, a musk of sea and land, salt and dirt.

Her sunken eyes remain glued to the stoned floor she kneels on, eyes darting all over the place. Her heart is a hard pound within her.

I know what she feels. It is a pain that calls out to my very being. Releasing a hunger in my wolf.

She is in a foreign land amongst beasts that could rip her to threads in a breath. Perhaps that is why she fails to breathe normally as one would.

Instead, it is a harsh wind against her dry torn lips, her hands shivering in her tattered lap.

"She can speak," I state, head tilting slightly, taking in the human.

"She has not spoken a word." Vaeln counters, starting at the small creature.

"She will."

I feel his eyes on me at my reply. It is not a promise, it is merely for telling.

"if she wishes to see the sunrise tomorrow." I finish.

The girl's eyes immediately rise at this, wide as saucers, her first mistake. Her eyes fall into mine, trapped in the abyss of chaos that lives in them.

Fear in return echoes in her eyes, so deep, I was certain it was the only reason she couldn't look away after. Paused treacherously, a way in which I was able to read her soul.

"Kayos," Mother whispers desperately beside me.

She has seen this one too many times.

"You're scaring the girl," she hisses, her voice a soft plea.

Mother's heart is soft. It is filled with light. Bitter when need be, strong when called upon. But she does not understand the chaos that lives inside me. She does not understand why I thrive on fear, why the wolf inside me stirs at its taste.

"She is better off scared, than dead, mother."

The girl's eyes widen ever so slightly ad my words. I keep her eyes hostage in mine, unwavering- pulling at the darkest memories that stretch deep within the outline of her soul. For these are the ones that hold pain, that hold fear, that draw chaos and calls out to the endless.

Her breaths deepen, then form into bare grasps as she struggles for air. It is not because she can not breathe.

Humans have no wolves to protect their souls, therefore stealing them is rather effortless. She is a meal presented before the endless, a soul to take, pain, fear, and heartache just there-

Waiting for it to feed.

She gasps because she can feel her soul slipping away, dissolved in the abyss of the endless that is carved in the eclipse of my eyes. The veins around her neck deepen to dark lines as she leans forwards, and I circle her slowly.

She is prey, and the chaos, the endless inside me wants to feed.

"Kayos!" Mother blurts, louder this time. She catches herself, swallowing deeply as she regains her posture, her tone lower and firmer, "This can not be necessary."

I ignore her concerns as the girl draws deeper gasps, enlarging her eyes.

She will never understand. She does not know the price of wielding darkness itself.

"Ancient forests are dying, wolves are missing, and there are no bodies to bury the dead," I coldly state, my head tilting to the side.

I watch the human for a few seconds knowing every word I speak sends a haunting shiver down her spine. She is human, unaware of what authority stands before her. One she senses but can not identify-

So much like-

I find myself slipping but I soon regain sanity, knowing my eyes are pits of flames now as my wolf shows forth I speak,

"You know of the threat human, and you refuse to speak," I taunt.

Her eyes watch me in pure horror, unblinking.

The endless inside me is delighted. It yearns for pain, it salutes chaos. It hopes for death, for a soul, small and innocent, pulling the darkness closer, and closer, and closer- soClose to consuming.

"You will kill her," Vaeln states quietly, as the girl becomes paler, her body a light breeze away from falling to the stoned floors.

I can not stop my wolf from growling when I speak, "Death will receive her with an open embrace."

I stop before her when she falls forward, her draws for air no longer gasps but empty attempts. Her eyebrows draw together, tears streaming down her already tear-stained face, terror in her eyes, not because of the soul I am taking, but because of death -lingering a shadow away.

"P-please!" she gasps, her words are a broken fountain of letters, her hands trembling outstretched toward my feet, bled by dark veins that have stretched up the length of her arms.

I am almost saddened by this. That her pain is to end so soon. It must be if am to gain the answers I seek.

A clench in my jaw. My dark-filled eyes turn to Vaeln, with a shrug, repeating my first statement.

"She speaks."

The chaos inside me lets go of her and she gasps for as much air as she can, her soul released from the grasp of the endless chord I had drawn back to me.

She stares at the floor breathing in deeply as fast and as hard as she can, her frail body still shaken in what could only be described as morbid disbelief.

She is in shock I assume. She does not understand what it is she has been through, though I am certain she knows death was a foot away, awaiting the moment the chaos inside me was released.

"Indeed," Vaeln replies, with a soft sigh, his gaze on the girl.

I stare down as she grovels at my feet for a moment until I pull up her chin so the fading life in her eyes meets mine.

She freezes once again drawn to my gaze, fear still locked behind them and I feel her wishing to close them and never open them again.

I know she feels how I invade her mind. She can not grasp that I am capable of such a deed.

"Name?" I growl.

She breathes low and quick, her lips trembling before speaks, but she knows she must, her voice is broken and small, "D-dula."

I search her eyes and she squirms. She speaks the truth.

I let go and her eyes immediately found the ground. They stay there, safe away from my gaze. I find it pathetic, perhaps I find it infuriating despite knowing why she can not.

I glance at Vaeln releasing myself from the fire lighting within me. The night is not easy to control. I do not desire to do anything to the girl- not yet.

I need only take what I need. She will be useful in the future but the night inside me yearns for more, more than the little I have given.

Vaeln nods in understanding, his gaze falling back on the girl.

"Where do you come from?" he asks.

The human's gaze remains floored, only rising ever so slightly in my direction, but her gaze reaches only my feet, before glancing in Vaelns.

"Nivera," she speaks.

"Across the sea?"

She nods, more times than is required and keeps nodding, a tremble in her voice, a shake in her body.

"You were found by the shore. A good way from a shipwreck. Were you on this ship?"

Vaeln paused momentarily, "Do you even remember?"

She paused, her gaze shifting about, but nodded, her eyes trailing to the cage before quickly looking away, blinking fast and blocking the memories that threatened to echo in her eyes.

"You know the creature?"

The sound of its voice causes her to stiffen for a moment before She nods once again, rubbing her arms as she sucks in a sob.

"Where does it come from?" I growl.

"I-I don't know," her voice skips as the creature hisses her way and she shakes again, her head turned away from the cage, biting her lips to stop a whimper, refusing to register the beast.

"Tell us what you do know," Mother says for the first time. Her tone is calmer, more collected now. A heavy authority laced in her tone.

The girl shivers as she speaks, her gaze always to the floor, her head turned away from the cage-

"T-they were f-first rumors. Just stories fathers told their children. I-I..." she trailed off shaking her head, "they're not supposed to be"

She gasped, tears streaming down her face, eyes still on the floor, she immediately slapped a shaken hand across her mouth as a sob escaped.

Once she collects herself as best as she can she speaks once more.

"they were supposed to be stories," she states, her eyebrows drawing together.

She seemed to be in shock.

"Silas said some villages had simply disappeared overnight. He said the Kings were hiding something, that things at night were taking people, drinking blood," she battled, sobbing, "that children were missing and someone was hiding the dead-" she froze for a moment, "they were stories! Silas always tells stories!" she huffed, hugging herself as she cradled too and for, "he's good at stories. Very good."

The hiss of the creature in the cage next to her sent her body frozen, her head shaking and eyes darting all over the place.

"And then they came," she freezes, staring at nothing for a moment, "and they just-" she blinks- she goes somewhere in her mind- she stays there for a few seconds, and then chuckles, "Just- dead, everyone...blood, everywhere"

She starts rocking back and forth lips trembling, "parts, everywhere, bodies, everywhere, everywhere, everywhere, everywhere-"

"Dula," I growl, and the sound of my voice snaps her into submission. Into calm, into nothingness.

Her gaze trails upwards, to no one in particular. She is not in the dungeons, she is not among beasts she hasOnly ever heard of, she is simply gone, "in the morning there was nothing- no bodies, no parts, only blood, only fire- only no one but us."

"Who is us?" Master Gregory asks.

Her eyes trail to him, ghostly, her eyebrows drawing together for a moment as if the memory was posted to her-

"I don't-" she pauses, blinking, her eyes falling to her palms folded in her lap, "Silas and I. My brother," her eyes water, "Us, him and I. To the sea, he said. We will be safe over the sea!" she mocks, tears stripping her eyes clean.

Her arms wrapped around her body, shaking her head as the sobs returned, as we, in turn, returned into the despair that echoed within her mind,

"but they were on the sea, Silas!" she screeched, "they were on the sea!"

My gaze travels to Vaeln and he holds it.

The monsters were on the boat. The massacre, the carnage there were no survivors but her.

The creature growls and the girl slaps her ears shut, rocking back and forth, "Make it stop! Make it stop!" she screeched.

Vaeln signals to the guards and the human is taken away. Weeping as she's dragged off into the dungeons.

She is no use to us in that state. Not at the moment.

"She says the bodies were taken too," Mother states, glancing among us.

"She also said the Men Kings may be to blame for this curse." Vaeln huffed, his gaze shifting to me slightly, "How did they get a hold of Adzar?"

"The Men Kings would not dare wage war against Valcane," I growled, eyes darting to him, "I am certain of that."

"Maybe then, when they were weak," Gregory replied, "but if they have found a way to wield Adzar, they are not what they used to be."

"Foolish is what they are!" I growled out, turning to him, "No one can wield Adzar. It is not force that can be wielded. Even if it foretells the illusion of it. No one can control it. It was not meant to be controlled. They will burn both our worlds if they do not stop."

"Can it be stopped?" Mother echoed, her gaze on the creature, she seemed out of it, "Look at it. It watches us like it understands us. How many of these...these things did it take to slaughter a whole ship? How many have escaped into our lands already and have poisoned our forests? How many more ships of humans are traveling across the turbulent seas seeking refuge in Valacane, but harboring this curse within their midst?" she huffed, "The curse is already here. How many ships have we missed?"

She was right. The plague was already spreading. If rogues were already missing then the threat was here and thriving.

"I will send my shadows across Valcane, see what they can gather. Meanwhile-" I dreaded speaking the next words, "we must speak with the others."

"We call the tribunal, now?" mother asked. "That will raise panic amongst the packs and the territories."

"We must move my ceremony sooner, then. We can not cause unwarranted chaos through Valcane by simply calling the tribunal. If it is under the guise of my mating, the wolves will not panic. They will think it is merely haste in my celebration. The people are anxious to see my soul tied toAnother, so their fears of another overnight will be quenched,"

Silence loomed among us as I spoke.

"They will not suspect a thing, only celebrate." My gaze traveled to Gregory, "Meanwhile, we need to set watches over every shore in Valacane in each of the four territories. Then we must send word to the Men Kings."

Gregory nods at this, with a low submissive hum.

"And the girl?" Mother asks.

"The human has more to say, she will remain here. We are yet to learn more from her."

"Do you think it is wise keeping her slaved to the Night Court? It goes against the treaty we have with the Humans," Gregory started.

"The treaty was broken the minute their threat crossed our borders. Make no mistake Gregroy," I growled, "We are at the brink of war."

He seemed to freeze at this for a moment before nodding, his gaze dropping to the floor.

Vaeln agreed with this statement, "War has always been inevitable. I shall call for my mate. She is best protected best by my side. Then I will reach out to the others. If there will be a war, I am certain Fir will take much delight."

He turned to Mother, with a bow, "I will see you soon, Grand Luna."

She nodded, as he bowed before her, before taking his leave.

"I will send word to the Men Kings, and set watch," Gregory added, bowing lo. He left soon after.

Mother and I stood in silence, my gaze trailing the creature trapped in the cage.

"Are you truly certain about pushing the date of your mating closer?" Mother asked softly, "You must know that I only wish you to be happy Kayos, I wish-"

"If only wishes were real, Mother," I grunted, my gaze held hers for a moment before I looked away-

"Sadly, they are not."

•|•|•Leave a comment and a vote if you're enjoying the story! Remember, comments make an author •|•|•